Murder in
Mykonos

Murder in
Mykonos

Jeffrey Siger

Poisoned Pen
PRESS

Copyright © 2008 by Jeffrey Siger
Cover and internal design © 2019 by Sourcebooks
Cover design by Nick Greenwood

Sourcebooks and the colophon are registered trademarks of Sourcebooks, Inc.

Published by Poisoned Pen Press, an imprint of Sourcebooks
P.O. Box 4410, Naperville, Illinois 60567-4410
(630) 961-3900
sourcebooks.com

Library of Congress Cataloging-in-Publication data is on file with the publisher

Printed and bound in The United States of America.
SB 10 9 8 7 6 5 4 3 2

*In Memory of Tassos Stamoulis,
the most beloved man on Mykonos,
and Ken, my brother.*

Acknowledgments

For all of you who helped me along the way, thank you.

Mihalis, Roz and Spiros Apostolou; Ersilia Bachauer; Olga Balafa; Tracy Beltran; Tonino Cacace; Cece Cord; Donald and Leena Crothers; Jody Duncan and Nikos Christodoulakis; Lori Estes-Markari; Donka Koleva; Andreas and Aleka Fiorentinos; Rebecca Friedman; Jane Gelfman; Susy Hammerson; Lillian Heiser; Nikos Ipiotis; Elizabeth Kabler; Nicholas Karahalios; Panos Kelaidis; Alexandros Kontogouris; Sharon Lock-Sikinioti; George Makrigiannis; Linda Marshall; Thomas and Renate McKnight; Leah Miller; Nikos Nazos; Wendy Popowich; Edward Prendergast and Roberto Mendes Coelho; Ellen Roth; Alan and Pat Siger; Jonathan (especially for his cover inspiration), Jennifer and Azriel Siger; Karen Siger; Peter and Joan Silbermann; George and Efi Sirinakis; Ed Stackler; Christine Smith; George and Theodore Stamoulis; Nolan and Chris Stripling; Hronis Taboulhanas; Margaret Wimberger.

And, of course, Aikaterini Lalaouni.

Prologue

Just past midnight the massive Rodanthi ferry silently made its grand entrance into Mykonos' narrow, crescent-shaped harbor. Though it was still a bit early in the season for the partying crowds that swelled this Greek island's population from ten thousand to fifty thousand in July and August, the harbor was wildly alive with lights and people.

It was exactly as the young woman had imagined—a blaze of white buildings under a diamond-studded sky.

She'd been standing inside with other backpackers on the third-level passenger deck watching the island's lights slowly envelop the horizon. Now she stepped outside and walked to the bow railing. Feeling the Aegean breeze in her face, she re-doubled the elastic band holding her blond ponytail in place. It was all so beautiful. She regretted only one thing: being here alone.

She felt as much as heard the thrusting power of the reversing engines as the ship began its graceful one-quarter pirouette toward the dock. Drawing in a deep breath from the wind coming off the sea, she picked up her backpack, headed for the stairs nearest the bow, and made her way down to the exit deck. The ferry had docked at its stern, and when she reached the bottom level she had to squeeze her way past a collection of beat-up island-hopping cars, trucks, and motorcycles waiting to disembark. She knew that at six feet tall her well-toned figure was attracting a lot of attention, especially in hiking shorts and a tank top. Several drivers along the way yelled out to her in various languages, offering her a ride anywhere she wanted to go. She acted as if she didn't understand but smiled to herself.

Most of the passengers were off the boat by the time she was at the gangway. Now she had to find a place to stay. That was not a problem. There were dozens of people offering accommodations, literally tugging at her for attention. She was inundated with photographs, brochures, letters of recommendation, all designed to funnel weary tourists into empty rooms.

The young woman spoke with the hawkers in English and picked what looked like a charming small hotel just above the town. The man, who claimed to be the owner, promised her a room with a private bath and a view of the town—at a "special price." He seemed very nice and with his gray hair was at least wise enough to mask any other interest he might have in her. Already, two couples from the ferry waited in his little van, so she wouldn't be going off alone with a stranger.

At the hotel she showed the owner her passport. He welcomed her in Dutch and told her he'd had many guests from the Netherlands, things that assured her she'd made the right choice. The room was as promised. She showered, put on her one sexy dress, and went out to wander the maze of winding, narrow paths lined by whitewashed buildings, adorned with brightly colored doors, shutters, and railings.

The town was awash in jewelry shops and bars. Vacationing families and pilgrims seeking early-morning connections to the nearby ancient and holy island of Delos were in their beds by now. Summer nights in Mykonos belonged to all-night partiers seeking their own sorts of connections. Bedtime could wait until a much later hour. No pretty woman ever needed to pay for a drink or dinner here.

At one of the bars she met a local Greek about her age. He introduced her to the owner who said the young man was his son. Then he introduced her to an "old family friend"—an American painter who told her he'd been coming to Mykonos every summer for more than thirty years. They all spoke in

English although the young man seemed to know enough Dutch words to use at the right time to be charming. By the time she left the bar it was nearly light and the young man convinced her to ride on the back of his motorcycle to a place where they could watch the sun come up.

She mounted his bike and put her arms around him; the engine vibrated between her legs. For twenty minutes she pressed her body against his as he raced toward the rising sun. At the beach—deserted, he said, except for a single small house owned by a priest from England—they touched and kissed through the sunrise; then took off their clothes and swam naked. He tried to make love to her, but he had no condom and she refused. He pressed her; she resisted. He pushed her down, yanked away his clothes, and stormed off shouting at her in Greek.

She heard the sound of his motorcycle as he drove away, leaving her alone to find her way back. She was thankful she hadn't been raped. Tipsy, tired, and angry at herself, she dressed and started up the steep dirt road toward what she hoped would be town. She had to take off her heels to walk, and the stones hurt her feet. She wasn't used to this. She wanted to cry but kept on walking. It was a dry and rocky road, like the island itself. After fifteen minutes or so she heard a motor on the other side of a hill. For an instant she thought it might be him returning. It wasn't. It was a car, a taxi bearing down toward her in a cloud of dust. She was surprised to see one out here so early in the morning but frantically waved for him to stop.

She spoke to the driver in English and he responded in English. She started to cry. He told her to get in and asked what happened. She told him the story as if replaying a video of her ordeal. He listened quietly, not saying a word. When they reached her hotel he said he knew the young man and she really hadn't been in any danger; but on an island filled with so many strangers she must be very careful who she trusts—especially when it comes to young men with motorcycles. That made her feel a little better, though she still was mad at herself for thinking she was the first one he'd taken on a romantic sunrise motorcycle ride.

She slept until about two that afternoon, then took a bus to Paradise Beach. She refused to talk to anyone there, but the young Greek men persisted. Eventually, she moved to the nude, gay part of the beach where macho Greek Romeos were afraid to be seen. She stripped naked and read a book, undisturbed. That night she went back into town and spent her time talking with jewelers and souvenir sellers. Enough bar boys. One of the jewelers invited her to dinner at a fashionable restaurant. She had a great time and he was a perfect gentleman.

He walked her to a taxi and invited her to attend a Greek festival to be held in three days to honor a saint. She thanked him but said she was leaving the island in two days and promised to stop by his shop before she left.

Then, like so many other backpackers, she simply disappeared. No one paid the balance of her hotel bill—also not unusual in Mykonos. The hotel owner simply threw out whatever she'd left behind, reported nothing to the police, and rented the room to a new pretty woman from another midnight ferry.

Chapter One

Andreas Kaldis knew why his six-foot-two-inch body was crammed into a midget-sized window seat on a plane to Mykonos, and he didn't like it one bit. He'd been "promoted" from the Greek police force's number one ass-kicker in central Athens to its chief dog-and-cat protector for Athenian weekenders. At least that's how he saw it. Thirty-four-year-old hotshot homicide detectives like one thing: catching killers. For them, the worst punishment imaginable was being taken away from the action. His promotion to chief of police for one of the smallest of the Cyclades islands meant just that: being as far away from what he was born to do as Andreas could imagine.

Ninety miles and less than thirty minutes from Athens by plane, or three hours by high-speed ferry, Mykonos was approximately one and a half times the size of the island of Manhattan and had become to Athens what Andreas understood "the Hamptons" were to New Yorkers. Rich and superrich Athenians—together with thousands of wannabe celebrities from all over Europe—flocked to Mykonos on holiday. Many built mega-million-euro summer homes on the island or paid London hotel prices for far less than English five-star service.

What the locals wanted didn't matter anymore—even though most didn't know it yet. The moneyed visitors now had a say in how Mykonos would be run, and they had their complaints. For one thing, they were tired of putting up with the old ways. They also groused about too many break-ins, too many crazy, drunken drivers, and too much local political influence over police enforcement practices. The wealthy were demanding better policing, and they had the political influence to get it.

Enter Andreas Kaldis. His move to Mykonos—or rather, his departure from Athens—was exceptionally good news to certain powerful people. His aggressive investigation into a series of murders over control of the Athenian drug trade had worried them. Promoting him out of Athens—and out of the investigation—was a political masterstroke that even Andreas could appreciate. It hurt no one and made everyone happy. Everyone but Andreas.

Officially, he arrived under a mandate involving the European Union's insistence that Mykonos show more evenhanded law enforcement toward non-Greeks. Andreas took that as a political cover story for Greece's Public Order Ministry, which oversaw the police, to guard against the inevitable griping by Mykonian locals that Athens was trying to control their affairs—a perennial complaint among islanders.

Also mentioned in the official announcement of his appointment was the fact that Andreas lacked family ties to any Greek island. That made him a particularly desirable choice for police chief because no one could accuse him of favoritism toward islanders—a perennial complaint on the part of mainland Greeks. The fact that Andreas had served his obligatory service in the military at an air force installation on Mykonos was not mentioned.

Off the record, Andreas had orders to tread lightly with the locals. As a young, single man wielding considerable power on a small island, he knew that word of his every move would get around fast. As far as he was concerned, Athens wasn't a much bigger place when it came to gossip—and he liked it that way. That was how he got some of his best leads. If the warning meant to avoid fooling around with the local women, he already knew better. Any self-respecting cop would. Besides, Andreas had no intention of incurring some local family's vendetta—or of tying his future to a Mykonos clan for the rest of his days.

His morning flight was packed with early-June tourists. He fit right in, except he already had his tan—it came, along with his dark hair and gray eyes, from his parents. So did his square jaw and decent good looks. The counterbalancing bump and slightly crooked tilt to his nose —the collective work of several folks who'd ended up looking a lot worse—let you know Andreas wasn't someone to mess with.

"Looks like it's going to be a busy season," said the guy in the aisle seat next to him. He was about Andreas' size but looked twenty years older.

Andreas hated talking to people on airplanes. Something about planes made people want to tell you things they'd never dream of talking about with strangers on the ground. Maybe it was something about being up in the air, above the earth and closer to God. Or maybe it was just nerves.

"You're Greek, aren't you?" The man was speaking Greek with what sounded like a South African accent.

Andreas had to respond in order to avoid seeming rude. He nodded.

"Sure hope it's busy. Business was slow last year."

This guy isn't going to stop, thought Andreas, nodding again. He turned his head and stared out the window.

"I'm a jeweler."

Andreas knew the man was just trying to be friendly and he didn't have anything against jewelers—someday he might even need one if he found the right girl. But this cheery nosiness was just the sort of thing he dreaded about being posted to Mykonos. Everyone wanted to know everyone else's business. Andreas turned back to the fellow and, with his most practiced, tired-cop look, said, "That's nice," and returned to the window.

The man took the hint and remained silent for the rest of the flight. After they landed and were walking from the plane to the terminal, he offered Andreas his hand, which Andreas shook graciously. "Enjoy your time here among the gods," the man said with a smile. "After all, they were our first tourists."

And, no doubt, those same gods knew that they wouldn't be the last.

As Andreas waited for his bags he looked around and saw a room full of excited, good-time-ready responsibilities. How would he possibly protect and police fifty thousand locals and visitors with only sixty cops—including the additional twenty-five assigned to him for the tourist season? He shook his head and chuckled aloud. Maybe he could summon a few of those gods from Delos in a pinch.

Outside the terminal he waited for whomever had been assigned to pick him up. The breeze felt good, but after five minutes of pushing his slightly too-long hair out of his eyes and over his forehead, he picked up his briefcase and walked the hundred yards to the police station abutting the airport. It had been relocated there from the center of town a few years before—perhaps to shorten the walk for stranded chiefs. Andreas didn't mind the walk, he ran regularly to keep fit—but he did mind the lack of respect.

The two-story, thick-walled building had the traditional whitewash with blue trim found in Mykonian architecture. Police and civilian cars, SUVs, and motorcycles as well as an assortment of vehicles mangled in road accidents were parked haphazardly along the front and left side of the building. Andreas wasn't in uniform, and the first things he noticed as he walked in were the ages and abrupt attitudes of the cops who got right in his face and asked what he wanted. All but a handful of the officers under his command were fresh out of the police academy, or still in it and assigned to Mykonos for the summer as part of their training. As green as green could be.

And their community-relations skills would need serious work. What would be even trickier was that, according to their personnel files, not one of these kids was from Mykonos. Mykonians were fiercely independent; they had no desire to be cops and little respect for those who were. Tourism had made Mykonians, on a per capita basis, the richest people in Greece. The financial benefits of police work—both lawful and otherwise—held no attraction for them. Besides, many boasted ancestors who had been unrepentant pirates.

One cop asked Andreas a second time—and more aggressively—what he wanted. Andreas couldn't help himself. "Would you be kind enough to pick up my bags at the airport? I left them with the Olympic ticket agent."

The young man, who was built like a bull, looked to his friends, then back at Andreas. "Listen, wiseass, this is a police station. So get the hell out before you find out what happens when you fuck with cops." He gave an "I showed him" smirk to his buddies.

Andreas fixed his steel-gray eyes on the young cop and let a "do I have your ass now" smile spread across his face. "So nice to meet you, Officer—what does that say on your uniform?— Kouros. I'm Andreas Kaldis, your new chief of police."

Someone should have checked Kouros' shorts at that moment, but there wasn't time. He proved himself smart enough to be out the door and in a car headed to the airport before Andreas could speak another word. Kouros' friends also jumped to attention, Andreas' point clearly made.

Chalk one up for the new chief. But there was no time to enjoy his little victory. He'd deal with Kouros and the man responsible for meeting him at the airport later, in private. For the moment. there was a lot of work to do. He just hoped to get half-accustomed to the job before all hell broke loose.

◇◇◇

By the middle of his first week Andreas knew his job was impossible. Everyone on the island did what they wanted. It was as if the police didn't exist. For now, he could only manage triage, prioritizing what could be done. The impossible situations would be left alone. The insignificant would too. He'd focus attention on what he'd been told was the most politically sensitive concern: danger to tourists. Mykonos thrived because of its tourists, and he had to protect them—if only from themselves.

By the beginning of his second week he'd set up a series of floating checkpoints for catching drunk drivers, reckless drivers, and helmetless motorcyclists. It was the sort of high-visibility, aggressive police activity that, by word of mouth, would change the behavior of far more drivers than they could ever arrest.

He also set up a special unit to back up the cops who worked undercover at the island's most notorious, late-night tourist spots keeping an eye out for pickpockets and drug dealers. If a tourist at any of those places was robbed or assaulted that unit would appear in force—and in uniform. It was a not so subtle way of sending word to the owners that they'd better take care of their patrons if they wanted their places to remain free of more intrusive police activity.

Thefts from unlocked hotel rooms and unattended bags were grudgingly accepted as an unpreventable fact of modern life. But unprovoked violence and robbery against innocent tourists enjoying the island's freewheeling party life threatened the economic heart of Mykonos. Andreas' message was clear: no such threat to its reputation would be tolerated—from anyone.

In less than two weeks, Andreas felt that he was having a positive impact on the community. The island's longtime mayor—a sturdy combination of political-machine boss and preening cock of the walk—even stopped by to compliment him. Things seemed to be working out. He thought if he made it through the summer without ruffling any feathers or stepping on any toes he just might be able to work his way back into the good graces of the folks in Athens—and get transferred the hell out of here.

He thought it might help him to stay cool if he tried a little harder to relax. Go to the beach and blow off some steam. Maybe even one of those beaches where the tourist women like to show off their lack of tan lines. He wondered if they were still as hot for Greeks in uniform as they had been when he'd served here in the air force. It was early afternoon and he was getting into the fantasy when Kouros hurried into his office—after knocking, of course.

The news was not good: an Albanian moving stone on some property way over on the other side of the island called to say he'd found a dead body.

Andreas didn't want to believe what he was hearing and his voice showed it. "A dead body, on Mykonos?"

"Yes, sir," said Kouros. He'd learned to treat his chief with respect. "He didn't say much more than that. Just the location. He was pretty frightened. I was surprised he even called. Most of them doing that sort of work are illegal and afraid of us."

Andreas paused for a moment and stared off into the middle distance, contemplating a decision. "Do you know how to get there?"

"Yes."

Andreas got up from his desk. "Well, let's take a ride over and see what he found."

"Uh, sir?" Kouros' voice was tentative.

"Yes."

In an even more uncertain tone: "Aren't we supposed to call Syros whenever there's a homicide?"

Central Police Headquarters for the Cyclades was on Syros, the political capital for the circle of islands spanning one hundred miles from Andros on the north to Santorini on the south. All homicide investigators and criminal forensic facilities were based there—less than an hour from Mykonos by police boat.

Andreas knew Kouros was right, but he'd be damned if he'd let Syros trample over a murder scene in his jurisdiction before he had a chance to look at it. So much for playing it cool. "Yeah, but let's just make sure it wasn't a dead goat he found before bothering Syros."

Kouros said nothing, simply walked with Andreas to the car, got into the driver's seat, and began driving east. Andreas liked the way the big kid knew when to keep his mouth shut.

"Sir, I understand you were with Special Homicide Investigations in Athens?"

Word got around. "Yes."

"How many murders have you seen?"

"Of goats? Or sheep?"

"Nice day, sir."

"Sure is."

The rest of their conversation was about Kouros' family back in Athens and his roots on the Ionian island of Zákynthos. It was a pleasant chat, but one that let Kouros know there would be no personal information coming from the chief for him to share with his buddies over coffee.

The twenty-minute drive took them along the road past the air force's mountaintop "secret" radar installation—the one everyone on the island knew about. Andreas had been stationed there twelve years ago. He couldn't believe how much that part of the island had changed. Back then there was virtually nothing to see from up here but dirt roads and endless rocky, barren hillsides crisscrossed with centuries-old stone walls. Now the road was paved and elegant homes sprouted everywhere on seemingly unbuildable sites. It was amazing what people with money could do when they wanted something.

The road turned to dirt, then drifted back down the mountain to the east before heading north and up again toward the most desolate part of the island. These steep, gray-brown hillsides once were home to goat herders who could afford no better land, but even they long ago abandoned their little stone-fenced fields in favor of other places. For almost a century no one had wanted to be here. Too far out of town, too much wind, too little—if any—water.

Now, a recent island-wide ban on new construction on land without an existing foundation made an even long-abandoned, goat herder's shed valuable. Using an appropriately connected contractor to obtain—for a price—the necessary permits, you could "finish" construction and truck in all the fresh water you wanted along the new road. All you needed was the money.

Andreas remembered old mines around here down by the sea. Some sort of mineral used in oil drilling—barite, maybe. He wondered if they still operated. Abandoned mines were great for hiding bodies. On an island like this, though, there had to be hundreds of places to get rid of one—if you had time to plan—but he knew murders rarely took place where the murderer would like them to. That meant moving the body or leaving it where the killer hadn't planned. Either way left clues. Most murders were poorly thought out beyond the decision to kill—unless, of course, professionals or terrorists were involved.

Then again, this was an island, and the best place to get rid of a body was the sea. No one would ever find one tossed in the sea if you knew how to keep it from popping up. Thankfully, most killers didn't have that skill—though Andreas was pretty sure that on an island of fishermen most Mykonians would know how or have a relative who did.

Just past a steep switchback, the road tied in to an older, badly beat-up dirt road coming around from the other side of the mountain. Andreas could see that it wound down to the mines and wondered if the body actually might be in one. This road was much worse than the other, and their car looked to be losing its battle with some deep ruts from winter-rain runoff. He was about to tell Kouros to call for an SUV when he saw a beat-up old motorcycle leaning against a boulder by the hillside. The bike was so dusty he couldn't tell its color. A slightly built man, more like a boy, was sitting in the dirt next to it. His dark hair, white T-shirt, and brown, coarse pants were as dusty as the bike. He jumped up as soon as he saw them. He must be their man.

Though he looked a good foot shorter and eighty pounds lighter than Andreas, the chief knew there was a good chance the man, like many of the Albanian laborers who worked like ants at tough, nasty jobs no Mykonian would ever do again, was stronger than he was. Building stone walls all day in relentless heat could do that, if it doesn't kill you. Andreas reached for a bottle of water from the backseat and got out of the car. He walked over and handed the water to the man without saying a word. The man thanked him and Andreas nodded but said nothing. Kouros kept his mouth shut.

From behind his sunglasses Andreas studied him. The Albanian was probably in his early twenties, but his hands and arms bore the bruises and calluses of a far longer lifetime of manual labor. A seriously distressed wedding ring faintly glistened on his finger as he held the bottle to his lips. His hand was shaking and he was frightened. He should be; that was normal. Now to see if there was anything about his story or behavior that wasn't.

He let the man finish drinking and stared at him for a minute longer without saying a word. Probably Kouros was right about the man being illegal. He must be scared to death he'll be asked to show his papers. Andreas decided to let that fear fester while he went after what he really wanted to know. Kouros could deal with his papers later.

"Did you call?" Andreas kept his voice firm but pleasant. He didn't have to say about what; either he'd know or he wasn't the right guy.

"Yes, sir."

"What's your name?"

"Alex."

He didn't need his last name for now. "Where are you from?"

"Ano Mera."

That was the other town on Mykonos, located in the middle of the island. But that wasn't what Andreas meant by his question. He let it pass. The man had to know Andreas knew he was from Albania, if only from his heavily accented Greek.

"So, Alex, why don't you tell us what you're doing up here."

"I was working here today."

"Doing what?"

"Fixing stone walls."

"Where?"

He turned and pointed two hundred yards up the steep hillside. "By the church."

Andreas looked where the man was pointing. All he saw were many muted shades of brown dirt, brown bushes, and brown rocks—though when he looked closer he saw the rocks were more gray and reddish than brown. The only church he saw was on a different hillside far off to the left. "Do you mean there?"

He pointed to the distant traditional, whitewashed, blue-doored, Mykonian family church with its distinctive terra-cotta-colored, horizontal half-cylinder shaped roof. They were all over the island, some no bigger than a hundred square feet.

"No, there." The man pointed to where he'd pointed before.

Andreas walked over and sighted down the man's arm as if it were a rifle. Out of the brown he could just make out rocks forming a wall, and behind the wall a structure of some sort—also made out of rocks—part way up the hill. He'd never seen an unpainted stone church on Mykonos.

"Who do you work for?"

The man gave the name of a well-known contractor on the island and said he was told to come here today to start rebuilding the walls around the church. As far as he knew, he was the first one to work here. Someone was supposed to help him but hadn't shown up. In fact, he hadn't seen anyone else around all day, except for an SUV or two that drove by while he was waiting for the police.

When Andreas asked why he called, the man got very nervous. Andreas pressed him. "I know you don't want trouble, so just answer my questions. Why'd you call?"

He was literally shaking. "If I not tell what I find, someone else come here and tell police, then you blame me when find I was here."

A rational reason, Andreas thought, possibly too rational. He'd better keep a close eye on the guy until he saw the body. A fresh one would make this guy suspect numero uno.

"Okay, then. Where'd you find the body?"

"In the church."

"What were you doing in the church? I thought you were working on the walls." Alex looked like he might run. Andreas moved to block off an escape down the hill. Kouros must have sensed the same thing because he moved to cut off a run the other way. Andreas wondered whether he should unholster his gun. Not quite yet.

The man dropped to his knees and began shaking his head. "I know I did wrong, I know I did wrong."

Andreas' hand was now on his pistol. Kouros' already was out of the holster.

"I want to see what inside church. It so old and different from others." As if to redeem himself, he added, "but door not locked."

"What was inside?" Andreas' tone was chillingly serious.

The man seemed afraid to look up from the ground. "Icons, candles…" He trailed off.

Just what you'd expect to find in a church, thought Andreas. "What else?"

No answer.

In a voice of unmistakable, ultimate authority Andreas said, "What else?"

The man was breathing quickly. "There a stone on the floor." He paused. "I want to see what under it."

Andreas and Kouros looked at each other. He saw Kouros immediately relax, smile at him, and holster his weapon. Even Andreas had to fight back a laugh. This poor bastard obviously didn't know much about island churches. Cremation was forbidden in the Greek Orthodox faith, and there wasn't enough cemetery space on most islands—even the mainland—for permanent burial under ground. So, the dead were buried in a cemetery only for three or four years. Then their bones were dug up and cleaned as part of a ritual before finally being interred in either the wall or under a floor slab in a family church—assuming the family had a church. Otherwise, they were stored in a building at the cemetery.

Alex probably was expecting to find some secret buried treasure and instead got the scare of his life when he opened a burial crypt.

Andreas wished he'd been there to see his face. Ah, what the hell, he thought; we've come this far and the guy did call us. Let's just play it out. "Okay. Why don't you just show us what you found."

The climb took about ten minutes for Andreas and Kouros, about six for Alex. No question who was in better shape for scrambling up hillsides, though Andreas tried to convince himself he was taking a bit longer to enjoy the view. And what a view it was. Each shade-of-brown hill faded into the next slightly darker rise until only a haze of retreating, graceful curves remained to vanish into a sapphire sea and slightly lighter sky. Salt-wind driven fragrances of wild rosemary, savory, and thyme seasoned the air. Whoever chose this site for looking out upon eternity knew what he was doing, thought Andreas.

From up here, he could see that the church was a testament to ancient craftsmanship in natural stone. But this was not an antiquities tour, and Andreas had a lot of work to do back in the office—boring things, but still things. He told Alex to lead the way inside.

Alex pushed open the unpainted wooden door. As usual for a church, the door faced west, toward the setting sun, and the altar at the other end faced east, and the rising sun. That meant there'd be no direct sunlight through the front door until late afternoon, but there was enough light to see. They followed him inside.

The church was smaller than it seemed from outside, prob-ably only about eight feet wide by fifteen feet long, including the small separated space in the rear reserved for the priest. Each side wall had a tiny, tightly shuttered window opening. Looming above them was the cylindrical dome. At its highest point this one looked no more than fifteen feet from the floor. The floor was made of some sort of hard-packed, dirtlike material, but not dirt. Probably ground seashells. A delicately engraved slab of white marble about four and a half feet long by two and a half feet wide sat flush with the floor, centered lengthwise in the middle of the main chamber. Obviously, Alex had taken the time to put it back in place.

As Alex had said, the interior of the church was neat and clean, with icons and candles in all the appropriate places. Andreas thought some family friend or neighbor must be look-ing after the place—unless the spirits were taking care of it themselves. There was no way the church could be in this condition without someone regularly caring for it. It was time to end Alex's ordeal and get back to planning the next traffic stop.

Andreas pointed to the crypt. "Would you please open it up for us."

Alex started to shake again. "No, please, I can't. Please."

Andreas was reluctant to force the man, but then again, cops don't bend over in the presence of suspects—however unsuspected they may be. "Sit over there in the corner." He gestured to the far left. "Yianni, move the slab so we can get the hell out of here."

Kouros walked over and put his fingers on a corner edge of the slab. It was a lot heavier than it looked, and when it didn't budge at his initial tug Kouros gave a quick look over at Alex—which Andreas took for a sign of respect—then gripped and pulled hard enough to send the lid across the floor and crashing into the wall. Neither man bothered to check for damage. They were too busy gagging at the stench from the decomposing body beneath the slab.

Chapter Two

Catia Vanden Haag was not concerned; just put off. Her only child, Annika, was away on holiday, and she'd heard from her just once since Catia and her husband returned home to the Netherlands after attending Annika's graduation ceremonies at Yale University. It was by postcard on her arrival in London to join her boyfriend, Peter, for the start of their six-week backpacking adventure through Italy and Greece—"Having a great time, glad you're not here." Catia knew her daughter well enough to know her note explained everything—she was too busy doing God knows what with her boyfriend to think of her poor mother.

A tendency to focus with single-minded determination on the matter at hand to the exclusion of everything else was a trait Annika inherited from her Dutch diplomat father. Catia smiled as she thought of a trait or two she'd passed on: the Greek passion for doing God knows what—and the physical stamina to recover afterward. Catia well remembered her own days of flitting through summers with boys in her native Greece. She was not worried one bit about Annika. Sooner or later she'd get a call.

It came that afternoon, but not from Annika.

Peter's father was calling to apologize.

"For what?" Catia had no idea what he was talking about.

"Peter told me what happened."

Catia felt the anxiety before knowing why. "Richard, what are you saying?"

"I just spoke to him in London and—"

It was so unlike her to interrupt. "In London? But they're in Italy...or Greece...or..." She realized she had no idea where they were.

"I thought that too, that's why I was so surprised when he called and told me he wasn't."

"He?" Catia's free hand instinctively went to her throat.

"Yes, that's why I'm calling. I couldn't believe my son would be so stupid as to allow your daughter to travel on holiday alone, no matter what the reason."

Catia didn't know what to say, so she said the obvious: "Why aren't they together?"

"I'm embarrassed to say, he won't tell me. All he said was they aren't traveling together and she's all right."

Her control was back and her voice abrupt. "Where's my daughter, Richard?"

There was surprise in his voice. "Haven't you spoken with her?"

"Not since she left for London."

He paused. "Peter doesn't know."

"Then how can he possibly know she's all right?" Her tone was angry and dismissive, but she didn't care.

"Catia, I'm sorry, I don't know what to say." His voice was sincere, but that wouldn't help find Annika.

Catia was silent for a moment, then asked, "Do you have your son's telephone number?" Her anger kept her from saying the boy's name.

"Yes," Richard said, and gave it to her. "Catia, I...I—"

She cut him off again. "I have to get off now, but thank you for calling to tell us."

"I really am sorry."

"Goodbye."

◇◇◇

It took Andreas only an instant to recover from the surprise of finding a body where only bones should be. He pulled his gun and ordered the wide-eyed Alex outside; then pushed a green-faced Kouros out behind him, yelling at him not to dare puke in the middle of a crime scene.

Andreas was pretty sure the laborer wasn't the killer—the corpse wasn't fresh—but he wasn't one for taking chances with murder suspects, and anyone who finds a body is a suspect until proven otherwise. He told Kouros to use the car radio to notify Syros of the body and to hold Alex at the station for further questioning but not to treat him as a murder suspect quite yet. In other words, no blowtorch and days of pain in a closet style interrogation. Andreas said he'd stay at the church until the Syros investigators arrived—but to leave Alex's motorcycle just in case he needed it.

Neither Andreas nor Kouros raised the obvious: another officer could be there in ten minutes to secure the scene and free up Andreas. Nor did Kouros ask what his chief planned to do out here all alone while waiting for the men from Syros. He just silently walked the handcuffed suspect down the hill, put him in the backseat, and got into the car.

Andreas watched them drive off and turned to study the crime scene—his crime scene.

He stood by the door and looked carefully down the hill. Nothing seemed out of place. Not a bush or a weed crushed by a tire or a single telltale sign of dragged or carried weight. Just endless gray-green-to-brown dry brush and brown rocky dirt mixed with wild-goat and donkey crap. The only tracks were Kouros', Alex's and his, and Alex's tracks bore out his story that he'd worked on the wall and walked to the church from there.

Andreas looked up toward the top of the hill and slowly scanned it just as carefully, moving his eyes back and forth in sections. He saw nothing unusual. He didn't expect to, because he couldn't imagine why someone would haul a body over the top of a mountain to get here. There was no more cover going that way than climbing up from the road below—and you'd be visible on the mountain for a lot longer to a lot more people if you did. Anyway, he expected Syros to go over every inch of the mountain looking for clues. Better chance at hitting the lottery, if you asked him.

As far as Andreas was concerned there were two conceivable explanations for the lack of tracks—and one was strictly for James Bond fans. It involved a helicopter dropping a body at a deserted church rather than into the deepest part of the sea. Not a chance.

No tracks meant only one thing to him: the body had been here for at least two weeks. Andreas had arrived in Mykonos the day after an unheard of early-June rainstorm. More like a deluge, he was told. Whatever tracks there were—and there must have been some—were wiped out by that rain. A bit of luck for the killer. Any other signs left on that hillside were long gone by now in the rough, northerly winds that regularly battered this part of the island.

If there was a clue, Andreas knew it had to be inside the church. He scanned the ground outside the door for tracks, scuff marks, any clue to how the body got there. Nothing but footprints he recognized. To be thorough, he checked outside the windows but, as he expected, found nothing there. The sun still wasn't throwing much light inside, and he thought about opening the shutters but decided against disturbing the scene any more than he already had. Even in this light, though, he could see the body. It was bent on its side, its back to him, bald and naked.

Andreas took a small flashlight out of his pocket and scanned the floor. He didn't want to step on anything important. He took three careful steps to the edge of the crypt by the front of the body and knelt down, all the time breathing only through his mouth. That cut down on the stench. He could never get used to that smell—and never wanted to.

The crypt was about four feet deep but about a foot longer and wider than the slab covering it. It was lined with the same sort of gray and red granite that made up the church walls. The body was crammed into a too small space for its height on top of a pile of bones—human bones. For an instant he forgot not to breathe through his nose and gagged on the stench. He turned toward the door to find a fresher breath of air, then back to study the body.

It was taller than five feet, probably closer to six, and slim. Because of the size and bald head, he'd thought from the door it was a man, but now he saw it was a woman; and her head was shaved, not bald. She just looked bald from a distance because the stubble of hair was a very light color, probably blond. Her ankles were bound together by thick hemp twine. A separate piece tied her hands crossed at the wrists, then looped a dozen times around her body, pinning her forearms and hands flat across her body at the bottom of her chest before ending leash-like about her neck.

He wanted to examine her face but didn't think he'd see much without moving the body or getting into the crypt. He couldn't do either until forensics had photographed, videotaped, and catalogued everything. He braced himself with one hand against the edge of the crypt and, with his flashlight in the other, held his breath and leaned in to see what he could.

Her eyes and mouth were closed. Nothing particularly unusual about that—perhaps the only thing so far that wasn't. As he lifted himself away from her face his flashlight caught a bit of white at one nostril. He leaned back in. It wasn't at the nostril, it was in it. It looked like cotton, and it wasn't in one nostril, it was in both.

Andreas got to his feet and walked outside. Like most Greeks, he smoked, but he liked to think he only did when stressed. He lit up. This was not a simple murder. There was a message to this one. He'd seen murders with messages before but not like this. This message was meant to remain secret to everyone but the sender.

He knew the word to describe this sort of preparation—the religious location, shaved head, bound feet, clasped hands, naked body, and whatever in the nostrils—but he couldn't say it until he had more proof. Suggesting there'd been a ritual murder on Mykonos wouldn't get him any more compliments from the mayor, or any closer to his old job in Athens. He would just wait for Syros to investigate and let them break the bad news to the town fathers.

He finished his cigarette and decided to have another look inside. Perhaps something about the church held a clue to why the killer chose this spot. Andreas wasn't very religious, but like virtually every Greek, he was Orthodox and he knew the basics. Everything looked perfectly normal. The candles were in the right places, as were the required four icons: the Blessed Virgin, Jesus, the archangels and the saint after which the church was named. He didn't recognize that icon and leaned forward to read the name. Saint Calliope. If he remembered correctly, she was a young woman tortured and put to death for her commitment to Christianity. That would fit.

He went outside again and sat in the shade of the church wall, waiting. Later, he heard the sirens. The boys from Syros were here.

◇◇◇

Although the call from Peter's father triggered her Greek temper, on balance Catia actually felt more relieved than worried by what she'd heard. She'd never liked Peter and had told Annika so more than once. She'd hoped the relationship would end when he left Yale to study in London but it hadn't. Something about him grated on her. She described him to her husband, Schuyler, as the quintessential pretentious Athenian braggart, consumed by appearance over substance. He pointed out to his wife that Peter came from an old-line English family and that bourgeois was a French word not confined to Greeks. She preferred her description.

Catia was sure their breakup explained why she'd not heard from her daughter. Annika didn't take well to "I told you so" scenarios—even if the actual words were never uttered. Still, Schuyler was right; a young woman should not be backpacking across Europe alone. She'd learned to accept in silence her daughter's assorted injuries and broken bones as part of the price for raising an independent, athletically gifted child. She no longer even winced when Annika described such things as hang gliding and skydiving as "too routine." But for Catia's own peace of mind, whether Annika wanted to talk to her mother today or not, she would have to. It had been too long—far longer than most mothers would tolerate.

She dialed Annika's mobile and waited for her voice to say "Please leave a message for Annika at the beep." Annika rarely answered her phone. That was a practice she picked up in college to cut down on distractions from studying. Every few hours she checked her messages and called back those she wanted to—or had to. Catia intended to leave a message, putting her at the very top of Annika's "must-call" list. Finally, voice mail picked up, but instead of her daughter's voice, she heard, "Sorry, this voice mail box is full and cannot accept additional messages. Please try again later." She tried again, and again, each time getting the same message. That was not at all like Annika.

She decided to call Peter in London.

"Hello."

Catia tried sounding warm and charming. "Hello, Peter, it's Catia Vanden Haag. How are you?"

He spoke abruptly. "My father called you, didn't he?"

So much for civility, she thought. "Yes, he did."

His voice became icy and distant. That old pretentious tone. "I'm sorry, but there's nothing I have to say."

"Excuse me, young man, but I expect a bit more respect from you than I'm receiving at the moment." She knew how to sound like a senior career diplomat's wife when necessary.

His voice wavered a bit. "I meant no disrespect, Mrs. Vanden Haag, I simply think that whatever is said to you on the subject should be Annika's decision, not mine."

That answer did not assuage her, but she sensed that if she got any testier, he'd probably hang up. "Peter, I haven't heard from Annika since she left to meet you in London. You certainly must appreciate that I'm worried."

He paused. "Yes, I do, but honestly, Mrs. Vanden Haag, I haven't spoken with Annika since she left, and I don't know where she is."

"Do you have any idea who may know where she is or how I can reach her? I've tried calling her cell, but all I get is a recording that her voice mail box is full."

"No, but the reason you can't reach her is she forgot to take her phone." Again he paused. "She was very angry when she left. She wouldn't talk to me, just threw her things in her backpack and walked out. I didn't find her phone until later. It was turned off and I left it off."

Catia shut her eyes to compose herself. If Annika called her phone to find where she'd left it, there'd be no answer. Was he just stupid or vindictive? Greek men were legendary for screaming at the drop of a hat; it was a cultural trait that serendipitously taught most Greek women patience. She let out a long, silent breath. "Thank you; and if you think of anything that might help us find her, please call me. And please, send me Annika's phone—I'll give you our FedEx number."

When she hung up, the word in her mind was asshole. Not very ladylike she knew, but accurate.

Her daughter's incommunicado jaunt around Europe must stop at once. No matter what the reason. The first thing to do was call Annika's friends and find how to reach her. Surely they'd know. No, she thought. The first thing to do was tell her husband. Oh boy.

◇◇◇

It was a virtually deserted, almost impassable road, but all three police cars arrived with sirens blaring. So much for keeping things quiet, thought Andreas. They're attracting the whole island. Sure enough, a gray Jeep Grand Cherokee and a beat-up black Fiat sedan pulled up behind them. Two guys got out of the Fiat and started up the hill before the investigators had their equipment out of the cars.

Andreas shook his head. Greeks—they were more curious than cats. He yelled at the two to stay on the road. They kept coming, as if they didn't hear or didn't understand. He yelled to one of his officers to arrest them if they didn't turn back immediately. That stopped them. He heard them mumbling questions about his parentage, but they were retreating back to the road.

There were eight men in the police cars: Kouros, three other Mykonos officers, and four strangers dressed in jackets and ties—in ninety degree heat. These guys were going to be a pain in the ass, he could just tell. He yelled to Kouros and another local officer to help the investigators with their equipment and told the other two to keep the curious off the hillside. He also told them to get the names, addresses, and phone numbers of everyone who stopped to watch—starting with the two in the Fiat. Andreas wanted them to know that he was particularly proud of his parentage.

Andreas took a schoolboy-like joy in watching the jacketed cops labor up the hill in twice the time it had taken him. It wasn't because of the equipment they carried but because three of the strangers clearly were deferring to the fourth—and much stouter—man's difficulty with the climb. At least now Andreas knew who was in charge. By the time they reached the church, the heavy one was sweating like the proverbial pig but still wore his jacket and tie. He stopped about five yards from Andreas and looked back as if reviewing his path. Andreas knew he was trying to catch his breath. He took that moment to step forward and introduce himself.

"Welcome to Mykonos."

The stout man turned toward him and nodded. He said nothing, just kept trying to breathe.

"I'm Andreas Kaldis."

The man nodded again and was able to say, "I know." He was about a half foot shorter than Andreas, with bushy, dark brown hair. From the almost pure gray of his eyebrows, Andreas guessed his hair was dyed.

Andreas was starting to enjoy this but decided he'd better stop. No reason to antagonize the man unnecessarily.

The man said, "I knew your father, good man."

That caught Andreas off guard. His father had been on the secret police force during the Junta or the Regime of the Colonels or the Dictatorship, depending on your point of view. Most cops avoided open discussions of those seven years and certainly wouldn't risk offering compliments on someone from that part of Greek police history to a stranger, even a son. Especially a son of his father.

Against his original instincts, Andreas thought he might actually like this guy. "Thank you for saying that," he said and extended his hand.

Taking off his sunglasses, the other man reached out and shook his hand. "Tassos Stamatos, chief homicide investigator for the Cyclades."

Andreas had heard of him, a real old-timer. One of those guys who'd never retire and had the political connections to keep his job. He probably was about sixty, but strangely, his weight and short, bulldog build made him look ten years younger. Andreas decided there was no need to mention his homicide background to Tassos. It seemed pretty clear he already knew it. Politically connected cops knew that sort of stuff. It's how they kept off the wrong toes.

"So, what do we have here, Kaldis?" Tassos asked, his tone crisply official.

Andreas took the use of his last name as force of habit more than an effort to show who was in charge. "A body in a crypt, female, probably between fifteen and thirty, Caucasian, light-colored hair, dead a few weeks I'd say." He stopped.

"That's it?" Tassos seemed surprised.

"No, not at all," said Andreas.

A glint of anger came to Tassos' voice. "What's this, a little test for the boys from the islands?"

So he knew Andreas' history. He tried putting the conversation on a more personal footing. "Not at all, Tassos, I just thought it might be better for you to look at this with fresh eyes and reach your own conclusions."

Tassos stared at Andreas for a moment. He seemed to be deciding whether this was just another—albeit former—Athens hot-shot putting on the local cops. "All right, have it your way. Show me what we've got."

Andreas pointed him toward the open door and watched as Tassos studied the room from the doorway, just as Andreas had, then carefully approached and methodically examined the body with his flashlight, just as Andreas had. Tassos walked past Andreas without saying a word. Once outside, he told the three men with him, "I want everything in there recorded and rerecorded. Get an ambulance here. We're taking the body and everything else in there back to Syros." Then he walked away from the church.

From their equipment, Andreas could tell one of the three was with the coroner's office and another was a crime scene technician. The third probably was one of Tassos' investigators. All three went inside. Andreas told them to let him know when they were ready to inspect the body—and told Kouros to keep an eye on them to make sure they did.

Tassos was sitting on a low stone wall in the shade of a wild fig tree looking at the view. Andreas sat next to him. A soft breeze was blowing in off the sea, mixing the scents of wildflowers and herbs.

"There are no views in the world like the ones from our Greek islands, Andreas." A bridge had been built.

"It's eternal," said Andreas.

Neither spoke for a moment.

"What are we going to do about this?" Tassos' voice was flat and serious.

"Do we have a choice?" Andreas used the same tone.

"A murder in paradise is bad. A tourist murdered in paradise is worse. But something like this…is unthinkable." Tassos was shaking his head.

"Why do you say she's a tourist?"

Tassos looked down and kicked at the dirt. "In thirty years on Syros I've only seen a few Mykonian or other local woman that tall, and she's not one of them."

Andreas smiled at the obvious—and Tassos' insight. "What's on your mind?"

Tassos looked down. "Something neither of us wants to say, and no one anywhere in Greece will want to hear."

"That's about what I thought."

"So, I guess we won't call it what it is, just use the clues to catch the bastard who did it." Tassos kicked at the dirt again.

"As long as we catch the bad guy," Andreas said.

"Yeah, as long as we catch the bad guy."

Andreas picked up a bit of something else in Tassos' tone. "What's bothering you?"

Tassos looked up and stared out toward the sea. "One summer, about ten years ago, an American girl working at a bar here in town didn't show up for her shift. A girlfriend went looking for her and found her room covered in blood but no body. Brutal thing. Another young woman, a Scandinavian, disappeared around the same time. The whole island went crazy."

A small lizard, as brown as the dirt, scurried out from the base of the wall, past their feet, and into the shade of a wild thistle. Tassos didn't seem to notice.

"We tied the American to an Irishman here on holiday. He'd met her at the bar. He was a convicted child killer released from an English prison after twenty-five years." Tassos paused long enough to shake his head, a disgusted look on his face. "On humanitarian grounds, because of a bad heart. We caught up with him by the Bulgarian border and brought him back to Mykonos for questioning. Had to get him drunk to talk—his heart wouldn't stand up to how I wanted to interrogate the bastard." He didn't have to explain to Andreas what he meant by that.

"He finally showed us where he'd buried the American's body—over there by Paradise Beach." He gestured south. "But he wouldn't say what happened to the other one. He refused to talk about it. Never denied it, never admitted it." Tassos took out his cigarettes and offered one to Andreas. They shared a match.

"We had the military, police cadets, Boy Scouts, farmers—anyone willing to help—out looking for the other woman's body. Never thought we'd find her, but we did."

Tassos took a drag on his cigarette. "She was in a shallow grave, right by a road not far from here—almost like she was meant to be found there, to end the search. The Irishman still wouldn't admit to killing her but everyone from the mayor on down wanted to pin it on him, mark both murders solved and move on to other things. One killer here was enough bad publicity—no reason to suggest another one might still be lurking around."

He paused to puff again. "Besides, if someone else did it, it had to be a tourist long gone by now who wouldn't dare come back—at least that's what the mayor said."

Tassos flicked the ash from his cigarette. "Before the Irishman could come to trial and maybe say which murders were his—and which weren't—he committed suicide in custody." He looked directly at Andreas. "I took that for a 'case closed.'"

Andreas shrugged. "We have to put up with that sort of cover-up shit all the time. Politicians don't like loose ends."

Tassos smiled. "Funny you should say 'loose ends.' The American was cut up, raped, and beaten to death in one place then buried in another, cleverly hidden location. The Scandinavian was full of crystal meth—the 'let's have sex drug'—but otherwise unmarked and died of suffocation—buried alive—under a virtual 'find me here' sign."

Bitching at bureaucrats was a hallowed police pastime, but that didn't seem to be what this was about. "How's all that tie in to this?" asked Andreas.

Tassos stared off at the horizon again. "Never thought the Irishman did the Scandinavian." Without looking back, he pointed toward the church with his cigarette. "She was shaved and tied up just like the one back there."

Chapter Three

Ambassador Vanden Haag's initial response to his wife's telephone description of their daughter's travel situation was predictable: ask the Queen to call out the marines. Then he took a more measured approach. His office contacted American Express for a list of Annika's recent charges. That should tell him where she was. But American Express wouldn't release the information to his office, to him, or to the American ambassador he asked to call on his behalf. It took some ingenuity from an old CIA friend to get the information, but he got it.

It showed no recent activity. The last charges were in Italy, indicating she had traveled from Sicily along the eastern mainland north past the heel of the boot. They stopped in Bari, with a payment to Superfast Ferries. He went online and found that it served the North Sea, Baltic, and Adriatic, but from that part of Italy the line had only two destinations: Igoumenitsa and Patras—both in western Greece. From there Annika could have caught any number of ferries to any number of places—or traveled some other way.

No doubt she was in Greece. That explained why the Amex charges stopped. Many businesses in Greece wouldn't accept the card—too slow paying, they claimed. Annika probably was using another credit card. He'd try to get that information tomorrow, but now at least they knew where she was—sort of—and the news was reassuring. She'd been to Greece more times than he could count, was fluent in Greek, and in a pinch, her uncle and aunt were there to help. Catia's brother was Greece's deputy minister for Public Order—the country's equivalent of the U.S. Department of Homeland Security. Catia would make a few calls tomorrow, and they'd know where Annika was in no time.

It was comforting to know their daughter was in a safe place.

◇◇◇

Andreas stood quietly listening to Tassos tell his three men where to place the lights in the church. The five of them were crowded together around the crypt when the lights went on, the videotaping began, and the coroner started his examination. It was not pretty, but the smell was worse—and more than a match for the drops of menthol gel on Andreas' upper lip.

The autopsy and serious forensic testing would take place at the coroner's lab on Syros, but there were crucial observations to be made here. The coroner spoke loudly and distinctly to assure that what he said was accurately recorded.

"Bruises on body are consistent with the shape and location of nearby bones," as if she had thrashed against them before she died. He couldn't be sure, but "eyes and mouth appear closed after death." "Rigor mortis appears cause of shift of body" onto her right side—from flat on her back, hands clasped by her chest.

"Cotton, probably tampons, in each nostril, will verify whether same in anus and vagina and—"

"Excuse me, I don't mean to interrupt," Andreas said, startled, "but aren't you surprised at finding tampons in her nose? And what's this about looking for 'same in anus and vagina'?"

The coroner did not look away from the body. "I both am and am not surprised. I'm surprised at finding it here, but not in a dead body." He was talking in riddles—like an academic lecturer.

Andreas hated the type but knew they were necessary. "Do me a favor, just tell me what the fuck you're talking about."

The coroner looked at Tassos.

"Costas, please tell the man what he wants to know." Tassos spoke like a man used to being in charge.

Without changing his tone, the coroner said, "Greeks bury their dead immediately and without embalming, but there is a viewing. In order to keep bodily fluids from leaking into the casket, cotton is shoved . . ."

Andreas knew about that part.

"These days, instead of cotton, tampons often are used. How many depends upon the size of the orifice."

"What about the throat and ears?" Andreas asked.

"Not in the ears, and the throat would depend upon the cause of death, but generally not. In this body, I saw nothing in the throat."

"Are you saying she was prepared for burial?" asked Andreas.

"From the position of her feet together, hands clasped at the chest—though hers actually are bound to the body just below the chest—eyes and mouth shut, I'd say yes, with one distinct difference."

"What's that?" He'd play along with the professor.

"I'm virtually certain this was done while she was alive."

"Sort of like a ritual." It was Tassos' investigator. He seemed to be showing off for the crowd. Andreas had better tell Tassos to shut him up. But he didn't have to.

"That will be enough of that sort of talk—from you and anyone else." Tassos stared at the faces around the crypt, the tone of his warning unequivocally menacing. "Costas, how long before you'll have forensics back on this?"

"How quickly do you want them?"

Tassos didn't respond, just stared at him.

Costas spoke quickly, nervously. "I'll call Syros and have them ready to start as soon as we get back with the body."

"And the bones?" added Tassos.

"Yes, of course. I'll have something for you by tomorrow."

"What do you think the chances are of a quick ID on the body?" Andreas' question was directed to the coroner, but Tassos answered in a tone Andreas knew was meant to make clear he was in charge of the forensic side of this investigation.

"I doubt she's local, but even if she is, depends on whether she's reported as missing. If not, as soon as we get Costas' results we'll check with Athens, and"—he was shaking his head—"probably the rest of the world, to get an ID on this one."

Andreas knew the most they could hope for was that someone somewhere had reported her missing because if no one cared enough to file a missing-person report, there was virtually no chance—outside of luck—of identifying her. Andreas couldn't imagine any police force in the world starting an investigation into a "do you know this body" request without—at the very least—knowing it somehow tied in to their jurisdiction. Each had too many of its own problems to deal with.

"Sounds to me like we should start looking at this end." Andreas was claiming his territory.

Tassos smiled. "I can just imagine all the screaming phone calls you'll be getting once you start flashing photographs of a dead body around Mykonos at the height of tourist season."

Andreas smiled back. "I thought I'd put up posters along Matogianni Street with her picture and your telephone number."

Tassos laughed and shook his head. "Mykonos and its politics shall be all yours on this one, my friend."

Territories were settled. They smiled at each other.

"May I get back to work?" asked the coroner.

"Yes," said Tassos, "and be sure you're your usual, thorough self. We need to know everything about how this woman died ASAP—and who she is."

Andreas wondered who else might want to know.

◇◇◇

Schuyler was right. Catia was relieved to know Annika was in Greece. But that made her a bit angry. Not at her daughter, at her relatives. How could they not have called and told her they'd seen Annika? Then again, how were they to know she hadn't spoken with her daughter in weeks? She took a deep breath and told herself to relax. She'd call Greece, and her relatives would find Annika.

◇◇◇

Quite a crowd had gathered at the bottom of the hill. An ambulance winding its way through Mykonos back roads was irresistible to the locals. It meant someone was ill, injured, or dead, and they wanted to know who. Andreas' officers were asking questions of everyone who stopped, but that didn't discourage a soul. The crowd knew by now there was a dead body in the church at the top of the hill and everyone was staying to watch it all. Cell phones were blaring out the news. Andreas always was amazed how fast word gets out. He wondered how it happened this time.

He just hoped Tassos could keep his men from any more mention of rituals. He had to be careful about that sort of talk from his own cops too. All it took was one trying to impress someone and all of Greece would be shouting "ritual murder on Mykonos."

Come to think of it, he was surprised an Athens TV crew wasn't here by now. There always seemed to be at least one somewhere on Mykonos during tourist season. TV viewers loved stuff knocking sexy, upscale places filled with rich people, especially on Mykonos. A murdered body being hauled down a hill out of an old Mykonos church was just the sort of story they'd run over and over again—not the kind of TV coverage Andreas was hoping after less than a month on the job.

Perhaps he'd get lucky and they'd be off catching live celebrity bodies on a beach somewhere and this dead one would be down the hill and off the island before they could film it. That's when he realized that most of the people on that road probably had cell phones with cameras—some even take video. Damn technology. He decided to leave the rest of the forensic examination to Tassos. He'd let the crowd know anyone using a cell phone camera would be arrested for interfering with a police investigation. Who knew—maybe the threat would actually work. It was worth a try.

The walk down was a lot easier than the climb up, but he took it slow. He wanted another glimpse of nature's take on blissful eternity after the time he'd just spent inside with the grim here and now. He looked straight up at the sky: bright blue, running off to almost white where it met the sea. It reminded him of the day of his father's funeral, on that hillside north of Athens. He hadn't thought of that day in years. He had only been eight. It must have been Tassos' mention of his father that brought it back. He shook his head and tried to think other thoughts.

When he reached the road he called his men together and told them what he wanted done about the cell phones; then he asked if their questioning had turned up anything interesting. Not really. He decided to talk to some of the curious personally—starting with the two men in the black Fiat.

The two had learned their lesson, or at least had enough sense to act as if they had. Both were very respectful to the chief of police. One was Alex's cousin and the other his friend. They said all three worked for the same contractor and, after Alex found the body, he first called the police on his mobile and then his cousin. They couldn't find the place until they heard the sirens and followed the police cars.

Andreas wondered how many others Alex had called. At least now he knew how word got out about a body in the church.

The guy in the gray Grand Cherokee was the contractor they worked for. He'd been sitting in it since he got there, running the air conditioner and watching. Andreas crossed in front of the Jeep and walked to the driver's door. The contractor never turned to look at him, just kept staring up the mountain as if Andreas wasn't there. Andreas knocked on the window with the back of his hand. The contractor still didn't turn to look, just pressed the button to roll down the window.

Andreas knew of him. He came from a very old Mykonian family, had once been mayor and now was the most successful contractor on the island. He'd grown very rich on the island's building boom and was said to believe his statue should be erected in the town square next to—and a bit larger than—Mykonos' legendary heroine of Greece's 1821 struggle for independence, Mantó Mavroyénous.

"Andreas Kaldis, chief of police."

No answer.

Andreas wanted to drag him out of the car and bang his head on the hood. "Mr. Pappas, I presume."

Slowly the man turned his head to face Andreas. "You are correct."

Now Andreas would settle for just ripping off the guy's sunglasses. "Would you mind telling me what you're doing here," then choked out words he sensed he had to say: "I mean no disrespect, but I can't help wondering why a man of your stature in the community is sitting in his vehicle at a murder site."

The man paused. "One of my men found the body and called his cousin—he works for me, too. His cousin called me, and I followed the police here."

Andreas had guessed right: kissing ass would make this pompous bastard talk.

"Thank you very much. Can you tell me why your man was working here?"

"He was repairing fence walls around the church. A client of mine is planning to expand the church's facilities."

In other words, someone was paying Pappas to use his influence to get around the building ban. With the right permits you were allowed "slight" improvements to existing churches. This church probably would be expanded "slightly" into a mega-villa dwarfing the original church. Pappas wasn't known for small-time jobs.

"May I ask you who owns the property?"

Again Pappas paused. "He lives in America. His family's from Mykonos, but they moved to Athens generations ago. My client started coming here a couple of years ago. Before then, no one from his family had set foot on the property since the war."

Andreas took that to mean World War II.

"He inherited the property surrounding the church. He wants to restore and renovate his family's ancestral church."

Andreas assumed he was hearing the pitch in the application for a building permit. "Thank you, Mr. Pappas. May I have the name of your client?"

"I'll have to check with him."

Andreas wanted to pull out Pappas' tongue, but instead, he held his own. "Thank you. I would appreciate any help you can give me. By the way, I noticed someone must be taking care of the church. Do you know who that is?"

Pappas smiled. "I know you're not from Mykonos. Otherwise you wouldn't be asking that question."

Andreas thought maybe he could grab him by his tongue, wrap it around his sunglasses, and then beat him against the hood. He forced a laugh. "You obviously have me at a disadvantage."

Pappas gave a self-important wave of his finger at Andreas. "Just remember who helped you, Chief."

Andreas kept smiling.

"Some say today there are 2750 churches on Mykonos. The church says it's more like half that number. Fifty years ago we only had about as many churches as there are days in the year—365." Andreas smiled and nodded appreciatively at Pappas' concern that Andreas might not know the number of days in a year.

"With that many churches and so few priests, some churches in deserted places like this"—he waved—"with no family members or neighbors to look after them, fell apart and mass was no longer said in them."

Andreas kept smiling, wishing he'd get to the point, but the lecturer was not about to give up his stage.

"Then along came the savior of all neglected churches on our island. He makes repairs, cleans them, replaces candles and icons—if they've been stolen—and says mass. He says it's his mission to protect them. The mayor even gave him a plaque for his work. A little weird—maybe even crazy—but harmless."

For Andreas, the word *harmless* hung in the air.

"Why do you say harmless?"

Pappas smiled again. "You really don't know, do you?" He paused for obvious effect. "He's a priest—not one of ours, Anglican I think—who's been coming here forever. He's from England and he lives over that hill." He pointed up toward the church. "In the only house on an out-of-the-way beach. Says he likes the solitude—and that every morning he can watch the sunrise from his front door. If you ask me, I think he gets more of a kick out of watching the ancient Mykonos tradition of local boys screwing tourist girls on his beach at sunrise." He laughed.

Andreas felt the need for a cigarette. A priest involved in a ritual murder—in a church. That's all he needed to make this the Greek TV media event of the year. He couldn't wait to pass the good news on to Tassos.

◇◇◇

It was late afternoon by the time the ambulance and the Syros contingent headed back to the port. Miraculously, no film crew showed up. It must have been a very busy news day somewhere—or one hell of a party—Andreas thought. Thank God for small blessings. Which got him thinking of the priest. He wondered if he should wait until forensic results were back before talking to him, but decided to try finding him for some light questioning. Just ask him what you'd expect to be asked if you've looked after a place where a dead body was found. He'd have other questions for him later. He was sure of that.

Andreas took one of the police cars and drove southwest along the narrow dirt road winding up onto the mountain with the radar station. Soccer-ball-sized rocks marked the edge of the road—and a straight plunge over the rocky, arid mountainside. Far down and off to the left he caught a glimpse of green and a small beach tucked alongside a crystal blue sea; that was where he wanted to be. He followed the road as it fell down along the mountain toward the sea. Just before winding back up again toward the radar station, a rutted dirt path dropped off to the left. That's where Pappas told him to turn.

It was scruffy and overgrown and looked barely passable except to motorcycles. Andreas bumped and battered his way down, all the while wondering if he'd have to make an embarrassing call for a tow truck to get out. Once at sea level the road smoothed out and he drove for another fifty yards alongside a phalanx of bottle-shaped, gray granite boulders carefully aligned at attention—to keep SUVs from driving onto the beach, he guessed. Someone very strong and determined had gone to a lot of trouble doing that.

Andreas parked at the end of the road and started walking toward the house on the far side of the beach. He remembered he hadn't told his office where he was going. He should have used the radio in the car. He tried his cell phone—no signal. Just his luck to be at one of the few places on the island still without service. He kept going. He walked along waves of light brown sand that seemed to rise and fall in pattern with the deeper brown, rocky ridgelines above the beach. The sand was of the pebbly sort, not the fine sugarlike stuff on the south-side beaches. The winds on this side blew away everything but the hardiest.

He noticed the beach was set so close to the eastern side of the mountain that it must be in shadows several hours before sunset. That must explain why this place was never popular with the late-rising Mykonos crowd.

He stopped about twenty feet from the front door of a traditional round-edged—but tiny—one story, box-shaped Mykonian house. There seemed to be no one around. Not a soul, unless a steady five-mile-per-hour northeast wind counted as a spirit. Suddenly, a man bolted around the far side of the house. He was completely covered in white and moving quickly toward Andreas with a rifle-shaped object in his hand. Andreas' right hand instinctively went to his holster.

"Welcome, friend. I'm Father Paul." The man spoke in Greek and seemed unaffected by Andreas' lurch toward his gun. He stopped and put out his hand.

Andreas took his hand off his gun but did not extend it. Instead, he nodded and said, "Hello." So far, it looked like Pappas was right about the guy. Definitely weird. What Andreas had thought was a rifle was a long-handled brush contraption the priest must be using to whitewash the thick exterior walls of his house—and himself, from the look of things. The man was wearing a pair of shorts, looked to weigh about one hundred-fifty pounds, five feet ten inches tall, and in terrific shape. Andreas guessed who'd moved those boulders.

"Andreas Kaldis, Father. I'm chief of police."

"Oh, yes, I've heard of you. Sorry, but I've got to finish this last bit before I completely lose the light," and off he ran to cover some spots by one of the small windows—and himself even more.

Andreas decided to wait until the man finished before asking any questions. He wanted to deal with him on a friendly basis, and sensed to do that it would have to be on the priest's terms. Andreas walked to the edge of the water and did what everyone else on this island did with a few moments to kill—he stared out to sea. Again his thoughts turned to his father. Damn it, why did Tassos have to mention him?

He was reaching for a cigarette when Father Paul went racing past him into the water. Ripples of white trailed behind him until he disappeared beneath the surface where, quickly, a film of white percolated above him, like an escaping halo. He must have been under for more than a minute before surfacing. He dipped his head back into the water and rubbed vigorously at his hair to get out whatever remained of the whitewash. Andreas saw now that his hair was almost as white as the paint. He was probably in his sixties, though you'd never think that if his hair were dark.

Father Paul emerged from the water as if born anew—and just as naked. He was holding his shorts in his hands, wringing them out. "Yes, my son, what can I do for you?"

The first thing Andreas wanted to say was "Put on your shorts," but hey, this was Mykonos and he didn't want to do anything to spook the guy. "I understand you look after some of the old churches on the island."

"Every one that needs my care." He was smiling, still squeezing and still naked.

"How many are there?" Andreas asked, his voice friendly.

Like a loving father proud of his children, the priest did not give a number. Instead he named and described each one in detail. Andreas did not interrupt, just took out his notebook and wrote what he was told.

"Thank you, Father. That's quite impressive. I have some questions about the church on the other side of this mountain." He pointed up the hill.

"Ah, yes, my beloved Calliope." Andreas noticed that before saying her name, he put on his shorts. "How can I help you?"

"When's the last time you were up there?"

"June eighth."

Andreas was surprised at how quickly he answered.

"With all the churches you look after, how can you be so certain of the date?"

"It was her name day. I always conduct mass there on her name day."

Andreas should have known that. "Are you the one who cleaned it and put in the candles?"

"Yes, I do that the week before celebrating mass."

Andreas remembered that the night before the name day, there's a celebration dedicated to the saint and the souls of the family members whose bones are buried there—though it's more like a big party, with food, dancing, and music. "Was there a *panegyri*?"

He shook his head. "No, not up there. I'd be the only one. I went to a *panegyri* at a different church honoring Saint Calliope."

"How often do you visit that church?" Andreas pointed up the hill again.

Father Paul looked Andreas straight in the eye. "The same as all my churches, twice a year—once to fix it up and once to say mass. I wish I could go more often, but I have so many to take care of and I'm only here for two months a year."

"Which months?"

"It depends, but always July and sometimes June—like this year—and sometimes August."

"How long have you been taking care of them?"

His eyes hadn't moved. "Twenty years or so. I started after I built this place and came across poor, neglected Calliope. I realized at that moment there was a need for me to fill, that God had brought me here to take care of his neglected ones."

Andreas was getting an uneasy vibe from this guy but didn't want to show it. The man didn't seem curious in the least as to why the chief of police was out here asking him all these questions. No reason to make him think I'm suspicious, he thought—at least not until I've had the chance to check him out, and the forensics are back.

"Thank you, Father. I appreciate your cooperation."

The man extended his hand, and this time Andreas shook it. Father Paul turned and started back toward his house. "Oh, by the way." He kept walking as he talked. "There is one thing I'm curious about, Chief Kaldis."

Ah, here it comes, thought Andreas. "What is it, Father?"

"Why didn't you ask me about the body?"

◇◇◇

Andreas kept yelling at himself as he drove back to town. He'd screwed up. In trying not to seem suspicious he'd made it clear to the priest that he was. Father Paul might be without a phone, but he was not without friends. Several had stopped by earlier in the afternoon to tell him about the body in "his" church. The priest was not mad. Far from it. The more appropriate word was eccentric. He claimed to know nothing about the body, adding that he had no reason ever to disturb a burial crypt—and regarded even an attempt as a sacrilege.

Andreas left it at that. He knew he'd better prepare a lot better for his next round with Father Paul. No more questioning until he heard back from forensics or—God forbid—something else went wrong.

◇◇◇

The first call Catia made that morning was to her brother's wife, Lila, in Athens. Her daughter, Demetra, and Annika were like sisters. Catia could not imagine Annika going to Greece without seeing Demetra. Her sister-in-law hadn't spoken to Catia since before Annika's graduation and wouldn't let Catia say a thing until she'd heard all the details about that. Catia gave the hurried version and, before Lila could raise another subject, asked if she'd heard from Annika.

"Yes, the day she arrived in Greece. She called me for Demetra's cell phone number—to make plans to travel the islands together."

Catia hadn't realized how anxious she was until hearing her sister-in-law's words. She let out a deep sigh of relief and smiled. Her daughter had once more shown good judgment. "Do you know where they are?"

"I know Demetra is still in Milan. She's not through with her work-study semester at the fashion house there. I think they made plans to get together when she gets back."

Every anxious thought came rushing back. Catia struggled for control of her voice. "Do you have any idea where Annika may be?"

"No, but I'm sure Demetra does. Here, let me give you her mobile number."

When Catia called no one answered and as instructed she left a message for Demetra. Something was wrong. She sensed she'd never find her daughter this way. There was no logical reason for her feelings, only a mother's intuition. For the moment, though, Catia could think of nothing else to do but tell her husband how worried she was, wait for a call from Demetra, and—probably—throw up.

◇◇◇

The phone rang and it was Tassos. He had some preliminary results for Andreas.

"I'm impressed, Tassos—answers before lunch."

"You'll be glad you didn't eat." His voice was grave.

"That bad?"

"Very."

"The woman suffocated to death…almost certainly right where we found her. She'd been prepared for burial while alive… tampons pushed very deeply into vaginal and anal cavities…far more than would be used for burial. Probably torture." Tassos kept pausing, as if trying to grasp the meaning of his own words as he said them. "As best as Costas can tell, she probably died somewhere between the seventh and ninth of June."

"Saint Calliope's name day!" Andreas blurted out.

"Yes." Tassos went silent for a moment. "He confirmed she was in her twenties, Caucasian, blond, blue-eyed, and almost six feet tall."

None of this was news. Andreas waited for the other shoe to drop.

"Preliminary pharmacology results show a strong indication of methamphetamine."

Instantly, Andreas felt he knew the reason for Tassos' mood. "Crystal meth! The same as in your body from ten years ago! The Scandinavian girl."

He didn't have to see him to know Tassos was nodding. "Yes… but I'm afraid that's not all of it."

"Not all of it? We've got two dead bodies ten years apart in what probably are ritual killings. How much worse can it be?" His voice exuded anxiety.

Tassos paused again. "In churches as old as this one there was no separation of the bones in a burial crypt; one generation was piled on top of the next. That's why it's not surprising we found the body lying on old bones." Another pause. "We know that the last member of the family who built that church left Mykonos more than sixty years ago. We should check to see if anyone remembers the last time someone was buried there."

"Why?"

"Well, we have a little problem, my friend." Tassos was using the sort of voice cops use when they're about to drop a bomb on a buddy. "The bones are too young."

"Are too what?" Andreas sounded truly puzzled.

"Young. New, not old, not ancient. Recent, recent, recent." Tassos seemed to be forcing himself back to cop-banter—a defense mechanism employed against the horrors of their job. Andreas let him go on.

"The bones don't belong in that crypt. Most of them were well over a hundred years old, some a little younger. Then we have the five-, ten-, and fifteen-year-old ones."

"The what?" Andreas' pulse was racing.

Tassos' voice was deadly serious. "I am afraid we have more than a ritual killing on our hands."

Andreas held his breath.

"The only information we have as yet on the three sets of bones is that they are skeletal remains approximately five years apart." Andreas could hear him drawing a breath. "And they most likely are all of young women...tall young women."

Andreas felt his throat closing. This was unheard-of. Greece had never had one of these before. Ever. "A serial killer," Andreas heard himself say, stunned.

"You and I must meet. Do you have time if I come over around four?"

Andreas thought it strange how someone as senior on the force as Tassos had put the question. He took it as a nervous courtesy intended to make things not seem as real and urgent as they were—as knights might have spoken to compose themselves before charging blindly into dark caves after monsters.

Andreas nervously tried to lighten the mood. "I'll try to squeeze you in between my motorbike-accident review and meeting with the hotel association's president over weekend parking restrictions."

Tassos chuckled. "Thanks. I know how busy you are." Then he added, "Welcome to Mykonos—isn't that what you said when we met? And I bet you thought it would be boring."

Andreas grinned. "Yeah, right." He paused and refocused. "Any luck with an ID on the dead woman yet?"

"We should have something by the time I see you. We think she's Dutch. A girl matching her description hasn't been heard from in weeks. Her father got Interpol involved, and we should have a positive ID by the end of the day. Her parents thought she was somewhere in the Mediterranean, possibly Greece, but no one knew just where."

"If you give me her name, I'll get someone started on trying to find a connection here."

"Sure, let me get it for you."

Andreas' head was spinning as he waited for Tassos to find the name. A serial killer in Greece—on Mykonos! The island and its reputation for tolerating all sorts of sinful behavior will be damned by the Greek Church and vilified in the Greek press as spawning this horror and shaming all of Greece before the world. *Shame* was the appropriate word, too, for now it was a world news headline story: SERIAL KILLER SECRETLY HAUNTS MYKONOS FOR DECADES. From fame to infamy in an instant. The hunt, the capture, the trial would be consumed by a crazed, feeding-frenzy media led by the European Union and Americans—which sent Greece its most sought-after tourists. And if the killer was never found…

"Here it is. Helen Vandrew. See you at four."

Chapter Four

Catia had not expected to hear back from Demetra so quickly. She'd just hung up with her husband—and alarmed him to no end—when Demetra called.

"Mother told me you're worried about Annika. Don't be. I spoke to her a few days ago. She's fine." Demetra sounded her typical, bubbly self.

Catia's heart felt lighter—but not completely relieved.

"Where is she?"

"Patmos."

Patmos was a beautiful, eastern-Aegean Greek island very near Turkey, reachable only by boat. It was a well-kept secret among the world's elite seeking seclusion and quiet, but not one Catia would have thought suited her daughter's mood after a breakup. Annika liked distractions when she was upset: parties, athletics—anything to keep her mind off what was bothering her. Patmos was not that sort of place. On its hillsides, Saint John wrote the apocalyptic Book of Revelations, and the island remained dominated by the church in more ways than just the massive mountaintop monastery named in his honor. "Why Patmos?"

"She said she'd never been there and wanted to go."

"Do you have a telephone number for her?"

Pause. "No. She called me."

Catia sensed a conspiratorial silence among cousins. Annika probably told Demetra not to give her mother the number. Catia thought of pushing the issue but decided not to. As long as Demetra and Annika were in touch, things were fine for now.

"Please, ask her to call me the next time you speak to her."

"Sure. I'll be seeing her the day after tomorrow."

Catia was relieved at hearing that but also surprised. "You're going to Patmos?"

"Oh, no, too boring," she giggled.

"Where are you meeting her?"

"Mykonos. I think she gets there tonight."

◇◇◇

Annika thought she'd never get over catching Peter in full thrust with that Bulgarian tramp——the one he'd dismissed as being as base and uninteresting as her bought-and-paid-for tits when she dropped her entire string-bikini-clad package next to them poolside their first day in Sicily.

She'd also never forget that bastard's words the next morning: "I'm not feeling very well, but don't worry about me, honey. Please, go out and see Siracusa. Call me when you're ready for lunch, and if I'm feeling better, I'll meet you." A very unladylike urge to inflict severe bodily harm raged through Annika each time she thought of the moment she swung Audrey Hepburn-like into their hotel room loaded down with food and wine for a surprise, romantic lunch together in Peter's sick bed.

She felt it all: betrayed, rejected, used, and victimized. Worse still, she felt somehow it was all her fault, that she must be a real loser as a woman if the man she thought her soulmate could so easily lie to her just "to fuck a tramp." She unconsciously said the last words aloud and quickly looked around to see if anyone had heard. She'd spoken in Dutch—perhaps that's why no one seemed to notice. Or maybe she didn't speak loud enough to be heard above the hum of the ferry's engines. She looked out toward the horizon from her seat in the protected, glassed-in section of the foredeck. They should be in Mykonos around midnight. She'd try to catch a little sleep. That might help her forget, or at least temporarily rid her thoughts of him.

She'd been trying to forget for weeks. First she tried a long ferry ride from Bari to Patras staring into the sea. That didn't work. Then a long bus ride to Athens across Greece's Peloponnese staring out at the countryside. That didn't work either. In Athens she'd hoped to surprise her cousin Demetra. They always made each other feel better. But Demetra wasn't there, and though they talked by phone, it wasn't the same thing.

Annika was too embarrassed to call her parents, and her mother would know instantly from her voice how utterly devastated she was. They would insist she come home immediately. She needed to get over this first—this bastard Peter. She went to Patmos thinking perhaps a spiritual place might help. It didn't. Then she called Demetra and they agreed what she needed was something quite different from spiritual comfort—and Mykonos was the perfect place to find it.

◇◇◇

Tassos was surprisingly prompt for a Greek. Only fifteen minutes late. He seemed agitated, preoccupied. Andreas led him upstairs to his second-floor office. It was bright and sunny and faced away from the road, but the view was not as great as the weather. It overlooked the backyards of Mykonos' working class—the people who never could afford to vacation here. Rusted skeletons of cars and trucks once kept for parts sat ignored in the midst of scratched-out gardens and scraggly goats. Stray cats ranged everywhere.

His office—like the rest of the place—was furnished with things from the old station. Tassos sat in a beat-up, brown leather armchair in the corner—the two of them fit together like old friends. Andreas sat behind his desk slowly swiveling his chair from side to side. It was only the two of them, but each seemed to be waiting for the other to speak.

Tassos started. "I thought it best we talk here, away from all the curious eyes and ears in my office."

Andreas kept swiveling. "How are we ever going to keep this quiet?"

Tassos fluttered his lips as he exhaled. "Don't know. Certainly not for long."

Andreas stopped swiveling, leaned forward, and put his forearms on the desk. "When it gets it out we're looking for a serial killer, all hell's going to break loose. There'll be a thousand reporters here making it impossible to catch the bastard."

"I know." Tassos nodded. "So far, only Costas, you, and I know about this—and he won't say a word—but, if we don't catch the guy soon, someone's going to put things together and"—he slapped his hands against the chair arms—"BOOM!"

Andreas grinned at the sound. "Is that meant to be our careers?" He lifted his arms and leaned back in the chair. "You know, the press will cut off our balls if we don't go public now with what we have." He paused. "And, come to think of it, don't you have to tell your boss?" For an instant, Andreas felt as if he were warning his father to be careful of cop politics.

Tassos closed his eyes. "We've worked together for many years. He trusts me not to tell him what I think he'd prefer not to know officially. This is one of those things—at least for now." He opened his eyes. "Besides, Chief, the murders occurred in your jurisdiction, and haven't you insisted on taking full responsibility for their investigation?" He smiled.

Well, so much for worrying about him, thought Andreas. Here was a political master offering Andreas what he wanted if he were willing to pay the price of assuming the political risk.

Andreas nodded. "Yes, but God help us if another woman's murdered." He paused. "I think we should go public with a physical description of the dead woman—it might make tall blondes more careful."

"And mention the crystal meth."

Andreas nodded again. "That too." He hoped they were doing the right thing.

Tassos asked, "What about asking Athens for help with a serial-killer specialist?"

Andreas gave a quick upward nod of his head—the Greek way of gesturing no. "There aren't any in Greece. Remember, we've never had a serial killer here, so no one's a specialist. We'd have to contact Interpol, and you know what that means."

"So much for keeping things quiet." Tassos patted the chair arms.

"We'll have to do our own research." Andreas opened his center desk drawer.

"How do we do that?" Tassos sounded surprised.

"The same way everyone else does these days, on the Internet." He lifted some papers out of the drawer.

Tassos waved a hand in the air. "You must be kidding."

"There's a lot out there. Here, take a look." Andreas handed him one of the papers. Across the top it read, "Characteristics of a Serial Killer."

Tassos looked at the list:

1. *Over 90 percent male.*

2. *Tend to be intelligent.*

3. *Do poorly in school, have trouble holding down jobs, and often work as unskilled laborers.*

4. *Tend to come from decidedly unstable families.*

5. *Abandoned by their fathers as children and raised by domineering mothers.*

6. *Families often have criminal, psychiatric, and alcoholic histories.*

7. *Hate their fathers and mothers.*

8. *Psychological, physical, and sexual abuse as child is common—often by a family member.*

9. *Many have spent time in institutions as children and have records of early psychiatric problems.*

10. *High suicide-attempt rates.*

11. *Many intensely interested from an early age in voyeurism, fetishism, and sadomasochistic pornography.*

12. *More than 60 percent wet their beds beyond age of 12.*

13. *Many are fascinated with starting fires.*

14. *Involved with sadistic activity or tormenting small creatures.*

Andreas put the other papers on his desk. "An FBI agent named Ressler came up with that list. There's a lot more, but this gives you the general idea."

"Why do I have the feeling we're trying to teach ourselves brain surgery?" Tassos reread the list.

Andreas waited until he finished. "I don't know what else to do. Do you know anyone we can ask for help we can trust to keep quiet?"

Tassos nodded no. "But how long do you think we can go on like this"—he waved the paper in the air—"before getting some real help?"

Andreas shrugged. "Let's play it by ear until one of us feels we have to go public."

Tassos stared at him. "All I'm risking is forced early retirement, but you…" He left the thought hanging.

Andreas looked down at his desk. "I know what you're about to say."

Tassos shrugged. "I really liked your dad and thought he got a raw deal, but if the press gets pissed off at you, they'll be screaming…" Again he hesitated.

Andreas finished Tassos' sentence without looking up, "'Like father, like son'?" He didn't wait for an answer. "I really don't like talking about this…" Andreas was surprised he'd made that admission to a stranger. "But I'll give you an answer."

He lifted his eyes and stared directly at Tassos. "I'm not going to stop doing what I think's right out of fear that the press might come after me like they did my father." They'd done more than just come after him—they'd crucified him—but Andreas had no intention of discussing it further. Besides, everyone from Tassos' era on the force knew all the details—up to and including the suicide.

Neither man spoke.

Andreas leaned forward and broke the tension. "Anything new?"

Tassos noticeably relaxed in his chair. "We've positively identified the dead body from dental records as the woman in the photo I faxed you, Helen Vandrew. Her parents are on their way to Greece to claim the body."

Silence.

Tassos continued. "The other three bodies probably were bound the same as Vandrew."

Andreas looked surprised. "How could you tell?"

"The twine." He folded the list and put it in his pocket.

"Twine?"

"Costas found deteriorated bits of hemp in the crypt that match the approximate age of the bones."

"He found twine that old?" Andreas gave a nodding look of admiration.

Tassos nodded with him. "The crypt was dry and the twine the heavy-duty, commercial stuff farmers use. It's made to survive all kinds of weather."

"Any idea where it came from?"

"Not yet, but doubt that would help much. It's sold all over the world. Nothing unique about it."

Andreas let out a breath. "All bound the same way…all killed in a church…" His voice drifted off. "The killer has to be acting out some sort of religious ritual—but what kind of ritual ever involved human sacrifice in Greece?"

Tassos shrugged. "There's always our myths. Look at Euripides' or Homer's account of Agamemnon."

Andreas shook his head. "I can't believe some myth about a king sacrificing his daughter so that the gods would send wind for his sailing ships is behind this."

"But a woman was at the center of the myth. They were warships sailing to Troy to rescue Helen." Tassos said the words without emotion.

Andreas said, "I just don't see it—two Helens or not—but who the hell knows. We're trying to figure out what twisted thinking is driving a crazy." He shook his head again and drummed the fingers of his right hand on his desk. "What about the drugs?"

Tassos lifted and dropped his hands. "Crystal meth? It must have something to do with getting his victim sexually excited. I don't have to tell you how tough that'll be to trace. It's everywhere. If we had a suspect, I could kick around some local dealers to try and come up with a match, but without a suspect, forget it."

Andreas let out a breath. "Could be homemade stuff. All he'd need is fertilizer, battery acid, and cold medicine."

"More Internet research?"

Andreas let the teasing pass with a smile. "I think there are three things to get started on right away, One"—he popped out a finger for emphasis—"identify the sets of bones; two"—out popped another finger—"find anyone who saw the Vandrew girl on the island and three—"

"Look for more bodies," Tassos interrupted.

Andreas hadn't intended to say that. He'd thought it, but that wasn't his third choice—his was checking out Father Paul. Finding more bodies would make it a hell of a lot tougher to keep things quiet—practically and morally.

Andreas shrugged. "You're right." He'd check out his original point three on his own.

Tassos said, "I'm pretty sure the bones we found were tourists because there are no women—Mykonian or otherwise—reported as missing from Mykonos even faintly resembling the size of the skeletons."

"How can that be? There are four women buried in a church on Mykonos. You'd think someone would have reported at least one of them missing."

Tassos shook his head. "That's why I'm saying we should widen the search, look for missing foreigners generally—or at least off-island Greeks—not just those who disappeared on Mykonos. Someone might have tried to file a report, but Mykonos has a long history of claiming 'nothing bad happens here.'" He emphasized the phrase with his fingers in quote marks and a look of disgust. "If someone tried reporting a foreign woman as missing on Mykonos, the police would say she must have left the island and no missing-person report would be tied to Mykonos. Only if a missing person were local or one with Greek friends or a family raising holy hell would there be a real push made." He grinned. "Isn't that one of the reasons you're its new chief—to change all that?"

There really were no secrets from this guy, Andreas thought. It reminded him of how his dad somehow always knew when he was hiding cookies under his pillow. "How do you suggest we get an ID on the bones without going through official channels?"

"I'll ask a friend at Interpol who owes me a favor for a list of possible matches."

Andreas leaned back in his chair. He knew any likely match meant DNA testing against family members. How the hell to keep that quiet? "My guys are checking the hotels, bars, clubs, taxis, tavernas, shops, and beaches for anyone who might have seen Vandrew."

Tassos nodded. "So, on to point three."

Andreas said, "How are we ever going to search all those churches?"

Tassos shrugged. "Good question. Even if we had the men, the families and the archbishop would be down our throats the moment we started. Trust me, our quiet investigation would end in roaring flames."

Silence.

Andreas swiveled again. "Maybe we don't have to go at it that way. If our killer's hidden other bodies," and it seemed painfully certain he had, "I think I know where to find them."

Tassos didn't seem surprised. "And where would that be?"

Andreas stared at him. "In churches looked after by Father Paul."

Tassos nodded and smiled. "You mean your original point three?"

"Wiseass." He really does know me, thought Andreas.

They spent the next several hours poring over Andreas' Internet research trying to agree upon a profile for their suspect. They concluded the killer was at least forty and acting alone. Based upon the sheer size of the victims, if their killer were female, she'd have to be tremendously strong or have help, and since statistically most were men acting alone, they went with the percentages. They pegged his age to the fact one victim was murdered fifteen years ago and most serial killers don't start killing until their mid-twenties.

How much older than forty he might be, they couldn't guess. The literature said serial killers act when they feel a "compulsion" they must satisfy—usually driven by "power-to-control or sexual urges." There are "cooling-off periods" of years or weeks between killings, but when they get the urge, they have to feed it—and the longer they kill without capture, the more frequent their need. The killer could go on killing for as long as he had the strength for it.

Much of what they read seemed consistent with what they'd seen. "The extreme, sadistic urges of many serial killers are typically expressed in bondage, mutilation, and torture of a sexual nature"—the twine, shaved hair, and tampons—"and killing victims slowly over a long period of time." Suffocation in a crypt was certainly that.

They agreed on a description to distribute to their cops, being as careful as they could not to make it sound too much like the list of characteristics in Tassos' pocket.

"A forties-plus male, in reasonably good physical condition. Intelligent, possibly a little kinky or sadistic, with a bad family history. May have a police record," read Andreas.

"Covers a lot of guys on this island," said Tassos.

"Let's add 'more than fifteen-year resident or tourist on Mykonos.'"

"Sounds good to me." Tassos looked at his watch. "It's almost eight-thirty. I better head to the port if I want any chance of getting back to Syros before it's totally dark."

"Thanks." Andreas reached out to shake hands but Tassos embraced him in the traditional Greek fashion of good-bye between friends.

Tassos gave him an extra pat on the back. "Speak to you tomorrow…my friend." Andreas sensed he wanted to say more.

After he left, Andreas looked over the notes of his conversation with Father Paul. He'd scribbled down the names of the churches the priest had rattled off, but he knew for sure he couldn't find all of them on his own. He'd have to come up with some innocuous way of getting that contractor Pappas to help him. For sure that would earn him a "favors beget favors" lecture, but what the hell, sometimes you have to deal with the devil to catch a sinner.

That was something he'd learned from his father.

Chapter Five

The massive ferry made its traditional, midnight grand entrance into the harbor. The town looked more alive than Annika remembered—lights and people everywhere. She couldn't wait to get off. As she stepped out onto the open deck, her honey-blond hair whipped across her face. She liked the way it felt: free and unhampered. *Meltemi* winds blew only on late-summer afternoons, she thought, but then again, this was the island with windmills as its symbol. She quickly ran her fingers through her hair to pull it off her face and thought to grab a sweater out of her backpack but didn't. Once out of the wind, she'd be fine.

She'd chosen a loose-fitting beige T-shirt, matching khaki cargo shorts, and sneakers for the trip. She wanted to look like every other backpacker. At just under six feet tall, that wasn't possible, especially when the straps of her backpack pressed her already ample bosom into the realm of *wow*. Nothing she could do about that. Nor about virtually every Greek man and adolescent boy around her taking part in a running gag all the way from Patmos as to how best to find and devour *karpouzi*. Since there were no watermelons anywhere to be seen, she had a pretty good idea of the melons that held their interest but acted as if she didn't understand a word of their conversations. She was being true to her father's favorite lecture: "Don't let strangers know you understand their language. It gives you an edge."

She'd decided not to let anyone but her cousin and aunt know she was here. She wanted to be anonymous for as long as possible—just a poor little Dutch girl in search of a good time on Mykonos. She'd let the Greek boys take a shot—maybe one would get lucky. No, maybe I'll get lucky, she thought. Time to take charge of my life and do what I want to do, not what pleases some dickhead. She knew she still was angry, but she couldn't help it.

She waited until the boat docked before going down the stairs. From experience she knew hurrying to get off in the first huddled rush meant a pressing crowd of anonymous groping hands. By the time she stepped onto the concrete pier a crowd had gathered about fifty yards away. That would be where the hotels solicited customers. She walked over and looked for someone holding a sign with the name of a hotel she recognized but where no one would know her. The one she liked had a Greek couple and a gray-haired, fiftyish man engaged in the traditional haggling over price. After five animated minutes they reached a deal. Now it was her turn.

The gray-haired man smiled and asked her in English where she was from.

"Holland," she answered in English.

He smiled wider. "Oh, we have many guests from Holland." Then he said to her in Dutch, "I have a wonderful room with a private bath and a view of the town, and because you are from my favorite country—next to Greece of course"—with a yet broader smile—"I will give you a special price."

She smiled courteously. "What is the price?"

"One hundred eighty euros."

It was more than twice what he'd agreed upon with the Greeks for a double room.

Annika replied in Dutch, "That's very kind of you, sir, but I can't afford that much." She turned to walk away.

He grabbed her arm. "No, no please, I understand. What can you afford?" He let go of her arm.

She smiled. "Oh, I'm sure it's far too little for such a wonderful room."

"I'll let you have it for a hundred euros." He looked at her in a way that made Annika wonder if more than the price of a room was on his mind.

She thought of walking away but decided to haggle. "Forty." If he accepted that lowball offer she definitely would walk away.

"Seventy-five."

"No."

He paused. "Sixty."

Sixty was a fair price, and it was late. "Including breakfast?"

A new smile lit across his face, and he gestured for her to come. "Agreed." He led her toward where his van was parked— with his hand ever so lightly pressing on her hip as if to steer her in the right direction.

She didn't make an issue about his hand even though she was pretty sure it wasn't offered purely for guidance. She smiled as she remembered overhearing her mother once tell a girlfriend, "Something about Mykonos makes every man think he has a chance at every woman."

He said the ride from the harbor to the hotel would be less than ten minutes and took the narrow two-lane road circling the original town. It was filled with partiers stumbling along the uneven concrete roadway trying to navigate a maze of illegally parked cars and motorbikes. Crowds constricted parts of the road down to a single lane, but the man didn't seem to care. He never slowed down unless forced to by an oncoming driver. Whether they knew it or not, these pedestrians were not protected by the gods of Delos; they were on their own, and for those not prepared to expect the unexpected from a Greek driver, there were ambulances.

Things came to an abrupt stop at a four-way intersection with an even narrower road. It was the busiest corner in Mykonos, for this was the main portal to the island's 24/7 lifestyle. To the left, the road went up a hill toward the airport; to the right, to what the locals called the bus station.

It wasn't really a bus station, just an area big enough for five buses and half-dozen taxis fifty yards into the old town. Buses going to and from the beaches, outlying hotels, and Ano Mera parked there. Crowds of rushing tourists funneling in and out of town were surrounded here by a bazaar of businesses catering to their holiday needs and fantasies: food shops for a fast meal and booze; kiosks selling cigarettes, postcards, phone cards, film, candy, gum, ice cream, condoms, and more; stands hawking last-minute souvenirs; motorbike and car rentals and ATM's. In quiet contrast to it all—unnoticed behind an unobtrusive wall on a eucalyptus-shaded knoll seventeen steps above the bustle—rested the recent, officially consecrated dead of Mykonos.

The van turned left up the hill. Two hundred-fifty yards later the road turned sharply to the left, then back to the right. As if by magic, the sights and sounds of the bus station disappeared. There was still traffic—and roaring motorbikes—but the crowds were gone and the view was picture-postcard Mykonos. The van slowed as if to take it all in but instead darted to the right through an opening in a low, white-capped stone wall and jerked to a sudden stop. It had to, because the parking area wasn't much deeper than the van and ended flush with the front wall of the hotel. No wasted space here. Four cars were parked in a line along the white-capped wall. Annika noticed that one was a police car.

She knew the hotel had two stories—the maximum allowed—but it was set down along the hillside and looked to be only one story from the road. Even in dim moonlight Annika made out bougainvillea and geraniums everywhere. She'd never been in the hotel, only seen it from the road, but she remembered the flowers and its view of sunsets over the bay by Little Venice, the area named for the dozen or so multicolored, three-story former pirate-captain homes on the northern side of the bay—the only such structures in all of Mykonos.

The gray-haired man quickly jumped out of the driver's seat and slid open the rear door as he said, "Welcome to Hotel Adlantis. My name is Ilias and I am your host." He spoke in precise English. Annika realized he hadn't introduced himself before. The Greek couple responded in Greek. Annika said hello in English and reached for her backpack.

"No, please, let me," Ilias said in Dutch. He took her backpack and lifted the couple's two sizeable bags as if they were empty. "This way, please." He gestured with his head in the direction of the lobby and waited, holding all three bags, until his new guests passed in front of him. He followed with the luggage.

The lobby was on the top, street-level floor and at the rear opened onto an open-air verandah overlooking the bay. The inside was unremarkable: standard-issue white stone floor, white walls with blue trim, and a few pieces of furniture upholstered in a coarse, matching blue fabric. A white marble countertop under a white arch on the south wall served as the reception desk. A painting of the hotel's exterior hung behind the counter. It looked like something painted by a guest in exchange for a free room.

A man sitting behind the counter smiled and said "hello" in English. Ilias put down the luggage and began talking to the man in Greek. Annika could tell from the other man's accent that he was Albanian. Ilias asked about the police car, and the man said that two cops were on the verandah. They wanted to talk to him. Ilias told the man to check everyone in "by the book" and take the luggage to their rooms. He then excused himself from his guests and went out to the verandah.

Annika gave the man her Dutch passport, paid cash in advance for her room for two nights, and waited for the Greek couple to do the same. She walked toward the verandah and saw Ilias in animated conversation with the police. He was looking at a piece of paper and shaking with his head. She decided not to go outside. Whatever the police wanted was no business of hers, and she didn't want to seem nosy. The man behind the counter said, "Miss," and she turned to see him holding her backpack and waving for her to follow him.

Her room was on the lower level. It was small but neat, with glass doors that opened onto a private balcony with the promised magnificent view of a rippling silver sea against far-off shadow-black hillsides. In the distant midst of the bay she saw three towers of the Cathedral of Notre-Dame—or, if you preferred reality, the lit-up riggings of three closely anchored, otherwise invisible sloops. The outside view was far better than the inside. Another of those paintings hung in her blue-and-white room. The artist must have slept here a lot.

The man pointed toward the balcony and said, "Keep locked at night," then showed her how to do it. She gave him a euro and, when he left, locked all the doors. She turned off the lights and fell onto the bed. From there, she could see through the glass doors to the sea. Her eyes started tearing. This was not a view she wanted to be seeing alone. She fell asleep.

"Miss, miss." She heard a man's voice in Dutch and quiet knocking. For an instant she wasn't sure where she was. It was still dark out. She looked at her watch. She'd only been sleeping a few minutes.

"Who is it?" Her throat was slightly dry from sleep.

"Ilias."

Her instinct was to be pissed, but it had only been a few minutes since she'd checked in, and how was he to know she'd fallen asleep? "Just a minute." She stood up, turned on a light, and looked quickly in the mirror before opening the door.

He was holding a basket of fruit and a bottle of wine. "I am sorry, I think I woke you up."

She forced a smile. "That's okay, I didn't mean to go to sleep this early."

He handed her the items without trying to enter the room.

She placed them on top of the dresser next to the door. "Thank you, that's very thoughtful." This time her smile was sincere.

"I wanted to welcome you to Mykonos. Is this your first time here?"

She decided to lie. "Yes."

"Ah, then when does your boyfriend arrive?" He laughed.

Even though she knew he was fishing, she was not going to lie about that. "I have no boyfriend." She realized that might have sounded as if she had a girlfriend and added, "We just broke up."

"I'm so sorry to hear that."

Somehow she didn't think he was.

He went on. "So, do you have friends here?"

"No, not yet."

"Well, now you do. Come, I make some dinner to properly welcome you to this island of my birth. I will answer all of your questions, and we will tell lies to each other of our lives and lovers."

He could be quite charming, but this was not how she wanted to spend her first night. "Thank you, Ilias, but not tonight."

He smiled his usual smile. "I understand. Perhaps tomorrow. *Yiassou*—excuse me, I mean good-bye." He reached to shake her hand. She reached back out her hand and he held it. "You are very beautiful girl, Annika Vanden Haag, do not be sad. Enjoy yourself." He then kissed her hand and left.

This is going to be an interesting few days, she thought. They're circling like flies and I haven't even tried to look hot. I wonder what would happen if I did? That's when she decided to go out for the evening. After all, it wasn't even two yet.

◇◇◇

She walked along the edge of the road, against the traffic, toward the bus station. Though dangerous, the other side was suicide, and besides, over there men could drive alongside her as she walked. As it was, she took hardly a step without hearing some comment. One man on a motorcycle did a U-turn wheelie trying to get her attention. A group of Italian boys walking into town caught up with her and tried getting her to talk. They wouldn't leave her alone but she ignored them and kept moving down the hill. She wasn't upset; after all, she was the one who chose to wear the form-fitting, sequined teal number Peter called her "second skin." He said he loved the way it "fired up the blue in her eyes" and its spaghetti straps fell from her shoulders in a suggestion of more to come. This time there wasn't much more to come. She wore only a thong underneath.

She'd learned that walking confidently—as if you know where you're going—is the best defense against hazing men. Once she passed through the bus station into the old town's maze of crowded lanes, they dropped away to pursue more willing, readily available targets.

Annika knew where she was headed. It was a bar in the center of town. She'd never been there but heard it was "upscale," which meant the men hitting on you pretended to have money and/or sophistication. At least it had a chance of being more civilized that the raging, dance-naked-on-the-table places that catered to most people her age. Tonight, at least, she was looking for conversational companionship. She also knew she was far too vulnerable to drink much. This would be an early night. She'd be back at her hotel no later than four.

The bar was at the end of a narrow alleyway filled with the sort of places she was trying to avoid. In keeping with Mykonos tradition—and a town ordinance—the alley's gray flagstones should have been outlined in glossy white paint, but here there were only shadows of an outline. Just before its front door the alley widened to accommodate a few café tables and chairs. She felt the eyes of the men at the tables but heard no comments. So far, so good.

From where she stopped it was two steps down into a wide open doorway. She could see that the room was only twice as wide as the alley, but beyond that was a larger room that looked to be a garden restaurant. A dark, well-worn wooden bar ran along the right side of the front room. Potted plants and hanging Chinese lanterns were everywhere. A dozen patrons of mixed ages sat at the bar, another twenty or so at the row of small tables across from it. All were well dressed and looked great in the complimentary dim lighting. The space between the bar and tables was crowded but not so much so as to make it uncomfortable for her to pass through, if she chose to.

She stood looking in and wondered what the hell she was thinking. This was not a smart thing to be doing alone. She should go right home to bed and call her mother first thing in the morning. She took a deep breath and mouthed silently to herself, "To stay or not to stay, that is the question." As if she'd spoken her question aloud, it was answered in welcoming English by a roly-poly, older Greek man seated on the single stool at the blunt end of the bar, closest to the door.

"Don't think, my dear, just come in. I need the business." He pushed someone who must have been a friend off the stool closest to him and waved her inside. "Come, my darling, you're in Mykonos. Jump in."

And so she did.

Chapter Six

The man at the end of the bar extended his hand, "My name is Panos and welcome to Panos' Place—the best place in all of Mykonos for making friends." A small crowd of middle-aged men around him parted as she moved toward the empty stool to his left.

"Thank you." She was about to add "sir" but caught herself. She sensed he'd be insulted if a young woman treated him with the respect due an elder.

"Would you like something to drink?" He waved to a very hot-looking young Greek behind the bar. He was about her age, tall with dark hair, dark eyes, a dark, well-toned body—she pulled her eyes off him. No need to inflame her need any further, especially since she was about to start drinking.

"As…" She caught herself about to say "aspró krasí"—"white wine" in Greek—"my friends back home would say, 'Wine would be fine'—white please."

"And where's home?" Panos' piercing blue eyes didn't fit his trusty, hound-dog face. His hair seemed just as confusedly located. Pirate-style, cascading dark brown curls should not share the same head with bushy, salt-and-pepper eyebrows and a drooping, even grayer, walrus mustache. Overall, Annika saw walrus.

"The Netherlands."

The men around them had been quietly listening but now exploded in Greek.

"Damn he's good. How's he do it?"

"I owe him another fifty euros. I'd have sworn she was American."

"My money was on Swedish."

"Panos always goes for the Dutch girls. He has a thing about them. He can smell them a mile away."

That brought out a few comments she wished she didn't understand.

Panos swung around on his stool to face the chorus. He held up his hands and cocked his head. "Never challenge the master," he said in Greek. Then he turned back to Annika and winked. "We have a little ritual here. When a pretty woman comes to the door, we try to guess where she's from. I won." He spoke to her in English.

She admired his honesty. "Am I that obvious?"

"No, that beautiful." He smiled at her.

It never changes, she thought. Greek males start learning to seduce as children and keep up with it to their graves. You have to admire them—unless, of course, you're married to one. She decided to subtly point out their age difference, though she doubted that would deter him. "So, how long have you been in business?"

"I was born here, but moved to Athens when I was a boy and started working there."

That was not what she meant but she realized he'd been drinking a lot longer than she. "No, I mean this place. How long have you owned it?"

Like many repeatedly asked the same question—and who drink too much—he responded with a stock answer not quite tailored to what was asked but that gives the requested information. "Oh, it's been thirty-five years since I moved back here. My family had a farm out there." He pointed over his shoulder in some vague direction away from the sea and took another sip from his drink. "Still does. I never much liked farming, so I opened this place. Last year was thirty years. *Yamas!*" He raised his glass and clinked on hers. Everyone around them did the same.

He ordered food brought to the bar and introduced her to the crowd standing around him, making clear to his friends that he was in charge of her attentions. Around three in the morning, dancing to a deejay began in the back room. The party was just getting under way. He ordered a round of tequila shots for everyone to bolt down together. A Mykonos tradition, he said. Then someone else ordered a round. And someone else did the same. She had a pretty good idea where this tradition was headed, so she did what she'd learned from her years at Yale: dump it on the floor and fake a chug.

The bar was packed and the back room was jumping. She was enjoying herself and getting buzzed from all the action, not the booze. She started moving to the music on her bar stool. Another round of shots. She'd lost track. She thought by now all the tequila at her feet must be marinating her Jimmy Choo stilettos. Better them than me. Someone from one of the tables came over and handed her another shot. She took it and smiled, but before she could fake her chug a hand grabbed her arm.

It was the man on the bar stool next to her. "I wouldn't do that, miss." He sounded serious. He looked about sixty, with blue eyes and neatly trimmed brown hair slightly graying at the temples. Handsome for his age, tanned, and if his grip was any indication, quite strong.

"I beg your pardon." She meant it. Who the hell was he to tell her not to dump her drinks?

"Sorry," he said, but he didn't let go. He reached over with his free hand, took the shot glass out of hers, and put it on the bar.

"I know that was very rude of me, but in Mykonos it's very dangerous taking drinks from strangers. You can't tell what may be in them if they don't come from behind the bar."

Of course the man was right, and obviously he hadn't noticed she'd been dumping her drinks. How nice of him.

"Thank you. That was very considerate. I'll remember that." The man nodded and went back to his drink.

"Annika, Annika Vanden Haag, sir," she said to him. It seemed appropriate and not offending to use "sir" with him.

"Tom. Tom Daly. Pleased to meet you." They shook hands. He didn't say more and kept his body facing the bar.

"So, Mr. Daly, where are you from?"

"The United States. New York. And you?" He only turned his head to look at her when he was speaking. Otherwise, he kept his eyes on his drink.

"The Hague."

"Ah, we may be distant cousins. My mother's side was Dutch—really Afrikaner Dutch. Part Greek, too, if you go back far enough."

"I'm only half Dutch myself." She didn't mention her own Greek roots.

"I guess that makes us two more in this world's litter of mutts." He laughed.

She smiled. "Are you here on holiday?"

"Sort of. I'm a painter and come for inspiration."

"Really? Should I know your work?" She realized the question was unintentionally insulting. She probably had had too much to drink, but the man didn't seem offended.

"I don't know. One of my pieces hangs in here."

She looked behind the bar. My God, she thought, it's one of those awful paintings from the hotel.

He must have noticed the look on her face, for he lifted his eyes to see where she was looking. He burst out laughing. "No, not that one—lord no—that one." He pointed behind him to a large oil painting in a place of prominence on the rear wall.

She didn't recognize his work but somehow thought she should. It was filled with nymphs and color and ancient ruins.

She decided to compliment him. "You're him?"

"Whoever 'him' is, yes." He nodded appreciatively.

"It's an honor to meet you, sir."

He turned his body and put up one hand. "Okay, Annika, don't bury me yet. Please call me Tom or else I'll never hear the end of it from all these youngsters at the bar." He smiled and pointed toward Panos and his crowd.

"Is he giving you that 'Don't take drinks from strangers' pitch again?" Panos asked with a wink, "He tells that to all the pretty girls. Our watchdog of virtue, we call him." Everybody laughed.

Tom shook his head. "Yeah, yeah, yeah," and went back to drinking quietly.

Annika leaned over and whispered in his ear, "Thank you," and kissed him on the cheek. He smiled without turning his head.

Panos said, "Annika, I'd like you to meet my son." She turned around to look in front of the bar but saw no one who looked like Panos.

"He's behind you."

She turned to see the dark-haired boy behind the bar smiling at her. "My name is Yiorgos—call me George. My father said I can talk to you." A chorus of Greek chants along the line of "It's time for the younger generation to have a shot at her" made her smile.

"So, let's talk," she said, and broadened her smile.

"Not here. There." He pointed to the dance floor.

She nodded, slid off the stool, and pressed through the crowd toward the rear. He walked in pace with her from behind the bar. They met at the end. He took her hand and pulled her into the crowd. It was body upon body upon body. She felt that, here, your body was no longer your own; it belonged to the crowd. His hands were around her waist, then on her ass. They were belly to belly moving to the music. The music pulsed and he thrusted. It felt good to have a man so close.

He dropped his hand to below her skirt and touched her bare ass. She let him. He moved his hand toward where only a bit of thong protected her and she twisted away. He persisted and she pushed him back. He gave a "can't blame me for trying" grin, and they went back to dancing. She let him grind at her crotch with his. She knew she was building expectations she was not prepared to meet—at least not tonight—but it felt so good. When he tried to move his hand inside her again she said she wanted to get a drink. He told her he'd wait for her and started dancing with another woman who appeared not to have Annika's reservations.

Her bar stool was still available. "I watched it for you," said Tom without looking up.

"Thanks." She let out a deep breath and reached for the wineglass in front of her. She paused. It had been sitting open at the bar. Anyone could have put something in it.

"I watched that too." He sipped his own wine without looking at her.

She smiled. "Thanks," she said, and took a drink.

"You're some dancer Annika."

"Thank you," she said, not quite sure what else to say.

He spoke softly without looking at her. "I once dreamt I lived on the edge of a wild amusement park, some place where any time I wanted, day or night, I simply stepped over the edge into the midst of my deepest fantasy, enjoyed my time there, and stepped back again unharmed."

Maybe he's had too much to drink, she thought.

"That's Mykonos—a mad fantasy. It's not real. You might think it is when you're here, but it's not." He sipped his drink again. "But, then again, it's not completely the place of my dream. There I wandered about invisibly, taking in only the energy I chose and returning safely and unharmed to my reality whenever I wanted. Be careful of this fantasy, Annika, for here there's definite harm afoot."

Before she could respond, Yiorgos was next to her, grabbing her arm. "Come, let's go."

"Go, go where?"

He seemed in no mood for talk. "To watch the sunrise." He pulled at her arm.

She pulled it away. "I'd rather stay." Her voice was sharp.

"We're going to close soon. It's after five." His voice was impatient.

"I still prefer to stay."

He tugged again.

"Yiorgos, stop." She looked around for someone to say something to him, but none of the once-so-attentive patrons seemed to notice.

He leaned over, kissed her hard, and tried to shove his hand between her legs.

She slapped his face. He slapped her back. His eyes were on fire. Still no one seemed to notice. In Greek, he called her a miserable, cock-teasing whore and stormed out of the bar.

Only then did someone speak. It was Panos. "I apologize for my son. He has a bad temper. Let me show you home."

She was shaking. She couldn't believe what just happened. None of these people who'd been so very nice to her had said a word or lifted a hand to help her. "No, no, thank you. Very kind, I'll get home okay." She was ready to cry.

"Please, let me take you home." Panos called to the remaining boy behind the bar for a glass of water. "Here, drink this."

Her hand was trembling as she took it and brought it toward her lips.

At that moment Tom said, "Good night, everyone," and got up from his bar stool. He stumbled and fell onto Annika, causing her to spill the water all over her dress. "Oh, I'm so sorry. I apologize. I had too much to drink."

Panos said nothing. Nor did he offer her another glass of water. He just glared at Tom.

"I better go too," she said. She quickly thanked Panos for everything and hurried out the door after Tom.

She fell into step beside him. "What was all that about? The speech—and the spilled water?"

"Nothing, just me rambling drunk and then stumbling drunk." He didn't seem that drunk.

"Where are you going?" She sounded anxious.

"To the taxi stand and home." He kept walking forward without looking at her.

"Where do you stay?" She kept talking and walking wherever he was headed. She didn't want to be alone right now.

"I rent a house from a farmer out beyond Ano Mera. Have been staying there summers for thirty years."

The taxi stand was by the harbor on the opposite end of town from the bus station.

There were a lot of people in line, and she stood with him while he waited. He talked about his art. She talked about growing up in Holland, her miserable boyfriend, and how she should let her parents know where she was. He said that was a good idea, but guessed she wasn't quite ready to give up on her "fantasy" search. She smiled and said he was probably right.

When it was his turn for a cab, he insisted she take it instead. He opened the door and told the driver in perfect Greek that she was a friend, and not to charge her like a tourist.

Annika said good night and got into the taxi, but she knew she was too upset over tonight's bad experience with another disappointing man to face going back to her room. She knew she'd fall apart.

The driver asked her in English, "Where to, miss?"

She looked out the window at the harbor and wanted to cry.

"Please, take me where I can watch the sunrise. I'll pay you double for your time."

"No problem. I know just the place."

◇◇◇

He was driving on a part of the island she'd never seen before. She'd thought he was headed east to Lia Beach, where her mother and she often swam, but he'd turned and headed north. He was on a mountain by some military installation. It was almost first light—that moment when the world seemed to come alive again with the seductive promise of a fresh start. She needed this. She needed this badly.

He turned onto a deeply rutted road and they bounced along for a few minutes until finding level ground. In a saner moment, she never would have dreamt of doing this—allowing a total stranger to take her to a deserted beach. Maybe the artist was right and she was ignoring reality in search of some fantasy. Too late now, but thankfully, the driver didn't seem interested in her. He hadn't said a word the whole time.

"Here we are, miss." He stopped and pointed straight ahead. "I'll wait here. If you need me, just yell."

He didn't get out of the taxi. She didn't mind.

The hard ground where he'd parked soon changed to sand. She almost broke a heel. She took off her stilettos and walked barefoot across the dunes toward some sort of structure at the far end of the beach. Dawn was about to break and she started running. Then faster and faster and faster. No goal in mind, no place in mind, just running to wherever the light took her. It was by the structure that she stopped.

She looked at the small, isolated house, totally dark inside, with no sign of life. Then she turned toward the sea and watched light fly at the horizon as if it were alive. Annika flung her shoes in the air and started running again toward the light. She pulled her dress over her head and let it drop to the sand as she ran. When she reached the water, she stepped out of her thong and threw it back in the direction of her dress. Naked, she waded out to above her ankles. She paused, and stood very still, her eyes fixed on the light spreading across the sea.

The wind was light, the air was warm, the sea cold. She shut her eyes. She needed release. She needed to feel free, in charge of herself, in charge of her body. She needed her life back.

Feeling the sun on her body, Annika gently lowered herself onto her back. She lay still for a moment in the shallow, lapping water—her eyes still tightly closed—then slowly rolled farther out. Over and over she rolled until it was deep enough for her to swim. For fifteen minutes she swam as hard as she could remember swimming. She burst back onto the beach and thrust a fist above her head. "*Yes!*" she yelled as if she'd just scored a goal. Her old self was back—enough with the fantasy and self-pity. "Yes!" she yelled again and thrust her other fist in the air.

Perhaps it was her renewed appreciation for reality, but whatever the reason, she sensed she wasn't alone—and hadn't been for quite some time. But where were the watching eyes? She saw no one on the beach or in the house. The taxi driver? Possibly, but it could be anyone, maybe a soldier with binoculars from the base on that mountain. Whatever, she couldn't do anything about it now, and besides, "I feel great!" she yelled to whoever was there.

She let the sea breeze dry her body, dressed, and walked back to the taxi. The driver was sitting where she'd left him. She gave him the name of her hotel, and he drove her there. She paid what she'd promised, and he said, "Thank you." The only words he'd uttered the entire trip back from the beach. Weird for a Greek man, she thought. But so what? She was back at her hotel, safe and sound at last.

Chapter Seven

Andreas had fallen into a routine. He'd wake an hour and a half before sunrise, dress in running shorts, T-shirt, and sneakers, do sit-ups and push-ups while his coffee brewed, gather what he planned to wear that day, and drive the five minutes from his rented house on the Paradise Beach road to police headquarters; where he'd park and jog the hundred yards onto the airport runway. At that hour only airport security and cleaning crews were around, and as chief of police, Andreas could go where he pleased.

He liked jogging inside the perimeter fence at sunrise. It gave him time to think, something you dared not do if you were crazy enough to attempt jogging on Mykonos roads—especially at sunrise. That was when the drunkest of the drunk returned from beach clubs and bars. The worst accidents took place during those hours, and heaven help the seriously injured awaiting an emergency helicopter flight to Athens. After his run he'd return to headquarters, shower, and ask the officer in charge to brief him on the "fresh hells" to confront from the night before.

For the moment, his thoughts were on the wonder of the Mykonos morning light. It never ceased to amaze him how its pale, rose-blue magic somehow brought the island's rock-edged hills and bright white structures into graceful harmony. If only it could last, he thought, but hard light always came, bringing on the heat. Later, when siesta was over and dusk had arrived, the light changed again, with every color competing for your eye. Every vessel, every soaring bird, every stroller in the port, and every lamppost lining the harbor seemed to stand alone and yet—somehow—fit together against the horizon.

Sort of like a 3-D movie, thought Andreas, bringing himself back to the reality of his day.

There hadn't been a break on the Vandrew case. His men had shown her picture at all the likely places, but no one had seen her—or would admit to it if they had. She wasn't listed on any airline passenger list, and ferries kept no records of passenger names. Nor had they turned up anything so far in any of the tourist logs hotels were required to maintain and regularly turn over to the police. That was no surprise. No one enforced the requirement. The bigger hotels complied, the unlicensed rooms didn't, and everything in between was a maybe. Besides, none of the records were on computer so no one ever bothered to look at them unless there was a reason tied to a specific person at a specific hotel. Many simply were tossed to make room for other things.

Andreas pushed himself a little harder on his second lap around the perimeter. He assumed Vandrew arrived sometime during the two weeks preceding what the coroner fixed as her latest probable time of death. With the average tourist stay at three days, and 30,000 licensed beds to report, there theoretically were 140,000, mostly handwritten hotel entries to review for that period—assuming she was reported. Good luck finding her that way. He jogged back to the station.

Andreas had showered, and dressed and was having his second cup of coffee when the officer at the front desk called to tell him someone was there to see him—an Albanian who said he'd "only talk to the chief." Andreas went down to meet him, a short, slim man, about thirty, dressed in a white T-shirt and jeans. He looked tired and nervous. "You want to see me?" Andreas used his official tone.

"Yes, sir." The man's eyes jumped back and forth between Andreas and the other policemen. "Cousin say to trust you."

"Who's your cousin?"

"Alex. He find body in church."

He had Andreas' interest. Andreas led him up to his office and had him sit across from his desk. He left the door open—just in case—and smiled to try to make the man comfortable. "So, why did you want to see me?"

The man's voice cracked as he spoke. "Alex say I can trust you," he repeated as if reassuring himself that he could. "He say you fair and did not hurt him."

Andreas just listened.

"I knew the girl."

Andreas hoped his expression didn't show his excitement. He let him go on.

He spoke quickly in broken Greek. "She stay at hotel I work nights. I know her from picture police show me."

"Why didn't you tell that to the police officer when he showed you the photograph?" Andreas already knew the answer.

"I afraid."

Andreas nodded. An honest answer.

"Because boss not want me say anything." A surprising answer. "I did not want lose job." He was shaking now. Andreas offered him some water, and he took a drink. "When police showed me picture I know it her but my boss not put her in book."

His boss was stealing from the tax office—another Mykonos tradition.

"Then police speak to boss and he say she murdered." He was rocking back and forth in the chair.

Andreas perked up but maintained his steady, official tone. "How did your boss know that?" His men had been instructed not to say she was dead.

"He say everyone on Mykonos know girl found murdered and if police show picture of girl it had to be her." His voice was slightly calmer though he continued to rock.

Sort of like trying to hide an elephant under a tablecloth, thought Andreas.

"He say he want no trouble with police and to say nothing." He stopped rocking and started clasping and unclasping his hands.

"Why are you telling me this now?" Andreas asked, looking for a motive.

"I like her, she nice to me," he said, his voice cracking this time.

Andreas knew there had to be more of a reason than that. Giving his best all-knowing look he said, "And?"

The man started rocking again. "I know Alex found her. I tell him what boss say. He say must tell you." He paused. "Because you will find out and I be in big trouble."

God bless those who overestimate how much police know— and can find out—Andreas thought. "And?" His voice was more forceful this time.

The man started to shake again. "No more, that only reason."

Andreas decided not to press him. He'd leave that to Kouros, who spoke some Albanian. He'd remain the good cop on this one. Andreas picked up the phone and called Kouros. He met Kouros at the doorway and whispered what the man had said and what he wanted Kouros to do.

Andreas introduced the man to Kouros as if the man were his friend. "Officer Kouros, this man has been a great help to us. Please take his statement and make sure no one lets his boss know he was here."

Kouros turned to the man and nodded. "Where do you work, sir?" he asked in Albanian.

"The Hotel Adlantis."

It took about an hour of good-cop, bad-cop to get the man frightened enough to tell what else he knew. Another hour until Andreas was convinced the man wasn't lying, and another thirty seconds for Andreas and Kouros to be out the door racing toward the hotel.

◇◇◇

Annika hadn't slept well. She felt uncomfortable in the room. She wanted to get out and decided to sleep on the beach. She threw her things into a beach bag, put on a tank top and a pair of shorts, and headed out the door, flopping along in her sandals.

It was still very early for Mykonos. She'd slept only a couple of hours. She couldn't believe how different this walk to the bus station was from her last. The streets were deserted. She laughed and shook her head as a police car went screaming by her. No one on the roads and still they drive with sirens blaring. Boys never grow up, she thought.

There was only one bus, marked "Paradise." She smiled. That's just where she wanted to be.

◇◇◇

Andreas was in no mood for niceties. He told the woman behind the counter he wanted to speak to the owner. She said he was out and wasn't sure when he'd be back. He told her that in ten minutes either the owner was here talking to them or his officers started knocking on doors and talking to every guest in the hotel. His choice. Ilias was there in five.

"Ilias Batesakis?" Andreas' tone was as stern as his look.

"Yes." His voice was neutral.

"Is there a place we can talk privately?"

Ilias showed him and Kouros into the small office next to the reception counter and closed the door.

Andreas stared at him, saying nothing. Without moving his eyes from Ilias he held out his hand, and Kouros handed him a photograph. "Have you ever seen this woman before?"

Ilias looked at the photo with no emotion. "As I told your officers last night, no, not in my life."

"It's time to rethink your answer."

"Who do you think you're talking to?" Ilias raised his voice. "You come into my place of business, frightening my help and threatening me. I am a cousin of the mayor."

"Fine. He can visit you in jail," Andreas said, and gave Kouros a take-him-away gesture.

Kouros motioned for Ilias to follow him. Ilias laughed, until Kouros grabbed him, swung him around, and cuffed his hands behind him. Not the usual treatment afforded politically connected Mykonians. Ilias no longer was laughing. He began to curse.

Andreas simply waited until he'd finished. "We came here to ask you questions. You're the one who's turned yourself into a murder suspect."

The color drained from Ilias' face. It was as gray as his hair. "Murder? I didn't do anything to the girl. I don't know what happened to her. She never came back."

There was no need to note he'd just admitted to lying—they were way past that point.

"Where are the tapes?"

The man looked as if he might faint. "What tapes?"

Andreas threw him into a chair. "Asshole, where are the tapes? You're the number one suspect in a murder case. Now try to change my mind."

"I want to speak to my cousin." He sounded frightened.

Andreas smacked him across the face with the back of his hand. "Take him out of here, Yianni. We'll get what we want from him back at the station."

Ilias was strong and tried to resist when Kouros took his arm to pull him out of the chair, but Kouros was stronger and enjoyed his work. The sound of Ilias bouncing off the walls got the receptionist yelling, "Is everything all right in there?"

Kouros had Ilias pressed against the wall with his arms locked behind him in cuffs. Breathing heavily, Ilias yelled back, "Yes, Roz. All is okay." Then he said quietly, "She came by boat."

Kouros didn't budge. "Keep talking," said Andreas.

"She was to stay four days but left before." It was a struggle for him to speak.

"What do you mean 'left before'?" Andreas' voice was merciless.

"She disappeared. We never saw her after the second day."

"What did you do with her things?"

"I threw them out."

All of that matched with what his night man had told them. Now to see if what else they'd been told was true.

"I want to see the tapes."

"I don't know what you're talking about," Ilias said, his voice cracking.

Andreas stepped forward so that his eyes were twelve inches from Ilias' and spoke in a precise, determined whisper. "Let me put it this way, you fucking pervert, we know you have a video camera hidden in your 'special room,' and frankly, I don't give a shit how often you beat off to those fantasies of yours, but if you force us to tear this hotel apart brick by brick until we find that camera and those tapes—and we will find them—you better pray hers is with them. Otherwise, we'll know you tossed it because you didn't want us to know what was on it."

Ilias was in full panic. "*No, no!* I had nothing to do with her. The tape is downstairs. You'll see what I say is true."

So, the night man was right about the tapes, too.

"I want to see the girl's room." Andreas gestured for Kouros to let him off the wall.

"There's someone in it."

"So what?"

"Please, this will ruin the reputation of my hotel."

Andreas couldn't believe the guy. He's a murder suspect and he's worried about disturbing a guest.

"We're going to take the handcuffs off, but if you even breathe funny, we'll drag you out of here by your balls. Understand?"

"Yes."

"Now show us." Andreas nodded to Kouros to take off the cuffs.

He took them first to a locked room on the bottom floor where he kept the tapes. Her time at the hotel was recorded on one of hundreds. They must go back years. Possibly decades. Andreas' heart was pounding. Could he be the one? "Where's her room?"

"Next door."

They knocked on the door but there was no answer. Ilias opened it with his passkey. It was tiny. Women's clothes were scattered as if the occupant had left in a hurry. Andreas looked at Ilias. "You have tapes of her too?"

No answer.

Andreas slapped him again. "I'm talking to you."

"Yes."

"Where is she?"

"I don't know. She must have gone out."

"How do you know?"

"I was taping her while she slept."

Andreas wanted to punch him. "Where's the camera?"

He showed them two—one in the bedroom, one in the bathroom.

"Yianni, get him out of here. Take him back to the station and let him call whoever the hell he wants. He'll need them all. Also, get someone over here to watch both rooms until forensics gets here from Syros. I'll wait for him."

Ilias started to object but Andreas gave him a warning look and he went quietly.

Andreas sat on the edge of the bed and called Tassos from his cell phone. Tassos sounded as excited at hearing what Andreas had found as Andreas was at telling him. Forensics would be on the way within an hour. Andreas hung up and stared down at the floor, thinking.

Why did speaking to Tassos make him think of his father? And why was that bothering him? He thought he'd gotten over the anger. Eight is a bad age to lose a dad. You're just getting to know him, appreciate him, learn from him, and *poof*, suddenly he's gone. It can make you a very angry young man, finding yourself instantly a fatherless, only son. Maybe that's why I've never married, he thought—to spare some other eight-year-old the pain. Nah, that's not it. Just haven't found the right girl yet. Thank God for my sister's kids, or I'd never hear the end of it from Mother.

He looked up. A pair of French doors opened onto a small balcony. The scene beyond was magnificent: a serene silver-blue sea and shades-of-brown distant hills dotted with tiny white houses under an Aegean-blue sky. He wondered how many other young women had seen that view as one of their last on earth.

Andreas couldn't believe his luck at finding the killer so quickly. It seemed too good to be true.

Chapter Eight

The early-morning bus to Paradise was filled with two types: the totally wasted who had not slept and were returning to the campgrounds by the beach, and the totally alert who had not partied. Annika felt closer to the former but tried acting like the latter. When the bus arrived, Annika followed the sober ones to the beach. She decided it was better to stay with that crowd because the others—and stragglers out of Paradise's notorious all-night dance clubs—were busy mating up for one last shot at whatever they hadn't quite been able to achieve by midmorning.

Her crowd headed to the end farthest away from the clubs, past the rented umbrellas and lounges to an open section of beach. She followed them. They put down their towels. She did the same. They took off all their clothes. She didn't know what to do.

Nudity was common on Mykonos, but these people were her parents' age. She looked back up the beach to see where else she could go, but something told her she was least likely to be bothered here. They all seemed to know one another, and the group kept growing. Before long she was surrounded by naked Karlas, Georges, Sharons, and Edwards from all over the world. As hesitant as she was to take off her suit, she felt she'd attract more attention in it rather than out of it; so with a "when in paradise" attitude she stripped naked as the rest. No one seemed to notice. They all seemed so nice. She fell asleep on her belly with a towel over her head to the sounds of old friends having a good time.

◇◇◇

Andreas told the officer watching the rooms not to leave the hotel until the woman staying in the Vandrew room returned. He wanted to know how she ended up in there. Then he left to see Pappas. There still was the matter of those other churches to follow up on.

Contractors, as a rule, aren't in their offices much, and Pappas was no exception. It took about an hour before Andreas found him, he was over by Elía Beach, where he was supervising the "renovation" addition of two dozen mountainside villas to an already huge hotel. There were mixed feelings over the effect those hotels had on the beauty of the island but not on how they affected the families who owned them. They made them very rich—and powerful enough to go on "renovating" away to their hearts' content.

Andreas met him in the hotel restaurant.

"So, Chief, how can I help you this time?" asked Pappas, from behind his sunglasses.

Andreas knew this was going to cost him. "I'm trying to locate some old churches."

"Which ones?"

Andreas handed him the list. Pappas looked at it. "These are Father Paul's," he said, his voice hard.

"I know. He gave me the names."

Pappas' voice grew loud. "You can't possibly think he had anything to do with the murder."

Andreas kept his cool. "I think it's best for your friend that you keep your voice down."

"Don't tell me what to do," he said in a quieter voice.

"I didn't say he's a suspect," Andreas said. "We found a dead body in an abandoned church. Now we're checking out other abandoned churches for clues."

"Why?"

Obviously Pappas didn't know about the other three bodies. If he had, he wouldn't be asking why. That meant word hadn't leaked out yet, because if it had, Pappas would be among the first to know.

"It's routine." Andreas was getting weary of playing up to Pappas' ego. "Look, if you want to help, fine; if not, I'll find someone else. I figured I could trust you not to start gossiping that your friend Father Paul might be a suspect just because I'm asking about his churches." Yeah, sure.

Pappas stared at him for several seconds. "You know, I'm getting a lot of grief about my trucks hauling concrete at seven in the morning through that neighborhood up there." He pointed north. "On the road to Aghios Sostis Beach, but it gives me the edge I need to finish my projects on time." The price had been set.

Andreas shrugged. "I don't see a problem with that, as long as your drivers aren't any drunker than the rest at that hour."

Pappas smiled. "Do you have a map?"

Andreas handed him one and watched Pappas make eight marks and write eight names before handing it back.

"Thank you."

"No problem, Chief. By the way…" Andreas couldn't believe he had the balls to ask for more. "Ilias is a pervert, everyone knows that, but he's no murderer."

How the hell does word get out so fast? Of course, Ilias' cousin's the mayor and Pappas is the former mayor. "What do you mean, everyone knows he's a pervert?"

Pappas gave his best "you should know this already" look. "Ilias is kinky, he films the women in his hotel, then watches the videos with his girlfriends. He gets off on having them imitate what he's filmed."

"How do you know all this?" Andreas' voice was official.

He snickered. "We have the same girlfriends. We all do. It's a small island."

Andreas took the *we* to mean the Mykonos powers that be.

"I'm not telling you how to do your job, Chief, but Ilias isn't your killer. Besides, he's probably out by now. The mayor's already spoken to Syros."

Andreas was certain his anger was showing now. "Anything else?"

Pappas obviously was enjoying this chance to lecture the new boy in town on how to get along. "No, but good luck in finding your killer. I'm sure it's some Albanian. Find one, and the whole town will support you."

In other words, if Andreas knew what was good for him, he'd stay away from the Mykonians. Andreas wanted to wipe the smirk off the asshole's face with a lecture of his own, on the perils of allowing a serial killer to run around his island paradise murdering tourist women, but instead he thanked him and left. He had churches to visit.

◇◇◇

Andreas' first call once he was back on the road was to Tassos. He wanted to keep Ilias in custody.

"Don't worry about it," Tassos said, his voice calm, reassuring.

"What do you mean don't worry, he's our number one suspect." Andreas was yelling in the Greek style.

"Andreas, relax. Where's he going to go? His whole life is on Mykonos, and we'll have him watched day and night. It'll be like house arrest—in a very big house."

Andreas knew Tassos was trying to put the best face on a politically impossible situation. It didn't make him any happier, but there was no way Ilias was staying in jail without solid evidence tying him to a murder. Showing he was a pervert wasn't enough of a reason for Syros politicians keeping the Mykonos mayor's cousin in jail. "Damn it."

Tassos must have sensed Andreas' tension through the phone. "I know." He paused until Andreas was breathing normally. "So, what about our former number one suspect?"

"I'm on my way to check out his churches," he grumbled.

"Do you really think he'd be crazy enough to name places where he buried bodies?"

"Who knows, he's damn smart, and if he didn't tell me, he knew we'd find out anyway. It was the savvy move." The anger had drained from Andreas' voice.

"Guess you're right. If you find anything, let me know and I'll send the forensic guys from the hotel over to meet you."

"Thanks. Any luck yet?"

"A lot of tapes of what must be five hundred women, indexed and cross-indexed by name, address, age, country of origin—the stuff off passports." He paused.

"And?" Andreas was not in the mood to enjoy Tassos' penchant for the dramatic.

"By body parts. Hair color—top and bottom—breast size, nipple color…need I go on? I think you get the idea."

"Fuck." Andreas shook his head. "Trouble is, unless we get a match to another dead woman, it's all consistent with what we already know—he's a pervert." He slowed down to turn onto the road leading to the old mines.

Tassos said, "I have someone trying to come up with a match, but I'm not sure we'll find one even if he's our guy."

"Why?"

"He could have destroyed tapes of girls he killed."

"But we saw Helen Vandrew on tape."

"Yeah." Tassos' voice was tentative, as if searching for an answer. "But maybe he hadn't gotten around to destroying that one yet."

Andreas was impatient—he knew there was something else. "What's bothering you?"

"My Scandinavian wasn't in the index, and it goes back years before we found her."

After a short silence, Andreas, clearly exasperated, muttered, "Nothing's easy. Well, maybe she's not in it, but they'll find her on the tapes."

"Maybe." Tassos didn't sound encouraged. "Good luck with your churches."

"I'll take that to mean 'May all the bones be old bones.' Call you later. I'm almost at the first one." Andreas hung up.

He pulled off the road at a place Pappas had marked on the map. He shut off the engine but didn't move, just looked up the hill at a ramble of dry brush and neglected stone walls and stared at the whitewashed church near the top. He still remembered standing in a museum as a child with his father, staring at the side of a famous sculpture and wondering what all the fuss was about. It looked so very simple and unremarkable—until he moved to face it and saw head-on all the terrifying power and complexity of snake-haired Medusa. Please, not again, he prayed.

◇◇◇

When Annika awoke there was a light, azure *pareo* draped over her body. It was not hers, and she had no idea who had put it there, but whoever did had spared her a horrific sunburn. She must have been sleeping for hours. She sat up, carefully folded it, and looked around. No one seemed to be paying attention to her except for a few young Greek men waving for her to join them.

An attractive, middle-aged woman on the towel next to her was reading a magazine entitled *California Living*. Annika asked if she knew who her Good Samaritan was. The woman pointed to a very fit, silver-haired man lying naked on his stomach two towels away. He was facing them but seemed asleep. Annika was sure she'd seen him before but couldn't place him.

"Just give it to me, darling, and I'll see that Paul gets it when he wakes up."

"Thanks," Annika said, and handed her the *pareo*. She was hungry and decided to get something to eat at the taverna on the beach. The Greek guys started calling to her, first in Greek and then in English. She ignored them as she dressed, gathered up her things, and walked to the taverna.

She chose the table closest to the sea and ordered water, a Greek salad, and grilled octopus. She felt at peace. She also felt someone watching her—but that wasn't unusual; the reason she picked that table was so she could look at the sea without someone in her line of vision trying to catch her attention. Not that anyone could have, for she was mesmerized by the endless stream of swimmers climbing onto a nearby reef running parallel to the beach.

Once on the reef, most preened a bit, as if they were walking on water. But their godlike experiences were not without risk, for the reef was covered in sea urchins—with porcupine-like spines. She watched one strutting, barefoot waterwalker after another suddenly jump in the air and grab a pierced foot. As for the occasional naked swimmer unwary enough to sit on the reef, all Annika could think of was "*ouch!*" She was feeling slightly guilty at her schadenfreude fascination but not enough to look away. After all, she thought, it's sort of their fault for not having the common sense to know better, and besides, it was very funny.

At around five, people started drifting in from the beach to begin their early afternoon partying. That was when the guys began bothering her again. It was time to head back to the hotel. She walked behind the taverna to the bus stop next to the campgrounds. It was just a wider bit of dirt than the rest of the road down to the beach.

She watched a faint-brown-and-green bus wind down the road toward where she stood. Brown and green were the colors of the hills. She wondered about the significance of Mykonos buses being land-colored instead of blue and white like the sea and sky. Probably just a practical one—light brown and green don't show the ever-present dust so much; when the winds are blowing it is like brown powdered sugar flying everywhere.

The bus at that hour was virtually empty except for a few older couples and locals lucky enough to squeeze in some time at the beach before getting back to their jobs. She decided to go into town rather than back to the hotel.

She had a coffee under a canopied taverna on the harbor and watched Pétros and Irini do their tourist thing—posing for pictures and giving the occasional nip at gestures deemed unfriendly—Mykonos' clipped-wing, pelican mascots, were direct descendants, some claimed, of the pair donated to the island by Mykonos lover Jacqueline Kennedy not-yet-Onassis.

Annika had seen this harbor from every approach and never tired of it. Her favorite vantage was the one she got when sailing between Mykonos and Delos, a sea view of the most famous church in the Cyclades, the fifteenth-century Paraportiani. It stood between the bays of Tourlos and Korfos on the outer edge of a jut of land at the southernmost side of the old harbor. Really a combination of five churches—four below and one above—its roots traced back the thirteenth-century when a portion of its structure served as part of a defensive wall for the protecting castle that once stood there. Paraportiani always made Annika think of a huge mound of sunlit marshmallows topped by a jumbo white cherry. The church was practically all that remained of the castle—that and the Kastro name for the area bordering Little Venice, where today's invaders sought their adventures in all-night bars and clubs.

Annika thought of the night before and how stupid she'd been. She must rid her mind of that memory. Tomorrow morning she'd catch an early boat to Delos. That should do the trick.

The holy island was only a mile from where she sat. She'd spent her college freshman summer there working at archeological digs begun by the French in 1873 and pitching in as a guide through its ancient ruins for VIP tours in one of her languages. She'd loved it. The uninhabited island was different from Mykonos in every way—though in antiquity Delos clearly had been the better place to party. Mykonos wasn't even on the maps of those times, and its name meant nothing more than "mound of rocks."

Annika tried to recall the words of the introduction to her tour: "Basically flat except for two hills, and only one twentieth the size of Mykonos, Delos in the ancient world was considered the center of Cycladic life. But its influence ended abruptly in the early part of the last century before Christ, when Delos backed the wrong protector and twenty thousand inhabitants were slaughtered, its physical and cultural landscape destroyed. The island was leveled, but its intense spiritual power endures to this day."

She repeated the last words aloud to herself: "its intense, spiritual power endures to this day." Yes, that's definitely what she needed, and she vowed to be on the first boat the next morning. She'd be back by four at the latest. Demetra was arriving tomorrow. Besides, she had to be—the guards allowed no one on Delos after sunset, and the last boat left at three.

But for now she was off to explore the shops just opening for the evening. Most didn't close until after midnight, some not until sunup. As if following Alice down the rabbit hole into Wonderland, Annika plunged through a break in a row of seafront tavernas, and—like magic—the harbor vanished. She was back in the maze of twisting, narrow stone paths that, for her, held the essence of Mykonos' charm; it was the labyrinth itself—not what it offered—that she loved.

Sure, Mykonos was famous for tantalizing tourists with brightly lit shops, colorful restaurants, roaring bars, and free-wheeling dance clubs, but this still was a town where people raised families and shared strong traditions. Down the less traveled lanes, children played their games oblivious to the occasional tourists squeezing through their four-, five-, or maybe six-foot-wide playgrounds. Pairs of grandmothers, all in black, did duty watching the children. They'd sit on stoops in front of their houses or, if a shop occupied the street level, on brightly painted wooden balconies outside their second-floor homes; balconies with gates guarding pets, pots of geraniums, draping bougainvillea, and—if rented to tourists—clothes left to dry.

As she walked, Annika's eyes drifted up from the rows of glossy green, blue, and red banisters to where the white textures of the buildings met the sky. So many whites: light white, dark white, sunlit white, shaded white, dirt-caked white, white over color, white over stone, white over wood, white over steel, white over rust, peeled white, fresh white, old white, slick white, coarse white—against so many blues: dark blue, pale blue, and all those blues in between. Annika smiled, took in a deep breath, and said softly, "I just love it here."

She wandered over to Little Venice and in a shop looking across to the windmills bought a blue-and-silver beaded necklace that reminded her of the sea. She was admiring her purchase in the reflection of another shop's window when a voice behind her said in English, "Great necklace, fits you perfectly." She could see in the reflection that it was an older man in the doorway of the shop behind her.

She turned and said, "Thank you." Her voice was courteous, nothing more.

"Is that one of Susy's?"

"Susy?"

"From La Thalassa."

She smiled and felt a tinge of pride at having something so recognizable. "Yes, it is."

"I thought so. She has great things. Glad her price point is different from mine. Couldn't stand the competition, especially from a fellow South African." He smiled.

Annika realized the shop was one of the premier high-end jewelers on the island—way out of her league. "That's very sweet of you to say."

"I like her, she has style. Would you like a coffee?"

Annika hesitated but caught herself. This is Mykonos, she thought, and jewelers are nice to everyone. She should stop being so paranoid over last night. "Thank you. That would be lovely."

She spent over two hours in the shop. The owner was a Greek born in South Africa and also a George—but very different from her George of the night before. He was raised on a farm "in the bush" and educated in Johannesburg. Although he missed the beauty of Africa—if not its politics—in Greece he'd been able to pursue an interest in ancient civilizations he'd picked up in college. He took great pride in showing her a small Corinthian vase he claimed predated the birth of Christ by more than five hundred years.

Even after more than twenty years on Mykonos, George still felt treated as a foreigner, but he accepted that as a fact of island life. Besides, there wasn't much choice because this was where his business was and where he'd made his life—though off-season he lived in Athens. He mentioned a few other old-timers, as he called them who felt the same way, including the artist she'd met the night before, and pointed to one of his paintings hanging in a corner.

"I admire how his style appeals to so many on so many different levels. It's not just for tourists." He pointed again and when he spoke, intensity came into his voice. "See how he weaves mythic Greek figures into his work."

Annika was tempted to add that somewhere in each painting lay the image of "a lost soul rebirthing out of darkness into light," but that inevitably would lead to explaining those were the artist's words to her—and a discussion of their meeting last night. She didn't want to get into that. Instead, she talked about her life as if she were a Dutch girl on her first trip to Greece; but mostly she listened. George liked to talk, and although he didn't say whether he was married, she assumed he was. She pointed to a photograph of a young girl and younger boy on his desk and asked if those were his children.

The question seemed to surprise him. He hesitated, as if searching for the right words. "No, it's my sister and me. In fact, you remind me of her." He smiled.

When she said she had to leave, he seemed disappointed but didn't push to see her again. They simply shook hands and said good-bye.

She walked back to the harbor and sat in a café to watch the sunset. For the first time in a long while she felt in control of her life. As far as she was concerned, Peter was now ancient history. She owed nothing to anyone but herself—and her family of course, which reminded her to call home the moment she got back to the hotel. For now, though, she wanted to enjoy her anonymity a bit longer.

◇◇◇

Andreas was getting used to climbing dry, rocky hillsides. It was his fourth of the day and so far so good—if not finding anything but very old bones was good. His fourth church of the afternoon was on the southeast part of the island, not far from some of Mykonos' most popular beaches. Sooner or later developers would bring a lot of company to this isolated tribute to Saint Fanourios. For the time being, though, it sat on deserted ground—the same as the three others he'd visited today honoring Saint Nicholas, Saint Barbara, and Saint Phillipos.

All four churches were several hundred years old. Andreas had been told that some went back to the 1500s, maybe even earlier, depending on who you talked to. Whatever their age, all were recently whitewashed, and their doors and shutters functioned properly. The roof of one could have used a paint job, but for the most part, they'd been kept up—just as Father Paul had said.

This church looked about the same as the other three: a bell tower above a west-facing blue door, one blue shuttered window on each side wall, a sacristy on the inside along the east wall, and a stone slab in the middle of a hard-packed floor. Newer churches built of concrete had hollow spaces in their walls for accommodating individual remains or steps beneath a floor slab leading to a cellar with places for the same purpose, but these old ones had only mass crypts in the floor—like the one where they found the Vandrew body. Aside from honoring different saints, the only real difference Andreas saw in any of them was that the church where they had found her was built of natural stone and never whitewashed. He wondered if that was somehow a clue.

He carefully examined the floor for anything that seemed out of place. Nothing looked unusual. He stood by the end of the slab nearest the door and gripped its edge. He took a deep breath to calm himself and forced a smile at the thought of how he was getting used to all this grave tampering. As he braced himself to pull at the slab, anxiety gripped the pit of his stomach—as it had each time before. If, God forbid, there weren't just old bones under here, he didn't know how they'd possibly keep things quiet. Another forensic team gathering bones from under another quaint Mykonos church was too much for the media to miss.

He wondered if he was up to handling the pressure of the press if it turned on him for doing what he thought was right. His father hadn't been. But he'd been set up and forced to choose between watching his family's reputation destroyed and…

"Damn it," Andreas said aloud. "Stop thinking about that."

He pulled at the slab until it moved enough for light from the doorway to shine into the crypt. He stared in for a moment, then walked outside and lit a cigarette. He took a puff, exhaled, and began to gag. He caught himself, took another deep breath, and wondered if he felt this way because of all the pressure he'd been under and those recurring thoughts of his father. That had to be part of the reason—that and the almost fully decomposed body he'd just found on a pile of not-so-old bones.

Chapter Nine

Andreas knew the mayor would not be pleased being summoned to the office of the chief of police. Dropping in once on his own for a visit was quite different from Andreas requesting his immediate presence. Still, Andreas had no choice but to insist; too many ears listened and tongues wagged in the mayor's office. Besides, by the time Tassos and Andreas were done with him, bruises to the mayor's ego would be the least of their worries.

Andreas wanted to inform the ministry in Athens immediately, but Tassos had convinced him that the politic thing to do was tell the mayor first. They still had to work with him, and the message would be bad enough without having it delivered by an elephant—Athenian no less—stepping on his toes. Andreas reluctantly agreed. They'd call Athens tomorrow.

Mayor Mihali Vasilas had been in office for almost two decades. He controlled the entire island. The island's two towns, Ano Mera and Mykonos, each had representatives on the island council but elected only one mayor. He was powerful and knew it. He also knew how to be gracious. This evening he was a combination of both. When he walked into Andreas' office he gave a charming hello followed by a searing look from deep-set dark eyes. He was a foot shorter than Andreas, and slim. It was rumored that he kept himself in shape by eating only those who got in his way. In other words, he ate very little. He looked hungry.

The three still were standing about an arm's length apart. The mayor looked at Tassos. "Tassos, why am I here?"

Andreas took the question for what it was: an effort to put Andreas in his place as irrelevant on Mykonos. He decided to let things play out. He knew where they had to end. May as well give him all the rope he needed.

Tassos looked at Andreas to answer. "Mr. Mayor," Andreas said, "we have a problem—a very serious problem—and we want you to know about it before we contact Athens."

The mayor jerked his head toward Andreas, anger glaring in his eyes. "You will do nothing without my approval, absolutely nothing!" he yelled. "Do you understand?"

"Beg your pardon, Mr. Mayor, but it's out of our hands." Andreas sounded as gracious as a headwaiter.

"Nothing is out of your hands where I'm concerned, absolutely nothing." The veins were popping in his neck, and he was waving his finger in Andreas' face.

Andreas wondered if something in their oath of office made Mykonos mayors—past and present—so arrogant.

"Well, this just might be the exception, Mihali." Tassos said, his tone telling him to get off his mayoral high horse and, by his nod toward Andreas, to show some respect.

But the mayor would not dismount. "I don't want to hear another word about that murdered girl and my cousin. *Not one.* Do I make myself clear?"

"It's not just about her. There's more," Andreas said, his voice coldly professional.

"More? More of what?"

"Murders," Andreas said the word softly. No need for more drama than that.

The mayor stared at him. His face looked puzzled, then he looked at Tassos and his expression strangely relaxed. "Let me guess, after all these years you think you've finally found a way to resurrect your theory that the Irishman didn't kill the Scandinavian. You think, because you found the new body bound copycat like one from ten years ago, everything ties together and vindicates your theory." His tone was derisive.

He certainly knew his facts, at least some of them, thought Andreas.

"I think it's safe to say I've more than proven I was right about that, Mihali." Tassos' tone was not appeasing.

The mayor pointed his index finger in Tassos' face. "If any of this bullshit gets out about the two murders being related—one word, a single word—you can kiss your pension good-bye, and"—turning to Andreas—"you, you'll never ever see anything but parking tickets for the rest of whatever career you have left."

If that's the way it's going to be, Andreas thought, he was prepared to play. "Okay, you've got a deal, Mr. Mayor." Andreas nodded in agreement, patted the mayor on the shoulder, walked around his desk, and sat down. Smiling, he leaned back and linked his hands behind his head. "Neither of us will say a fucking single word to anyone tying those two murders together. We'll leave that to the press to figure out on its own when we tell them about the other sixteen bodies we found—some still bound like the two you don't want us to talk about." He leaned forward, dropped his hands to the desk, and looked at Tassos. "Am I right that it's eighteen in total? The seventeen we found in four churches plus the Scandinavian."

Tassos gave Andreas a quick look of admiration and turned to the mayor with a deadpan expression. "So far. After all, we've only had time to look in eight churches."

They both stared at the mayor. His mouth was wide open but not a word came out.

After allowing the stew to simmer for a moment, Tassos added some spice. "The murders appear spaced at the rate of one per year." He paused. "And roughly span your term in office, Mr. Mayor." Tassos smiled broadly and dropped into his favorite chair.

The mayor was seething. He pulled up a straight-back wooden chair and sat so he could see both men. Then he demanded details. Andreas delivered them matter-of-factly. "We found the remains of seventeen bodies, all tall females, in the floor crypts of four churches. Preliminarily, forensics show no evidence of clothing or hair more than stubble on any victim, but hemp twine was found at all locations, and remains of at least one body in each crypt were found bound in the same manner as the Vandrew woman."

"And the Scandinavian," Tassos added with a glare at the mayor.

Andreas continued, "Remains of four bodies each were found in Saint Kiriake, Saint Marina, and Saint Calliope—including Helen Vandrew's. Five bodies were found at Saint Fanourios. No bodies were found at Saint Barbara, Saint Nicholas, Saint Phillipos, or Saint Spyridon."

Visibly shaken, the mayor tried sounding imperious. "You're the professionals. You should know what to do. Do you have a suspect?" It wasn't working. It was obvious to everyone in the room that his fate was in the hands of the men he'd just threatened with destruction.

Andreas smiled. "Yes."

The mayor looked like he was about to say "Who?" but he stopped. "Do you have any proof tying your suspect to any of the other killings?"

"Not as yet."

The mayor put his head down and ran his hands through his hair. "Do what you have to do, but I don't think he's your man." He'd abandoned all pretext of not knowing his cousin was who they had in mind. "I've known him all my life. I know how badly beaten he was by his father—the drunken bastard—and when he drowned no one blamed Ilias, but I can't imagine him being involved in…in this."

Did I just hear him say his cousin might have killed his father for abusing him? Andreas thought. *Damn, we're checking one box after another on this guy's list of major, serial killer-traits—male, intelligent, a voyeur, abused, drunken father—and we're just getting started!*

"Anything else unusual about your cousin's behavior or background?"

The mayor took in and let out a deep breath. He now was being interrogated by the chief of police. He raised no objection. "You mean other than the tapes?"

Andreas nodded.

"I don't know…" The mayor's voice drifted off. He sounded lost, not in control. "What are we going to do?"

"Not much we can do, Mihali, we have to tell Athens," said Tassos.

The mayor nodded and clasped his hands together. "I have a suggestion." He seemed to be pleading more than suggesting. "This is a disaster for Mykonos. We all know that."

The two policemen nodded.

"It would be better if when we announced the terrible news we also announced the capture of the killer." He was looking at the floor as he abandoned his cousin.

"I don't know how we can do that. We don't have proof yet," said Andreas.

"I'll give you whatever help you need. If we have no killer, we have no tourists and we have no island. It's as simple as that."

"Mr. Mayor—"

"Call me Mihali, Andreas." He really was politicking now.

Andreas nodded. "Mihali, I don't see how we can keep this quiet until we find the killer. It puts too many people in danger."

"But I thought you said it's one victim a year and he's already murdered once this year."

Tassos answered. "It just looks that way, but we can't be sure and we've only been to eight churches."

The mayor put his head down again. "I understand, but is anyone missing who meets the description of his victims?"

Andreas said, "Not that we know of, but that doesn't mean much. You know how that sort of thing goes unreported." Andreas diplomatically did not add "because of your insistence on keeping such things unreported."

Again the mayor nodded. "What if we wait a few days and you spend the time looking into every shadow of Ilias' past, and if he turns out to be the one, well, so be it."

Andreas looked at Tassos. It would be impossible to do that sort of investigation with media running all over the island, and if they kept a tight rein on Ilias, there'd be no risk to anyone else. Perhaps the mayor's suggestion wasn't so bad. Unless, of course, the killer wasn't his cousin—but, then again, the mayor was correct in saying the killer seemed to get his urges only once a year. The risk of a few days might well be worth it.

As if reading Andreas' mind, Tassos said, "Okay, Mihali, three days, but you must give us your complete cooperation—"

The mayor cut him off. "Done."

Tassos smiled, "And—"

"I was afraid of that." The mayor grinned.

"Sign a letter on your official stationery acknowledging what we've told you and assuming full responsibility for directing us to keep that information from Athens until we've completed our investigation."

It was two political masters at work. All three of them knew the letter would mean nothing to Athens. Tassos and Andreas were toast if this deal ever got out. All it did was keep the mayor from throwing them to the wolves. He didn't even attempt to argue. "Done."

They told the mayor to tell no one—something he'd no doubt figured out for himself—and although they wouldn't be arresting his cousin just yet, they'd be closely watching his every move. Mihali assured them he'd handle any complaints of police harassment from Ilias.

When Mihali stood up to leave, he told them not to get up. He walked over and shook Andreas' hand. "Sorry about all that before, Chief. Sometimes my head gets a little too big for my own good."

Andreas nodded. "Thanks. I appreciate that."

He also apologized to Tassos. No wonder this guy's stayed in office so long, thought Andreas. He knows when to cut and run—and change horses in midstream.

After the mayor left, Tassos smiled and said, "I see you're pretty good at taking care of yourself with political types."

Andreas nodded.

Tassos lightly smacked the arms of his chair. "So, where do we go from here?"

"Why are you asking me?" said Andreas, looking puzzled.

"Because, I'm hoping you'll say 'Out to eat.' I'm starved."

Andreas smiled and with a come-along wave of his hand got up and said, "Good idea. Let's go to town for some dinner among those we've sworn to serve and protect."

◇◇◇

Annika wondered why her evening seemed headed toward ending at a gay bar in Little Venice. Sunset at the harbor had started out nicely, but when the wind picked up, and she went looking for a more sheltered spot, Little Venice was the natural choice, as it offered perfect sunset views. She didn't want to go to one of its popular straight bars and run into someone she knew—and the absolute certainty of being hassled. Then again, the wrong sort of gay place was likely to get her hassled by suitors of another persuasion.

She peeked inside a bar called Montmartre. It had an English pub-style front room and a larger, table-filled, back room lined with rear windows opening onto the sea. The place seemed cozy and not that busy. The two guys behind the bar—one blonde, one dark—were talking with a group of male customers and one very large woman. The dark one was telling a story in Greek and looking very serious. As Annika waited for him to finish, she looked around at the artwork on the walls. From the scenes she could tell it was local but way better than the stuff at her hotel. She liked the feel of the place and asked for a table overlooking the sea. The blonde smiled and told her in English to pick any one she wanted. It seemed the perfect, unthreatening place to spend an hour finishing the contemplation she'd begun at the harbor.

Before her hour had passed the place started filling up, with gay men and older, straight couples. She'd been staring out the window nursing her wine and hadn't noticed the piano tucked away in a corner by the front room until someone started to play. He was good, very good. The place kept filling up. The table she'd had so long to herself she now shared with six others. She didn't mind. They all seemed to be there for the music. Just when Annika thought the place couldn't get busier, the very large woman she'd seen earlier walked into the room and began to sing.

She was terrific. Before long it was standing room only in the front room. At a break, Annika ran to the toilet just past the bar—after making sure her table mates saved her seat. She was having the best night she could imagine and was working her way back to her table through the bar crowd when she felt a tap on her shoulder.

"So, we meet again, Annika," a voice said in English.

◇◇◇

One of the advantages of being police chief was that you didn't have to park in the public lot over by the ferry landing, a pleasant but ten-minute walk from the main part of town. Andreas nodded as he passed the officer assigned to keep all but taxis and official vehicles from mixing with the crowds milling along the old flagstone road down to the harbor. For part of the way, the road ran at tabletop height above and beside a tiny beach used more by pets than people, that ended abruptly at the north wall of the town's oldest hotel. As the road passed the rear of the hotel it began funneling down between buildings until it was only inches wider than Andreas' car. He had no choice but to crawl along at the pace of the crowd in front of him.

Andreas poked Tassos and pointed at two young women just beyond the front bumper. They were walking—more like staggering drunk or drugged—as if the police car didn't exist. Their tight skirts ended where their thighs began, and except for thin halter strings around their necks, their backs were bare, adorned with matching tattoos at the base of their spines. Two local boys walking with them noticed the police car and hurried them into the main square where the road opened up again into the taxi stand. Andreas nodded to the boys as he passed—it made them look important. It was a man thing.

"And they'll wonder why they wake up feeling sore in places they never knew they had," said Tassos, sounding disgusted.

Both men were quiet for a moment. "Do you think ours were like them?" asked Andreas. The victims were personal to him. That happened to cops.

"Don't know," said Tassos, shaking his head. "Don't think so, but I'm not sure why." He paused. "Maybe because there were no signs of rape with any of ours, and"—he gestured over his shoulder back at the women—"with that sort I'd expect to find some evidence of sexual activity."

Andreas parked beside a port police SUV, and they joined the crowd packing into the narrow main shopping street of Mykonos. It was still early, not yet eleven, and Matogianni Street was filled with young people trying very hard to look different from one another—so hard, in fact, that they all ended up looking alike. Andreas pointed to a side street, and they moved out of the crowd, heading to a restaurant that was surrounded by bougainvillea and geraniums, filled with white linen-covered tables, and watched over by an owner whose personality gave Greeks a good name.

Andreas didn't go here simply because Niko wouldn't let him pay—no restaurant would take the chief's money—but because he liked the place. Good food, no attitude, and a garden out of sight from the street. There was a lot to talk about and he wanted no interruptions.

They chatted at the bar for a few minutes with Niko and his wife, then Niko led them to a table in the rear of the garden. He left them for a moment and came back holding, in one hand, a plate of *mostra*—fresh made toasted bread, spread thick with homemade Mykonian *kopanisti* cheese and covered with olives, fresh tomatoes, and olive oil—and a bottle of wine in the other. He poured each a glass and said he'd already ordered for them. They smiled, thanked him, and watched him leave to greet other guests.

Andreas was in a serious mood. "Our careers are over if we don't catch this bastard in three days."

Tassos shrugged. "Even if we catch him, Athens will be pissed." He reached for his wineglass but didn't pick it up. "They'll say we were grabbing the glory for ourselves by not telling them sooner, and if he gets away…" He let his words drift off and a devilish smile formed as he lifted his glass. "*Yamas*, Chief Dead Meat."

Andreas smiled and picked up his glass. "*Yamas*."

They clinked and tasted the wine.

Andreas put down his glass. "So, why are you risking your pension for just three more days?"

Tassos took a longer sip and put down his glass. He tasted the *mostra*. "If we don't catch him now, he'll just fade away. Once this gets out, everyone on Mykonos will be a suspect watched by everyone else. He'd have to leave the island—if he wanted to keep killing—or just stop. Either way, he'd get away."

Tassos picked up his glass again but just stared at it. "He'll have murdered all those young women and walked away as if nothing happened. The three days are our last shot. Had to take it." He extended his glass toward Andreas.

Andreas picked up his and again they clinked.

More food arrived—*taramosaláta, tzatziki, salata horiátiki, kalamárakia, keftédes, dolmades, barboúnia*—and they jumped right on it. Neither spoke for a bit. Andreas seemed to have something else on his mind.

"How well did you know my dad?"

Tassos kept on eating and answered as if he'd been expecting the question. "He was a respected man on the force when I joined. I knew him by reputation more than anything else, though I met him a few times." He paused to take a sip of wine.

"When was that?"

Tassos stared at him. "1972."

Andreas nodded. Tassos just admitted to serving the dictatorship, but unlike Andreas' father, he'd survived Greece's return to democracy in 1974.

Andreas smiled. "I was still in diapers."

Tassos gave a dismissive wave. "He was a tough cop in those days, no doubt about it. He did what had to be done to enforce the law. No *fakelaki* for him. That made him enemies."

Fakelaki, that simple Greek word for "little envelope" had a secondary meaning burned into Andreas' memory.

Tassos looked down at the table. "Do you really want to be hearing this?"

Andreas paused, as if wondering whether he did. "It wasn't easy for him after 1974."

Tassos looked up and nodded. "No, it wasn't. The new regime didn't want him—if you ask me, because he was honest." He paused. "Then he hooked up with that bastard—"

Andreas put up his hand to stop him. "No need to go there." Andreas remembered the headlines, Ex-Secret Police Captain Leads Massive Bribe Operation. "I know all about it," said Andreas.

Silence.

"My dad," Andreas said slowly measuring his words, "loved being a cop. When that…deputy minister gave him the chance a few years later to be one again, he jumped at it." He let out a breath. "He had no idea he was being set up. I think that's what devastated him more than anything else—that he didn't see it coming." He picked up his glass and took a sip of wine.

Tassos spoke softly. "That deputy minister was a shrewd bastard."

This time Andreas didn't object. "Sure was. Getting my father appointed head of his ministry's security detail made Dad loyal as a puppy. Never questioned all those *fakelaki* pickups and deliveries…that bastard had him make." Andreas reached for his water glass. "Told him they were 'top-secret ministry documents.' He'd deliver a demand for a bribe in one envelope and bring back the cash in another. When someone complained to the press about all the bribes involved in getting business from the ministry, he was fingered as the one demanding and getting the payoffs."

Andreas didn't say any more. No need to. Tassos already knew. Within a week of the story breaking, his father was dead. "Accident while cleaning gun" was the official finding, but everyone knew that was so he could be buried in consecrated ground. Suicides weren't allowed that rite by the church.

"You do know what happened to him," said Tassos, "the deputy minister?"

Andreas looked at him. "He was killed about a year later in an automobile accident."

Tassos stared straight into Andreas' eyes. "It was on a mountain road in northern Greece. A blowout. His car went over the side. He was the only passenger."

Andreas kept his eyes on Tassos. "I know."

"Remember when I said your father made a lot of enemies in his days on the force?"

Andreas nodded.

"He made a lot of friends, too. Friends who weren't happy with the way he was set up by that bastard, that dead bastard."

Andreas didn't blink. "Yes, I've heard that, too."

Tassos looked away, and neither said another word on the subject. They ate in silence for a few moments.

"I think you asked me, 'Where do we go from here?' How about back to the night manager at Ilias' hotel?" said Andreas.

"Why him?" Tassos was enjoying the food.

"He's the one most willing to talk. Maybe he'll remember something." Andreas reached for the bread. "Can't hurt—as long as his asshole boss doesn't find out who snitched on him."

"I wouldn't worry about that," said Tassos, taking a piece of bread from Andreas. "Ilias probably can't find better or cheaper help. Besides, the worst he could do is get him deported to Albania. Even if that happened, he'd be back in Greece in no time."

"I guess you're right. And he'd be nuts trying to mess with the guy. He must know how tough the Albanians can be at protecting their own from legbreakers."

"Mmm," Tassos agreed through a sip of wine. "He knows. And without his cousin the mayor backing him up, Ilias is a bit of a coward." He took another sip. "You still think it's him?"

"Don't know, but there's something about Father Paul that's not right."

"I'll ask a friend in London if they have a file on him."

"Good idea." Andreas was into the octopus and salad.

Tassos lifted his fork to his mouth. "Any other suspects?"

Andreas gave the upward head gesture for "no" among Greeks. "Not yet," he said, then took a sip of water. "I think I'll stop at the hotel after we're done. Where are you staying?"

"Just outside of town, at the Rhenia Hotel. I'm catching the first morning boat to Syros."

Andreas pushed his plate forward. He was finished eating. "I meant to tell you, your forensic guys did a great job."

"Thanks," said Tassos.

Andreas was sincere. Tassos' men had agreed to no suits, no sirens, no marked cars, and whirlwind stops at the churches. Andreas had left them with the body at Saint Fanourios while he went on to the last three on Father Paul's list. His first stop, at Saint Spyridon, yielded an empty crypt and hopes of no more bodies. Forensics caught up to him before he'd opened the crypt at Saint Marina's. There they found another decomposing body on another pile of bones. Andreas waited until Tassos arrived from Syros, and together they went to open the crypt at Saint Kiriake's. From the edge of that crypt Andreas called the mayor to come to his office for their meeting and Tassos called forensics to come for its fourth pile of bones and another body.

"They're excited about this. It's the biggest challenge of their professional careers. I told them, if one word of this leaks out, they'd find whoever's responsible under a Syros church someday."

Andreas smiled. "Do you think they'll keep quiet?"

Tassos paused, his fork held midair, and stared at him. "You think I'm kidding. They know better."

Perhaps they do, thought Andreas.

Over coffee, Tassos said he'd get his men looking for every official and unofficial detail on Ilias—and the death of his father. He'd also call the mayor in the morning for everything he knew about his cousin.

As they walked back to the car, Tassos put his arm across Andreas' back and rested his hand on his shoulder. It reminded Andreas of how his father used to walk with his friends in the evening through the square by their home in Athens. Both the memory and the arm were comforting. When they reached the car, Tassos refused a ride. He wanted "to walk off the meal." Andreas said something about the Balkans being pretty far away and Tassos gave him a less-than-pleasant one-finger gesture. They hugged good night and agreed to talk again at ten the next morning.

As Andreas drove to the hotel he thought about the death of the deputy minister who'd set up his father. Over his years on the force, Andreas had reviewed and investigated—unofficially—every bit of information surrounding his father's death. He also knew his father had friends "from the old days"—and some probably were responsible for getting Andreas into the police academy. As for whatever else they did—or might have done—out of loyalty to his dad, Andreas had no interest in finding out, from Tassos or anyone else. His only interest was in being a cop who would honor his father's memory. He always had been, and he hoped he always would be.

Andreas pulled up to the hotel and got out of the car. Damn, he thought. I hope the night guy's in a cooperative mood. I've no time left to fuck around and make nice.

Chapter Ten

The lobby lights were dim and a muted TV was flickering with a rerun of a soccer game. The night manager was lying on the couch dozing. He jumped up when he heard someone and forced a smile through sleepy eyes. He didn't recognize Andreas at first, but when he did the smile disappeared.

"Mr. Ilias not here." He was nervous.

"I'm not here to see him. I'm here to see you." Now the man was very nervous. "Where can we talk?" Andreas' voice was crisply official.

The man showed him to the office by the reception counter.

"I have a few questions for you." Andreas said.

"I told you everything," the man said, his body shaking.

Time to make him shake more, thought Andreas as he shook his head and said, "I don't think so."

Andreas made him repeat everything he could remember about Helen Vandrew. Nothing new. Andreas raised his voice a few notches. "Okay, now tell me anybody else you can think of who might know something about her. Anybody you saw talk to her, anybody you saw with her, anybody you saw near her!" His voice had risen until he was yelling.

"I don't know."

"Think, damn it! Did you ever see her with anyone?"

"No, like I said, never." The man looked hysterical with fear.

Andreas softened his voice a bit. "Look, she was pretty and alone here for two days. Someone must have tried to talk to her. At breakfast or when she was going out."

"Honest, there no one. She never come to breakfast. She never come back second night, and first night she go out of taxi alone."

Andreas heard a new word.

"Taxi? You never said anything about a taxi."

"It just Manny. He bring her in morning."

Now Andreas was yelling for real. He grabbed the man by the shirt. "Listen, you bastard, I told you I wanted the names of everyone you ever saw with her. Even Jesus Christ himself! If I even think you're holding back or covering for someone, I'll find so many ways to keep your ass in prison the only way you'll ever get out is in a coffin! *Understand? Now tell me everyone!*"

The man was probably frightened enough to wet his pants. He was in tears. "I no think you mean taxi drivers. Sorry, sorry, sorry. There no one else, no one. On my mother's grave no one else."

Andreas kept scaring the life out of him for another fifteen minutes until he was certain the man was telling the truth. All that work for the name of one lousy taxi driver

◇◇◇

Annika wasn't quite sure why she agreed to leave the piano bar with him to get something to eat, but he knew everybody there, was interesting, and behaved like a gentleman. It seemed harmless enough—and it wasn't as if he were a total stranger. He suggested a place out of town, a local Italian restaurant on the road to Kalifati Beach, southeast of Ano Mera. She'd been there before and liked it but didn't tell him; after all, she wasn't supposed to know the island.

The place was full when they arrived, as if no one knew or cared how late it was. He acted shyer than she expected, often pausing thoughtfully before speaking. In academic circles, taking such time to collect your thoughts was known complimentarily as taking a "Harvard pause"—though Yale kibitzers said it meant waiting for the voices inside your head to tell you what to say next.

They sat outside, just off the beach, at a shaky wooden table barely covered by a plastic, blue-and-white checkered tablecloth. The ground was hard-packed and sandy, but the nearby fig trees and geraniums seemed to like it. So did the mosquitoes. The owner brought Annika some repellent and a wrap for her shoulders—the night air was a bit nippy for beach wear. She wasn't dressed or in the mood for a romantic dinner, which made this all the more perfect a choice. The only thing romantic about this place was a funnel of rippling silver moonlight coming at them across the sea between two matching hills locals called "the breasts of Aphrodite."

They ordered pizza and chilled red wine. It was great, and reminded her of a late night food-run in college.

"How do you like the place?"

"I love it." She took a bite of pizza.

"I thought you would." He sipped his wine. "It's more relaxed than most places in town. Seems more real to me than there." He gestured toward town.

She nodded in agreement as she picked up her wineglass. "Absolutely. It's crazy back there."

"Bet you can't wait to leave." His voice was calm, matter-of-fact.

"Oh, I like Mykonos. Just have to find the right crowd to share it with." She sipped her wine.

"No luck yet?" He put down his glass.

She nodded again. "For sure on that score." She put down her glass and excused herself to go to the bathroom.

When she returned a chocolate soufflé was on the table.

"Surprise. I thought you could use a pick-me-up and the chef has a secret recipe for the absolutely best deep-dark chocolate soufflé in all of Greece."

"Wow, I never knew that." That was true, but she didn't mean it to sound as if she'd been here before, so she quickly added, "Greece really has soufflés?"

He looked at her, paused, and smiled. "Yes, Greece has soufflés."

It was delicious. They finished it and their wine. He went to pay the check and returned with two *sfinakis* on a silver tray. He handed one to her.

"A Mykonos tradition. *Yamas.*" He lifted the other glass to clink with hers.

She smiled and decided not to dump the drink. She was headed straight back to her hotel for the night; this would be her very last one. "*Yamas.*"

Clink.

◇◇◇

All Andreas wanted to do when he left the hotel was head straight home to bed, but he called the taxi dispatcher instead. She said Manny wasn't due to start his night shift for another half hour but as soon as he signed in she'd tell him to meet Andreas at the police station. Not even enough time for a quick nap, he thought.

◇◇◇

Annika didn't realize how tired she was until they were in the car headed back to her hotel. The music on the CD player was soothing, and he wasn't forcing her to talk. She tried to stay awake but was too exhausted. She leaned her head back against the seat and shut her eyes. Only for a moment, she thought. Only for a moment.

◇◇◇

Andreas was downstairs by the front door talking to Kouros when a silver Mercedes taxi slid into the lot. There was space by the front door, but the driver parked away from the building, beyond the reach of its floodlights. He looked like most Mykonos taxi drivers—dark hair, swarthy complexion, light colored short-sleeved shirt, dark slacks, and dress shoes. They tended to take themselves seriously.

Andreas assumed this was Manny. Their file on his taxi license listed him as forty-five, and he looked about that age. The driver walked over to them and asked if the chief was in. "I was told to meet him here."

"Hi. Andreas Kaldis." He extended his hand. "Thanks for coming over." Andreas noticed that for a man of average height and weight, his forearms were massive.

"No problem." They shook hands. Despite his obvious strength, Manny's handshake was exceptionally weak.

Andreas took him up to his office and closed the door. The man appeared calm, not concerned in the least as to why the chief of police had summoned him at one in the morning.

"Any idea why I asked you here this late?" Andreas began.

"No, sir." He answered like someone used to talking to police. He's probably had his share of run-ins over tourist complaints, Andreas thought. Andreas gestured for Manny to sit in front of his desk, then walked around to its other side and picked up a photograph of Helen Vandrew. "Ever see her before?"

Manny looked at it carefully. "I think it's the same one another officer showed me," he said, and handed it back to Andreas.

Clever answer. "I meant while she was alive." No need to hide the fact that she was dead—everyone knew.

"Not that I can recall."

Another clever answer. "I don't know how to tell you this, Manny, but you're one of the last people to see her alive."

Manny twitched but kept his composure. "Why do you say that?"

"Because," Andreas said, speaking slowly and deliberately, "I have a witness putting her in your taxi." He paused for a few seconds and continued with a shrug. "If you want a lot of cops asking a lot of people a lot of questions tying you in to a murder investigation, just keep answering like you think I'm a fucking idiot."

Manny sat silently.

"Why don't I start with a call to your dispatcher asking for your location around sunrise on June third?"

Andreas could tell he'd surprised him, but still Manny said nothing. It was the savvy way to behave around questioning cops.

Time to turn up the heat. "Okay, if that's the way you want to play it, let me tell you how it's going down on my end. You'll make me waste my time checking out my witness' story, and if it checks out, I'll make your life on this island a living hell. My men will stop you a dozen times a day. There won't be a U-turn you'll get away with, and heaven help you if a tourist ever makes a complaint against you. My purpose in life will be to yank your taxi license the very first chance I get. So, either talk or get out of here so I can stop busting my balls and start busting yours." He put the photograph back on his desk and stared at Manny.

Manny sat perfectly still for a moment, then leaned over and picked up the photograph. "Now that you remind me, I think I did have someone who looked like her as a fare. I dropped her off at the Adlantis Hotel that morning." He remained calm, eerily so.

"Where did you pick her up?"

"Walking along a road on the other side of the radar station."

Andreas' pulse jumped. "What was she doing out there?"

"How would I know?"

"Don't start up with me again. A pretty girl walking alone on a road in the middle of nowhere at sunrise, and you didn't ask her why?" He raised his voice.

Manny let out a breath. "Okay, she said a boy took her on a motorcycle to that beach where the priest lives. He got a little aggressive, she said no, and he left her there to walk home. I saw her on the road and picked her up."

Andreas nodded. "Good. Now tell me what you were doing out there at sunrise."

It was the first time he looked uncomfortable. "I dropped off a fare."

"Really? Who and where?"

"I don't remember?"

"You'd better start to, unless you want to be my number one suspect in her murder."

Manny's breathing quickened and he looked down at the floor. "He's my cousin."

Andreas was puzzled. "Who's your cousin?"

"The boy on the motorcycle. He called me on his mobile to tell me he'd left a girl alone on the beach. He wanted me to pick her up. He's not as bad a kid as he seems. Just a little hot-blooded at times."

"What's his name?"

"Yiorgos Chanas. His father owns Panos' Place. That's where he met her."

"Did you ever see her again?"

Manny paused—that had to mean yes. Andreas waited.

"The next night. I saw her getting into a taxi at the stand by the harbor."

"Was she with anyone?"

"Yes, but he didn't get in with her."

"Who was it?'

"George, I don't know his last name, he's that South African jeweler who speaks Greek with the big shop over by Alpha Bank. I swear that's the last time I saw her."

Andreas knew who he meant. He asked for the name of the other taxi driver, but Andreas didn't recognize it. He called Kouros into his office, and together, they pushed Manny through his story a half dozen times, banging away at every inconsistency and hesitant gesture. When Andreas finally told him he could leave, he warned him to keep his mouth shut—unless he wanted to become the island's poster child for efficient taxi law enforcement. Manny left in a hurry with Kouros right behind him on Andreas' order to find out ASAP what the other taxi driver knew about the girl.

Andreas sensed there was something Manny wasn't telling them. He couldn't put his finger on it, but the man was far too calm for all the pressure he'd been under. Perhaps Tassos knew something about him. He'd ask when they spoke at ten. For now, he needed sleep.

◇◇◇

She'd fallen asleep slumped over on the front seat. At the rotary where the road to her hotel branched off he went around and around until they were headed back toward Ano Mera.

He was taking her elsewhere.

Chapter Eleven

When Tassos finally called Andreas that morning, his voice was grim. He had nothing new on Ilias but had probable IDs on eight victims and none of them was listed on Ilias' tapes. All eight were tall blondes traveling alone from Holland, Scandinavia, or Germany and disappeared during the summer months of different years. Each was last seen or heard from on or near Mykonos.

They'd made the identifications with help from his friend at Interpol, but there'd be no more help from him on the subject of missing women without a formal request—and explanation of what the hell was going on—from the ministry.

"As it was," Tassos said, "my friend pressed me for why a homicide detective on an idyllic Greek island was so interested in all eighteen- to thirty-year-old, tall, blond women reported as missing in Europe over the past twenty summers."

"Not a bad question," said Andreas.

"He said my answer—'statistical reasons'—didn't pass 'bullshit' on his snifftest meter, but he'd let it pass because he owed me." Tassos paused before continuing. "My favor wasn't big enough for him to keep it to himself if we ask for DNA comparisons of our bone collection against their list of missing blondes. He won't miss what that means—no one could miss what that means."

Andreas figured "no one" included tourists, travel agents, parents of young women and everyone else in the world with a TV. Their time was running out.

Sounding slightly less grim now, Tassos said, "I also spoke to my friend at New Scotland Yard. He should have something for us on Father Paul by early afternoon—if there is anything."

"Thanks." Andreas said without enthusiasm.

Forcing a note of lightness into his voice, Tassos said, "OK, Chief, I showed you mine, now show me yours."

Andreas smiled and played along. "Mine's bigger. I spoke to the taxi driver who picked up Vandrew the morning of the day she disappeared. She was on the road from the beach where Father Paul lives. Said she'd been taken there by Yiorgos Chanas, son of—"

"Panos." It was an edgy interruption.

Andreas was surprised at his tone. "Yes."

Tassos said, "His whole place is dirty, and I don't mean just the kitchen."

"What's dirty about it?" Andreas hadn't heard it called that before. Overpriced and filled with aging girl-chasers, yes, but not dirty in the cop sense.

"It starts at the top. I've no problem with older guys chasing young girls, but Panos takes it too far. He and his buddies do the usual big-money flash and brag about their boats and planes—you know, that 'mine's bigger than yours' sort of thing."

Andreas laughed. Tassos didn't miss a trick.

"But when that doesn't work he takes a nasty turn." There was an unmistakable anger in Tassos' voice. "He drops a little date-rape shit—probably Rohypnol—in the girl's drink, and it's on to party time."

"I can't believe it," Andreas said, outraged. "The son of a bitch is…how's he get away with it? Why do you let him?"

Tassos' voice showed frustration, not offense, at the question. "Never touches locals—or Greeks for that matter. Always ends up the same way, some young—and therefore obviously promiscuous—tourist girl's word against a 'respected Mykonian businessman' and his 'respected witnesses.' Besides, date-rape drugs have a nasty habit of producing a degree of amnesia in their victims. Like an alcohol blackout, but worse. They can't remember events that took place while under its influence. And for those who do, it's usually too late to make a difference."

"Christ, how many other sinister little secrets are going to pop up in the middle of this investigation?" Andreas knew that his own frustration was beginning to show.

Tassos wasn't reassuring. "And he has this weird competitive thing with his son over who gets first shot at the girl. Panos had a really fucked-up childhood—his sister died in some almost-too-freak an accident to be an accident, and, if you ask me, he's trying his damnedest to pass his craziness on to his kid." He sounded like an angry father.

"Great," Andreas said, "now we've got two suspects sprouting serial-killer characteristics."

"And we're just getting started. Any other possibilities?"

"Aside from the son?" asked Andreas.

"I doubt he was killing in diapers. Too young to be our man. If he's involved at all, it's through his father, but it seems unlikely. Remember your list—serial killers are loners."

Andreas didn't disagree. "The taxi driver said a South African jeweler—a guy with a shop over by Alpha Bank—was with her the night she disappeared."

Tassos paused. "I know the guy but have nothing on him. Respected businessman as far as I know, but I'll see what there is."

"Then there's the taxi driver, Manny Manoulis."

Tassos' voice jumped at the name. "Christ, Andreas, you aren't making this any easier."

"What are you talking about?" Andreas felt a headache starting above his left eye.

For a few seconds Andreas heard only Tassos' breathing. "When Manny was a kid he was raped. It was horrible. He was only eight. Some drugged-up degenerates caught him in town late at night over by the Kastro. He was hanging out waiting for his father to close his shop. The rapists never made it to trial, if you know what I mean, but the kid was never the same."

Andreas' headache took aim at a spot right between his eyes.

"He tried to kill himself three times before puberty," Tassos continued. "Finally, some psychiatrist from Athens got through to him and he's been pretty much under control since then. I think he's on medication."

"What do you mean 'pretty much'?"

"His father was a nice guy—dead now—and considering what happened, we tended to cut the kid some slack." Tassos sounded defensive.

Andreas knew he wasn't going to like what was coming.

"Every once in a while a female tourist has complained that she thought her taxi driver was masturbating in the front seat."

"Jeezus, Tassos."

"We never had to ask who it was." He paused. "It's always the same story. The driver would never say anything to any of them or expose himself—certainly he never tries to touch them—and the few who've leaned over the front seat to check him out have seen a lot more dicks than his." He paused again. "We've treated it as harmless." His words hung in the air.

After a pause, Andreas asked, "How long's this been going on?"

"Hmm. I'd say about twenty years."

Andreas' head was pounding, and he rubbed his forehead. "Now we've got three meeting the profile, plus a priest my instincts scream is dirty, a jeweler we know nothing about, and who knows how many more suspects from the date-rape-drug crowd over at Panos'."

Tassos said nothing. Andreas tried to ease his headache with less serious thoughts, and he burst out laughing.

"Are you okay?" Tassos asked.

"You remember the name of that Agatha Christie murder mystery about all those people on the train?"

"Yeah, I saw the movie, *Murder on the Orient Express.*"

Andreas caught himself nodding into the phone. "That's it, the one with a dozen suspects, each one looking guiltier than the other."

"Do you remember who did it?" Tassos asked.

Andreas laughed. "Yeah, they all did—with only one body to work with and stuck on a train. Here we have eighteen, maybe more, and a whole island—more than enough for all our suspects to have killed at least one."

"I really hope you're kidding," Tassos said, his voice serious.

Andreas sighed. "I'd like to think I am." The whimsy of the moment was gone. "I think I'll stop by to say hello to your friend Panos."

"He's probably at his farm. It's out by the reservoir in Ano Mera."

Andreas rubbed his eyes with the heel of his free hand. "Time to get back to work." He was about to hang up but didn't. He knew Tassos hadn't either. There was something else he had to say, something he'd been meaning to say. "I don't know where all this is headed, but I want you to know I'm praying for something."

Tassos spoke softly. "What's that?"

"That nothing bad happens to some other poor girl because of what we're doing." There was a long pause.

"Amen." Tassos hung up.

◇◇◇

Demetra looked forward to seeing her cousin. It was a terrific day, bright, sunny and not too hot. She had a surprise for Annika; she was moving her to a different hotel. The parents of one of her friends owned a new five-star hotel on a beach made famous for unexpected, transforming romance in the movie *Shirley Valentine*—just the sort of atmosphere her cousin could use.

Demetra took a taxi from the airport to Annika's hotel. She told the driver to wait while she ran in to speak to her cousin. He grumbled, but after a "Greek-to-Greek" conversation—at all appropriate decibel levels—agreed to wait "a few minutes." Demetra had tried unsuccessfully for more than a day to reach Annika after getting her message that she was staying at the Hotel Adlantis, but none of Demetra's phone calls to the hotel had been returned. That wasn't like her cousin. She assumed Annika hadn't received her messages.

As she got out of the taxi she noticed a police car parked by the entrance. A young policeman was leaning against the hood, smoking and smiling at her. She smiled back. He was cute. Once inside she heard shouting. It was a man's voice yelling about "police," "lousy cousin," and "useless mayor." When she reached the counter, she saw that it was a gray-haired man screaming into a cell phone. She stood looking at her watch and the taxi outside while the man behind the counter seemed oblivious to her presence. After a minute she said in Greek, "Excuse me." He waved her off.

Wrong move. "Excuse me."

No answer.

"Excuse me," she said a little louder now.

Still no response, but an angry look.

"*Excuse me.*" Demetra banged on the bell on the counter.

The man swore at her in Greek.

She swore back and banged louder on the bell, yelling "Excuse Me Excuse Me Excuse Me."

Finally, the man put the phone against his side and cursed at her for two or three seconds. "What do you want?"

She smiled. "I am looking for my cousin, Annika Vanden Haag."

"She's not here," he said, and he put the phone back to his ear.

"Where is she?"

He looked at her with hate in his eyes. "I don't keep track of my guests. Now leave before I get really angry." He went back to his conversation.

She screamed, "Help! Police! Help! Police!"

The man's face turned white. He dropped the phone and told her to shut up.

She smiled. "Now, where's my cousin?"

He swore a few words at her but answered, "I don't know. She hasn't been in her room since yesterday morning and she was going to leave today. She probably moved somewhere else."

"Did she take her things with her?"

"How should I know?"

Demetra smiled, turned toward the front door, and waved at the policeman who looked as if he'd heard someone calling for him. He waved back. She turned back to the gray-haired man. She thought he'd be seething. Instead he looked scared to death.

"Her things are still here. It happens all the time. A girl meets a boy and leaves her things. All the time."

Demetra was getting nervous. "I want to see her room."

"I can't allow it," he said seeming almost to tremble.

She just stared at him. He came from behind the desk and led her down the stairs. She'd forgotten all about the taxi driver.

The room looked as if Annika had left in a hurry, but with clothes and toiletries there—as if she'd intended to return. Demetra left the room and headed upstairs toward the taxi. She thought of saying something to the policeman, but what was there to say? She'd call Annika's mother as soon as she reached her hotel and let her decide what to do.

The only thing she knew for sure was that something was very wrong.

◇◇◇

Catia's relief at Demetra's voice was very short-lived. She expected Demetra to tell her that she was with Annika or at least had spoken to her. Instead, Catia heard panic. "I don't know where she is, Auntie, I don't know."

All her life Demetra was the tough-mouthed little kid who tended to lose it a bit under pressure, just the opposite of Annika. Out of habit, Catia spent most of their conversation calming her niece and ignoring her own anxiety. That changed as soon as they hung up and Catia called her brother, Demetra's father—the deputy minister. He tried treating his younger sister as she'd just treated his daughter, but Catia would have none of it.

"Don't patronize me, Spiros, I'm not Demetra," Catia said, her voice steely.

He sounded slightly annoyed. "I understand you're worried about Annika being out all night, but let's be realistic, she just broke up with her boyfriend, she's on Mykonos, and…uh—"

Catia cut him off. "This is not about that. I know something's wrong. I sense evil." With those words she let her brother know further argument was useless because, among Greeks, a mother's sense of evil lurking about her child was taken very seriously.

He sighed. "Okay, what do you want from me?"

It wasn't exactly the marines she asked for, just a call from the person in charge of all police in Greece to the chief of police in Mykonos to find her daughter ASAP.

Another sigh. "Okay, little sister, I'll call as soon as we hang up."

Catia thanked him, sent him kisses, and hung up feeling much better. She was certain her brother would find Annika. After all, wasn't that what police did all the time?

Chapter Twelve

Panos' farm lay at the base of one of the barren, brown-gray hills north of Ano Mera along the west side of the well-worn dirt road to Fokos Beach. Between his farm and the sea were a mile-long rainwater reservoir, a daytime beach taverna, scraggly brush, wandering goats, and not much else. The last time Andreas was out this way a bit of the island's Eastertime cast of green—peppered with bright floral dots of red and yellow—still covered the hills, but that short-lived color was gone by now.

Dust from the road caught up to Andreas' car as he slowed to make an awkward, almost U-turn over a mattress-sized concrete slab. It bridged a dry creek bed separating the road from a rocky, rutted path running up to the farm. In all that dust and heat it was hard to imagine enough rainwater raging through this area in the winter to overflow the reservoir's seventy-five-foot high dam and flood the beach. Then again, what worried farmers here wasn't a lack of water, it was the relentless, drying winds.

Panos' farm used stone walls and close-packed, tall bamboo windbreaks to protect his crops. The thick bamboo plantings ran uninterrupted inside a low wall along the north side of the path, perfect for screening out wind—and the curious. Andreas didn't see a structure until the windbreak ended and the wall turned north. Then he saw two.

He parked by the closer one, next to a rough, unpainted wooden gate at a break in the wall. It was a one-room shed made of the same sort of stone as the wall; both looked centuries old. Equipment was strewn everywhere. Andreas couldn't tell what was being used and what had been left to rot.

He stood by his car for a moment and listened. He heard no human sound but sensed someone was around. A light brown van sat parked about forty yards away, up by the other structure. Whatever it was, it was made of the same sort of stone as everything else on the property and built into the hillside like a mine entrance. Andreas walked to the shed and looked inside. It was a mess: hoes, rakes, shovels, pots, hoses, cement, gasoline, seed, fertilizer, wire, rat poison, rope, twine, batteries. Everything you'd expect to find on a farm—or with our serial killer, Andreas thought. Only thing missing was cough syrup for the crystal meth.

As if on cue, he heard a loud cough followed by a shout. "Can I help you?" It was Panos. He was standing at the entrance to the other structure holding something in his right hand.

Andreas was not in uniform—he rarely was—and could tell the man didn't recognize him even though they'd met once in his restaurant. Andreas gave a friendly wave and started toward him. "Hi, Panos, Andreas Kaldis." Still no sign of recognition. "Police chief."

That got an immediate response. Panos gave his biggest restaurateur smile and hurried down to meet him.

"Hello, Chief, nice seeing you again." It was a water bottle Panos held, and he switched it to his left hand and reached out with his right hand to shake with Andreas. Andreas noticed only a bit of water remained in the bottle. "How can I help you?" Panos seemed nervous.

"Nice place you have here." Andreas fanned his head from left to right.

"Thanks. Been in my family for generations."

"What do you grow?" Andreas wanted to see if Panos would raise the subject of Helen Vandrew. By now, one of his friends must have told him the police knew she'd been in his bar.

"Zucchini, tomatoes, eggplant, onions, purslane…" As Panos recited the list his voice became calmer.

"You must have a lot of help," Andreas said.

"No, just me. I like doing the work myself." He shifted the bottle back and forth between his hands.

"Then you must spend a lot of time here," Andreas said matter-of-factly.

Panos seemed unsure how to respond. "Only what I have to." He paused. "That's why the place is such a mess. I spend all my time working my crops and none cleaning up." He seemed to like his answer.

Andreas switched to a sharp, prosecutorial tone. "And just what sort of crops do you work in there?" He gestured with his head toward the stone entrance at the hillside.

"Where?" Clearly he was stalling.

Andreas put his right hand on Panos' left shoulder and slowly but firmly spun him toward the hill. With his left hand he pointed. "There."

Panos answered nervously, "Mushrooms. I grow mushrooms there. It's an old mine. Perfect for mushrooms."

"What's a mine doing over here? I thought they were over there." Andreas pointed past the mine entrance to the northeast.

Panos waved his arm toward Fokos and back toward Ano Mera. "This whole area's filled with mines, from the sea just east of Fokos all the way to Ano Mera. Miles and miles of tunnels."

That surprised Andreas. He dropped his arm from Panos' shoulder. "But why an entrance here?"

Panos spoke quickly. "They never mined here. I think it was for emergencies, maybe just ventilation. I don't know. They're all over the hills. Some bigger, some smaller, some just holes in the ground. My grandfather built this." He pointed at the stone entrance. "To hide the hole. He didn't like the way it looked."

Andreas reached back and patted Panos on the shoulder. "Always wondered what an old mine looked like. Mind if I take a peek inside?" From the way Panos started breathing, Andreas thought he'd die at the question.

"I was just heading back to town, but if you'd like to come out tomorrow, I'd be happy to show you around."

"Do you mind if I take a look around on my own?" Andreas left no doubt it was not really a question but a command.

"It's really not safe to go in there alone." Panos' voice was desperate.

Andreas took off his sunglasses and stared at him. "Don't worry, I can take care of myself." He started toward the entrance.

Panos touched his arm to stop him. "So, why did you come out to see me?"

Andreas just smiled and put on his sunglasses.

Panos stared at his feet. "It's about the girl, isn't it?"

Andreas said nothing, just continued to smile.

"Yes, I knew her. I said I didn't to your man because I didn't want to get involved. You know how it is." He gave a nervous grin, as if talking to a friend.

Andreas had stopped smiling now and returned a cold stare. "No, I don't." He paused for a few seconds before pointing his finger dead center at Panos' chest. "Now tell me everything you know, everything you think, everything you guess about that woman."

Panos started to object, but Andreas pressed his finger into the man's chest. "I don't want your bullshit. Just tell me what I want to know or get a lawyer to get your ass out of jail."

Panos looked down and glanced toward the mine entrance. He let out a deep breath, lifted his head, and started talking. He told what he swore was everything he could remember about the evening they met and everyone who spoke to her. He swore that was the only time he saw her and that he had no idea what happened to her. He swore to a lot of things but the only thing Andreas hadn't heard before was that she'd spoken to an American artist at the bar. Andreas asked what Panos knew about him.

"Tom's a famous artist. He's in his early sixties and been coming here two, three months every summer since the seventies. Nice guy, but acts like he's everyone's conscience."

"What's that mean?"

Panos hesitated. "He doesn't like the way we treat women, says we show them no respect."

Now, there's an understatement, thought Andreas. "Anything else?"

"No, but one of his paintings hangs in my bar, if you want to see it. Why don't you come by tonight? We'll have dinner. On me." Panos was trying to make friends again.

"No, thanks. But why don't you run along. I'll see if there's anything else for us to talk about after I've had a look inside the mine." The color drained from Panos' face. "You don't look too good—better take a drink." He pointed to the bottle in Panos' hand. "I'm going to get one myself," he said, and headed back to his car.

When he got there he saw Panos hadn't moved. He looked frozen in place. Andreas was pretty sure he knew why. It all added up. The mine, the almost-empty water bottle meant just one thing to him: inside the mine was a lot more than mushrooms, and whatever was in that bottle wasn't just water. He picked up the phone to call for backup. Andreas wasn't a fool. There was no telling who else might be inside the mine or what Panos might try when faced with heavy prison time for whatever drugs he was cooking up in there.

As soon as Andreas reached the station, he was told Kouros must speak to him immediately. Andreas started to say he had no time, but his call already was on hold. As he waited for Kouros to pick up he watched Panos walk toward the van. He looked like a condemned man.

"Chief, I've been trying to reach you for half an hour." Kouros sounded anxious.

"I was out of the car. Next time try my cell phone. What's got you so excited?"

"The ministry called, the deputy minister wants you to call him immediately. He said it's of the 'utmost importance.'"

Andreas' heart jumped to his throat. "Which ministry?" He held his breath as if in prayer.

"Ours."

So much for prayer. He and Tassos were dead meat. He wondered if Tassos knew yet. He needed time to think and wanted to talk to Tassos before calling the deputy minister. He watched Panos empty the water bottle onto the ground and get into the van. You lucky bastard, he thought. "Okay, I'll be right in." Andreas had no choice but to go. He had bigger things to worry about at the moment. Like his career.

Andreas thought of telling Kouros to send someone here to keep everyone out of the mine until it was checked out—probably by a new chief from the way things looked—but he guessed Panos had other ways of getting into the mine and getting rid of whatever he was hiding. He smacked the steering wheel hard with the heels of his hands and cursed aloud as he watched Panos drive away. "Why do motherfuckers like him have all the luck?"

◇◇◇

Andreas drove slowly back toward headquarters. No need to hurry to his own execution. Besides, Tassos was busy on another phone call and Andreas wasn't going to call the ministry until after they spoke. At the crest of a hill overlooking Ftelia Beach and the foot of Panormos Bay, Andreas pulled off the road and waited for Tassos to call back. Far below, windsurfers slid gracefully back and forth across the bay. Their work seemed effortless from this distance; not at all like the instant-to-instant reality of their up close battle to stay afloat in relentless winds and driving seas.

His cell phone rang. It was Tassos.

"Sorry, I was on the phone with my friend at New Scotland Yard. Have some news for you on your priest." Tassos sounded excited. Obviously, he hadn't heard from the ministry. "Father Paul won't be up for sainthood anytime soon."

Andreas decided to hear him out before dropping the bomb. "What do you mean?"

"His story was he'd been 'called' to the priesthood after his sister died in an accident. About ten years ago he left the priesthood—actually was forced out. It involved young girls in his parish."

"I knew there was something dirty about him," Andreas said in a detached way.

"Nothing was proven. His family had a lot of money, and—with the church's help—they paid off the kids' families and kept everything out of the papers. He quietly resigned and moved to a different part of England—probably to prey on someone else's kids." There was anger in Tassos' voice.

"Damn," Andreas said without emotion.

Tassos paused. "That's not the end of it. A few years later the parish church he'd been forced to leave burned to the ground. Arson, but couldn't tie it to anyone."

"Just what we need. Another prime suspect with serial killer characteristics." Andreas was trying to sound interested. "Anything else?"

Tassos didn't answer right away. "We've identified two more of the victims, both Dutch. Still no Greeks. I think our killer's careful to stick to tourists."

Silence.

"Andreas, is something bothering you? You don't seem right."

Andreas shook his head and let out a breath. "Do you have that letter from the mayor?"

"What are you getting at?"

"I have a message from the office of the deputy minister for Public Order for me to call him ASAP."

Pause. "Shit," said Tassos.

"That's one of the words that went through my mind. I take it you didn't get a call."

"Me? What do I have to do with this? It's all a Mykonos problem." Tassos forced a laugh.

"I admire your sense of humor."

Tassos sighed. "I don't like crying so close to the end of my career."

"I wonder how he found out."

"I think we've been kidding ourselves thinking we could keep this quiet. Who knows, that asshole mayor might have burned us for some bullshit political reason. And, yes, I have the letter." Tassos was sounding more defiant, and it was helping to pick up Andreas' spirits.

"Maybe it's about something else?" Andreas sounded hopeful.

"When's the last time you got a call from a ministry-level member of government?" Tassos didn't wait for an answer. "Let's just figure out what we're going to tell him and…and…"

"I think the word is *duck*." Andreas paused. "But even if he's calling about something else, it's time to tell him. There's too much for us to run down on our own. We need help before someone else gets killed." He waited for Tassos to say something. After all, informing Athens would end more than just Andreas' career as a cop.

Tassos spoke softly. "I'm not going to try to talk you out of it. If you think it's time, fine. The hell with our deal with the mayor—he's probably the one who told the deputy minister anyway."

Andreas let out a deep breath. "How do you think I should I handle it?"

They talked for a while and agreed he'd tell the deputy minister everything in the most politic way possible—then duck.

◇◇◇

Annika was cold. That was the first thing she noticed. Her head was aching, but she didn't notice until she tried sitting up. She was on a floor on what felt like a chaise longue mattress. The room was completely dark—at least she thought it was a room. She pushed out with her hands to feel in front of her face. She touched nothing. Then she felt out around her as far as her arms could reach. Again nothing. She realized why she was cold: she was naked.

Her chest was pounding and her breathing was running away from her; she knew that meant panic. "*No!!*" she yelled to herself. I'm still alive, no matter what this is. I'm still alive, she kept thinking over and over again. She thought of her mother and her father. They'd find her. She just knew they would. She fell back down on the mattress, curled up into a ball, and started crying quietly.

◇◇◇

He stood still as a granite wall, sharing nakedness with her in the dark. But only he could see. The night-vision goggles added a green cast to her body but did nothing to conceal her beauty from him.

This was his favorite moment: the instant of a tribute's first tears, when she realized she was no longer free. The drug had worked again; it always did, bringing on panic at no memory of how she'd fallen from paradise to here. He carefully moved his right hand to where he could touch himself and quietly began pulling—gently at first, until her crying ended and she finally slept—then fiercely, to the point of pain and beyond, until finally he came.

At last he felt the chill of the room again. It was always this way with a new one; just the thought of her fear drove him to fever. For now, this moment of relief was enough. Later, he'd need much more.

He stared at her for a bit longer. Reluctantly he turned to leave. There were other things to do.

◇◇◇

"Good morning, Deputy Minister Renatis' office."

"Uh, good morning, this is Andreas Kaldis, chief of police on Mykonos. I'm returning the minister's call."

"Oh, yes, Chief, the minister asked that I give you a message. He had to leave for a cabinet meeting."

I guess I'm not even worth firing personally, Andreas thought. He's going to have his secretary do it.

"He's spoken with the mayor…"

So, he is the one, that miserable two-faced bastard, thought Andreas.

"…and understands you're in the middle of a murder investigation."

Andreas felt he should jump in before she reached the punch line. "Yes, but I think if the minister understood the circumstances—"

She cut him off curtly. "Chief, I'm reading the minister's message. Please let me finish, and then I will take down whatever it is you want me to tell him." Obviously, she was experienced at keeping the condemned at bay. He was about to be drawn and quartered without getting a chance to speak. "As I was saying, he understands you're in the middle of a murder investigation, but this matter really can't wait."

Andreas held his breath.

"His sister is worried about her daughter, the minister's niece. She's on Mykonos and he'd like you to find her to tell her to call home."

At first Andreas thought she was talking to someone else on her end of the line.

"It's only been a couple of days since she's been heard from, but the minister's sister is anxious. We know where she's staying, so it shouldn't be too much of an inconvenience for you to find her right away." Her words were courteous but her tone made clear he had no choice but to act immediately.

She was the sort of condescending bureaucrat who angered Andreas—but not this time. "Sure, no problem. Glad to help out. Can you give me the details?" He reached for a pen and wrote the deputy minister's name across the pad of paper on his desk.

For a secretary used to aggravating people, the tone of relief in Andreas' voice must have had her wondering whether she'd lost her imperious touch because she paused for an instant before responding. "She's twenty-two years-old, five feet eleven inches tall, blond hair, blue eyes…"

Andreas' heart skipped two beats. Thank God she's Greek, he thought.

"Her name is Annika Vanden Haag—"

"But she's Greek?!" he said, practically screaming the words.

His interruption clearly surprised the secretary. "Uh, yes, Chief, her mother's Greek but her father's Dutch. They live in the Netherlands."

Andreas thought he'd throw up. He didn't hear her next few words, and when he tuned back in it was to "She's staying at the Hotel Adlantis."

Andreas had never fainted in his life and wasn't about to now, but he suddenly felt that he knew just what it would feel like.

The next thing he heard was the secretary practically shouting, "Chief, Chief, are you still there?"

"Yes…yes, thank you."

"Do you need any more information?"

He paused; his mind was jumping among a thousand thoughts and settling on none. "Uh, yes. Could you fax me her photo and her passport and address information?"

"Certainly."

He took a deep breath. "I must speak to the deputy minister." His voice had lost its vigor.

"He's not available."

"I understand, but the moment he is, please tell him it's critically important he call me at once."

The secretary's tone turned icy. "If it's that important, you should tell me what you want to tell him. That way I can get a message to him."

Bureaucrats—all of them want to know everything. "It's something very personal."

In an even icier voice: "I see. Very well, I shall give him your message. Good-bye." She hung up before Andreas could return her courtesy.

He put his elbows on his desk and his head into his hands. Andreas was certain their killer was at it again.

Chapter Thirteen

Annika didn't know how long she'd been sobbing or falling in and out of sleep, but she'd not heard a sound other than her own crying. She took a deep breath and got to her knees. Slowly, she stood up, raising her hands above her as she did to find what was above her. At her full height she felt the ceiling. It was about two feet above her head. Smooth but hard, like concrete. She carefully shuffled her feet along the mattress, touching her hands along the ceiling as she did. It felt the same everywhere. She thought of stepping off the mattress but had no idea what she'd find. It could be a floor, a pit, anything.

She went to her knees and inched her way forward off the mattress. The floor felt the same as the ceiling, smooth and hard. Before every move, she reached out to feel in front, above, and below her. Her feet were about three feet off the mattress when she touched a spot of something wet. There were several more spots near the first, as if something had dripped from the ceiling. They were slightly sticky, and ever so tentatively she lifted her fingers to her nose to smell what she'd touched.

She recoiled and nearly threw up. No doubt now what it was. He'd been there, only feet from her. He could be standing right next to her now and she wouldn't know it. All she could think of was finding her mattress. It was the only place of any comfort in whatever hell this was. Frantically, she probed out behind herself with her feet until she found it, and retreated like a frightened dog to shelter.

◇◇◇

Hours seemed to pass before Annika worked up the nerve to leave her mattress again, and when she did, she used it as her safehaven, always mindful of where it lay. Quickly she determined a few things. The space's floor and ceiling were square, with about fourteen-foot sides. There was nothing on the floor other than the mattress, but near the center of the ceiling were three one-foot-square surfaces, one smooth, two louvered. She assumed one was a light fixture and the others vents. This meant there had to be electricity. The walls were made of stone, with all the expected ridges, gouges, odd-shaped protuberances, and crevices, but they felt strangely smooth and cool to the touch—as if coated with plastic or Teflon. It made no sense to her. There was not a single interruption in the walls. Not a door or a window—nothing but stone. How was that possible? She wanted to pound on something and shout for someone to come but sensed that was what her captor expected. She decided to wait and see. That was all she could do. Wait and see. Sooner or later someone would come. She was sure of that.

◇◇◇

He had many places from which to watch her. He'd built his dungeon that way, dug it out of an old mine tunnel and fashioned it himself, taking great care to fit its wall flush with the existing tunnel wall. It represented years of work, started decades ago, lugging all the stone, cement, and everything else without help. But there was a benefit to building it as he had: it was virtually invisible to anyone who might happen by—as unlikely as that was. Locals were superstitious and many viewed these old mines as haunted.

As far as he was concerned, they were right; for this was the realm of the ancient Egyptian gods that he honored: Serapis, ruler of the underworld, and Anubis, its gatekeeper.

◇◇◇

Andreas knew there was no time left for civilized tactics. It was bare knuckles from here on out—starting with Ilias. He told his man at the hotel to bring Ilias in to headquarters immediately. Then he called Tassos. His reaction to the conversation with the deputy minister's secretary was equally severe. He said he'd leave for Mykonos as soon as he could get to a helicopter. That's when Andreas decided to have them all brought in: the priest, Manny, Panos, and the jeweler. Panos' son too.

Additional bad news started coming in almost immediately. The officer at the hotel couldn't find Ilias, and no one there had seen him for hours. Their best guess was that he'd gone out the back and down the hill behind the hotel to the road below. He could be anywhere by now—on or off the island.

By the time Tassos called to say he'd landed, the only suspect Andreas' men had been able to locate was Manny—and that was because the taxi dispatcher said he'd come to the station as soon as he "finished his current job." The priest was nowhere to be found. Nor were Panos or his son, and according to an employee in his shop, the jeweler was away in Athens for a few days and couldn't be reached. Great, thought Andreas—a missing tourist and a batch of unaccounted-for suspects.

◇◇◇

Annika had no way of telling how long she'd been asleep. All she knew was she was cold—and thirsty. She also needed a toilet. She felt no hunger, at least not yet.

Her mind kept racing over the same thought: Why? She couldn't bring herself to think it was random, unrelated to something she'd done. That would mean…she stopped herself. Such thinking would lead to panic. There must be a reason. If she could think of the reason, she could think of a way out. She kept saying to herself, "This is just a problem-solving exercise, a pure and simple problem-solving exercise." There has to be an answer, a reason. There must be.

More time passed. She decided to move about, get some exercise. She had to do something to keep from losing her mind. She stood and stretched, then stepped across the cell. She determined she could take three long steps in one direction before having to turn. She found her stride. One, two, three, turn, one, two, three, turn, she counted to herself, then started counting aloud: "One, two, three, turn, one, two, three, turn, one, two, three, turn." She was moving faster and faster, almost running—almost running into panic. She had to stop. She was dizzy and bent over, resting her hands on her knees. She drew in a deep breath, let it out, and shook her head. "Think," she said to herself. "Think."

She leaned against one of the walls. It felt cool against her skin. She'd forgotten she was naked. Not important anymore. She ran her hands over the wall; it was the same wherever she touched. Hard and smooth. She walked beside it, rolling the tips of her fingers along as she did. They rolled so easily, as if on wet, smooth, shaped glass, filled with hidden textures. She was growing accustomed to the darkness.

Her hands moved onto the second wall. The sensation was the same. There was now a rhythm to her walk. She felt a comfort in the walls. Around and around the cell walls she went. She was drifting into her third loop when it happened: "*Clang, clang, clang, clang, clang.*" Whatever she'd kicked was bouncing across the room. It hadn't been there before—she was certain of that. Her heart started pounding and her stomach churning. She wanted to throw up. It was fear. He was back. Invading her space, again.

She sensed she'd started to laugh—a rolling, building laugh she could not stop. Had she lost control of her mind? She had to do something. She screamed, "*My space. My space?*" I must be going mad, she thought. She forced herself to think of her parents. They were real, this wasn't. She had to deal with what was real. She took a deep breath and another, then stepped forward toward where she'd heard the sound. Two tentative steps ahead, she stepped on something. It didn't clang. It gave under pressure from her foot.

She knelt and reached out slowly, as if putting her hand into the murky bottom of an unknown pond. It was cylindrical and flat at one end with circumferential ridges and indentations midway along its body. At its other end she felt…"a bottle cap," she said aloud. It was a plastic bottle of water, or at least felt like one. A liter bottle. She clutched it in her hand, stood up, and stepped forward again, this time more boldly.

Her foot struck a new object. This one clanged against the floor and she reached for it without hesitation. She knew what it was. A bedpan. She wanted to throw it at a wall. But she needed it. And she needed the water, if it was water. She wondered what else—what other kindnesses, she snickered to herself—her tormenter had in mind for her.

As if he'd read her mind, she heard a sound. He was here, she thought. She heard it again. It sounded like a mail slot swinging open at the bottom corner of the wall behind her. Then she heard a rough scraping along the floor coming from the same direction. Something was moving toward her. She turned and backed away from the sound. It kept coming. Now she was against a wall. Annika knew she had to fight—she had no choice. She leapt forward screaming, "Bastard!" throwing the bottle and bedpan at the sound. She lashed out scratching and punching in a wild chase around the room, searching for confrontation, some physical body to attack. All she found was a wall with one of her punches. The pain was instant. It felt like she'd broken her left hand, maybe her wrist too.

She screamed and clutched at the pain. That made it hurt more. She stumbled into another wall, then tripped over the bedpan and instinctively thrust her injured hand out to break her fall. She screamed again and rolled onto the floor and into a ball, clutching again at her hand. "*Why? Why? Why?*" she shouted. There was no answer. She started sobbing.

Annika had no idea how long she'd lain there feeling sorry for herself—maybe minutes, maybe seconds—but she knew she had to regain control. She turned onto her right side and slid backward along the floor. She had to find the mattress, to find some way to use it to ease the pain. Suddenly, something touched the back of her thigh. She screamed and jerked away. A minute passed. Nothing moved. Slowly, she brought herself to a sitting position facing the thing she'd touched. It had to be what made the sound. Carefully, Annika cradled her left hand across her lap and reached out with her right. She found it.

It was about the size of a shoebox. It wasn't very heavy and— her heart plunged—it was tied with a ribbon. It was a gift. She stared straight ahead into the darkness. The man was mad.

Now she knew she was going to die.

◇◇◇

He never quite understood why the scraping sound of a long-handled, wooden pizza-oven paddle delivering a gift box of chocolates created such panic. But it always did, and so he used it as a tool for conditioning his tributes to accept the unfamiliar. That was important, for there were many more unknowns yet to come.

◇◇◇

Annika sat on the bare floor, the water bottle held tightly between her thighs. She moved her good hand along the bottle, checking for anything unusual. Finding nothing, she fingered the plastic cap. It seemed anchored to the bottle and unbroken. She carefully twisted it and heard a snap as it separated from the bottle. Slowly she removed it and sniffed the contents. No odor. With her good hand she poured a little on one thigh. No pain. She rubbed at the liquid. It felt like water. She sniffed again and tentatively took a sip. No taste, no pain. She drank.

Chapter Fourteen

Tassos was pacing in front of the arrivals entrance when Andreas pulled up beside him. He opened the cruiser's front door and dropped himself onto the seat. "I can't believe this."

Andreas didn't respond, just drove out of the airport and past the police station.

Tassos looked back at the station. "Where are we going?"

"There's nobody to question in there, so I thought we'd take a ride out to Ano Mera to check out Panos' little mushroom mine and then see if we can find that artist Daly. Besides, we can talk just as well in the car as in my office." Andreas was in an even fouler mood than Tassos.

"It looks like we fucked up big-time," Tassos said, letting out a breath.

"And it's probably going to cost another woman her life." Andreas sounded angry at himself.

"Any ideas?"

"I'd like to pull the covers over my head and say 'Go away, bad dream, go away.'"

"Now, there's an idea I can relate to." Tassos grinned and gave a quick, hard left jab to Andreas' right shoulder. The car swerved into the path of a very panicked-looking couple coming at them on a rental motorbike.

Andreas jerked the wheel clockwise with his left hand to pull the car back to his side of the road and put up his right to block any further punches. "Hey, take it easy. I don't need more dead tourists." He was smiling.

"Like I said, any ideas?"

Andreas glanced at Tassos' fists. "Okay, okay, are we done with the shock treatments?"

Tassos smiled back at him. "For the time being."

"So, why did he go after the Vanden Haag woman a month after he killed Vandrew? It breaks the pattern of one a year."

Tassos sighed. "I'm afraid it doesn't. One of the victims we think we just identified disappeared a month after we found the Scandinavian linked to the Irishman. Looks like he killed again—to replace the one we found. He must have put the Scandinavian where we'd be sure to find her once he thought our search might get to a church where some of his other victims were buried."

"And now he's replacing Vandrew." Andreas' voice was rising.

"Or one of the sixteen others," Tassos said it without emotion.

"My God, do you think he'll try to replace them all?"

They were silent for a few moments, then Tassos said, "Why do you think they're all blond, tall non-Greeks?"

Andreas shook his head. "I don't know, but he's obsessed with the look. Must tie in to someone from his past: a mother, sister, wife, relative, friend—maybe even a movie star or model." He reached for a cigarette in his shirt pocket. "One thing's for sure; he knows how the system works here because, except for this one, every victim he's chosen traveled alone, was a foreigner without local friends, and spoke no Greek." He found a cigarette, and Tassos reached across and lit it for him.

"Yeah, just the sort of invisible, transient tourist no one looks very hard to find on Mykonos."

Andreas drew in and let out a puff. "He sure screwed up this time."

Tassos tried to sound a bit more upbeat. "Maybe he didn't take her. It makes no sense for him—after twenty years—to change his choice of victims."

"Unless he didn't know who he was snatching." Andreas was back in his foul mood.

"You know what that means," Tassos said flatly.

"If he realizes his mistake she's probably dead on the spot. No church burial, just a toss in the sea."

Tassos nodded. "How much time do you think we have?"

"I wish I knew. There's a key here somewhere. Must be." He turned left onto the road toward Panos' farm. Now that he knew the way, it took only five minutes to get there. This time he drove right up to the mine entrance.

"Here we are," said Andreas.

"I suggest we bring a shotgun," said Tassos.

"Good idea. I'll get it out of the trunk."

Tassos walked to the entrance and shone his flashlight inside. "Never liked mines."

"Think of it as a mushroom farm," said Andreas, coming up behind him. "Don't worry, I'm right behind you." He gave Tassos a gentle prod in his backside with the butt of the shotgun.

Tassos gave a quick, one-finger fuck-you response, then carefully stepped inside. About fifteen feet from the entrance, the tunnel made a sharp right into total darkness. Tassos aimed his flashlight up-ahead. Not only was it pitch-black, it was cramped and a mess.

"You'd think the guy would clean up some of this shit," said Tassos. "Just so he wouldn't trip over it."

"I don't think cleanliness is one of his virtues," said Andreas, shining his light along the base of the wall. "Well, here are his mushrooms."

"I'm not sure I'd want any of those in my salad," said Tassos, directing his own light along the wall. "They look like the 'let's take a trip back to the sixties' kind."

"Doesn't surprise me."

They walked another twenty feet or so, to a point where the tunnel turned left. Andreas' shotgun went around the corner first. Just in case.

"My oh my," said Tassos. "What do we have here?"

"Looks like our buddy likes to play with chemistry sets," said Andreas.

"A crystal-meth lab. Son of a bitch."

They did a quick search of the rest of the tunnel. It ended about thirty feet from the lab at a cave-in. "Dead end," said Tassos.

"But we have a possible source for the meth in the bodies."

Tassos nodded. "Yes, but even if it was meth from this place, it doesn't mean Panos killed them—or even gave it to them. We've always known he was into this shit. It's no surprise."

"Christ, you're a downer. Fine, maybe it's not enough to get him on the murders, but we've got him nailed on the drugs."

Tassos shrugged. "You know, now that you mention it, I don't see any roofies here."

Andreas nodded. Roofies, the date-rape crowd's street name for the prescription drug Rohypnol, would be a much more damning find. They continued to look everywhere but found nothing more than methamphetamine.

"I don't understand this," said Andreas. "You said he uses Rohypnol on women at his bar, so why the meth?"

"Meth's the drug of choice for a cheap way to a long lasting-sexual rush. He probably supplies it in return for a bit of the action. Doubt he uses the stuff himself, though. Once the excitement's passed you crash into an intensely deep sleep. He's too busy during tourist season to sleep that much."

"But why meth in the victims' bodies?"

"I don't know, maybe the killer wants to keep them deeply asleep or sexually aroused."

"Hard to imagine how he'd get a terrorized girl to do the meth or—even if he could—how it'd get her aroused."

"If she was out on Rohypnol—like our friend here uses—he could shoot her up with meth while she was under and have her right where he wanted her."

Andreas looked disgusted. "Bastard sure knows his drugs. That would explain why the only traces found in the victims were methamphetamine. The Rohypnol wouldn't show up—it passes through the victim's system too fast."

Tassos moved his light along the base of the wall. "Who knows, maybe he adds a bit of mushrooms, too."

Andreas waved toward the entrance. "Let's get back to the car and call for someone to watch this shit-hole until forensics gets here."

◇◇◇

Andreas made his call and began driving back to the main road. "Do you still want to look for the artist?" asked Tassos.

"It beats banging my head against my desk trying to figure out what all this means."

Andreas made a left onto the main road and turned left again just beyond the gas station in Ano Mera. It was another narrow dirt-and-gravel road winding north through old, scratched-out farms. He lit another cigarette.

"They all were found in the same four churches. That must mean something," said Tassos.

"But what do they have in common? All four were kept up by Father Paul, but he took care of four others with no bodies." Andreas looked for the road Panos had described. "And the bodies were found in churches named after male as well as female saints."

Tassos said, "What do Saints Kiriake, Marina, Fanourios, and Calliope have in common that makes them so different for our killer from Saints Barbara, Nicholas, Phillipos, and Spyridon?" He shook his head. "I think we need a priest."

"Right now I'm looking for an artist." Andreas tossed his cigarette out the window and turned right onto a dirt road leading to a two-story, white house with blue trim that sat just below a hillside church with a blue roof.

"Must be to Saint Nicholas, the patron saint of sailors," said Tassos. "They're the only churches with blue roofs."

Andreas parked next to an SUV by the front of the house. They walked to the door and knocked. No one answered. They called out again, but still no answer. Andreas tried the door. It was unlocked. He pushed it open and called out again, "Hello, anybody home? Hello."

They looked at each other and walked inside. They'd explain later. The front room was neatly furnished and clean. Everything seemed to be right in its place. They walked into the kitchen and found it just as neat. They went upstairs and Andreas once more said, "Hello, anybody home?"

There were two rooms and a bathroom upstairs. They looked in the rear bedroom first. Not a thing out of place. A photograph in a silver frame sat on the nightstand next to the bed. It was of two blond and smiling children, a boy and a girl. The other room faced south and was bathed in light. It had to be his studio. What looked like finished paintings stood lined up against the wall closest to the door. Unfinished paintings were everywhere else, all neatly arranged according to their relative stages of completion.

"Looks pretty normal to me," said Tassos.

"Me, too," said Andreas. "And I recognize his stuff. He is famous."

Tassos walked over to the line of finished paintings and began looking through them.

Andreas was standing in the middle of the room looking at all the unfinished works. "Tassos, do you notice something about his paintings? Something every piece seems to have." His voice was excited.

Tassos kept looking through the finished ones. "No, what?"

"Turn around. I'll show you."

Tassos turned and watched as Andreas pointed to every visible canvas. "Look there, there, there and there. They all have the same thing."

Andreas walked over to the finished paintings and Tassos moved aside so he could get to them. Andreas scanned them quickly, then looked up and stared in disbelief at Tassos. "My God, there's at least one in each of his paintings—a tall, blond, naked nymph."

◇◇◇

As if crazed, Andreas had them search every drawer, every corner, every inch of the house. They found absolutely nothing incriminating. Not even a pornographic magazine or drug harsher than Advil.

Dejected, Andreas and Tassos were sitting on the wall outside the house smoking when the call came through from the station. Manny had shown up, and Kouros wanted to know what do with him.

"Hold him!" Andreas shouted, then calmed his voice. "Until I get there."

He looked at Tassos. "I thought we had our killer."

"Yeah, but when you think about it, the only thing that made it seem that way was his paintings."

"You mean the only thing so far." Andreas was ornery.

Tassos shrugged. "So, let's find him and talk to him."

Andreas picked up a stone. "Yeah, but we can't fuck around with him. He's a famous American artist. All we can do is talk." He threw the stone and stared after it. "For now."

Tassos nodded.

"It seems too much of a coincidence that all the victims are tall blondes and all his paintings have tall blondes," Andreas said.

"Perhaps we're looking at this the wrong way," said Tassos. "What if the killer knows this guy's work? After all, he's been painting on Mykonos longer than the killer's been doing his thing here—and that's why he's going after tall blondes?"

Andreas picked up on Tassos' thought. "Yeah, maybe he's a fan of the artist or someone inspired by his paintings, or maybe it's somebody who hates the artist and is trying to assassinate his nymphs." He was seriously caught up in his thoughts.

Tassos rolled his eyes. "I get your point, but do me a favor, don't tell anybody else we're looking for a nymph assassin."

Andreas let out a quick laugh and looked back at Tassos. "I guess he's not coming back."

"Probably at the beach, like every other self-respecting tourist. Let's take a look in the church." Tassos stood up.

They walked up the hill to the church. It was relatively new as churches went and, like the house, was neat and well maintained from the outside. The front door was locked and the side windows were shuttered and latched from the inside. Again, nothing out of the ordinary. Rather than breaking into the church, they decided to head back to the station and talk to Manny the taxi driver.

It seemed the right decision at the time.

◇◇◇

The first thing Andreas did when he returned to the station was check to see if the deputy minister had called. He hadn't and Andreas wasn't going to call him. He was prepared to put his head in the guillotine by telling all, but he wasn't about to chase down his executioner. Until the blade fell, Andreas intended to do exactly as the deputy minister's office said—find his missing niece "right away."

◇◇◇

Spiros Renatis loved his sister. He also loved his niece. What he didn't love—but had learned to live with—were the bureaucracy and favor traders plaguing his ministry. Although telling a local police chief to drop everything to find his niece didn't approach the sort of abuse of power that bothered him, asking this particular police chief that favor was about the last thing in the world he wanted to do. He knew all about Andreas' unwanted "promotion" to Mykonos for pushing an investigation too close to the powers that be—and Andreas' rumored anger at being booted out of Athens for being too good at his job. He also knew the police legend about what happened to the deputy minister who assassinated his father's reputation. Regardless of how much any of that was true, he didn't want to do anything that might draw him into a potential mess—such as speak with Andreas. That's why he had his secretary make the call.

He knew he'd made the right decision when his secretary told him Andreas insisted he call back at once on a critically important matter too personal to describe to her. He was certain it tied in to Andreas' efforts to get back to Athens. My God, he thought, who knows what information he intends to tell me that I don't want to know? He left instructions with his secretary that she was only to take messages from Chief Kaldis and never—under any circumstances—put him through.

◇◇◇

With Tassos in the room Manny was even calmer and more cooperative than before. He acted as if in the company of a beloved uncle—until Andreas showed him Annika's photograph. "Ever see her before?"

Manny's eyes seemed to double in size. He said nothing.

"Manny, do you recognize her?" asked Tassos.

Still silence.

Tassos tried again. "Manny, what's wrong? Do you recognize her? Tell us, it's important."

"I want to see Katerina."

Katerina was Mykonos' number one criminal defense lawyer. Andreas was caught off-guard and looked at Tassos. His face looked just as surprised. Andreas spoke softly. "Manny, this is serious, but if you want us to help you you'll have to help us."

No answer.

Tassos spoke affectionately, in a fatherly tone. "Manny, we've been through a lot together, and I've always been straight with you. You have to trust me now and tell me what you know about her before whatever trouble you're in gets worse."

Manny looked at Tassos with tears in his eyes. "I want to speak to Katerina."

Andreas wanted to hit him but knew Tassos wouldn't let him. "Put him in a cell and get Katerina over here now," he barked to Kouros.

"She might be in Syros. It's a court day. What do I tell her?" asked Kouros.

Tassos answered. "If she's in Syros, I'll get her back here by helicopter. If she's in Athens, I'll get her back by air force jet.

If she's in one of her boyfriends' beds, I'll drag her here myself. Just find her and tell her that I—and the Chief—want her ass in here *now! Or else!*"

Andreas presumed she'd know what "or else" meant, coming from Tassos.

The instant Kouros left the office Tassos banged his fist on Andreas' desk. "Damn, I'd have sworn on my mother's soul Manny wasn't our killer. I just don't understand this." He banged his fist again.

Andreas shook his head. "It doesn't make much sense to me either. I don't see a killer with the balls to walk in here on his own—after snatching, maybe even killing, another one—falling apart when he's shown her photograph. For sure he knows her, but if he's our guy…" His voice trailed off.

Tassos dropped into his chair. "That means someone else has her. Any word on the others?"

"*Kouros, get in here!*" Andreas yelled.

Thirty seconds later, Kouros appeared. "Sorry, Chief, I was on the phone with Katerina. She's on the fast boat from Syros. Gets in at five. She'll be here as soon as she's off the boat."

Andreas looked at his watch. Five was only twenty minutes from now. "Good. Any news on that other cabdriver, the one who picked up Vandrew at the taxi stand?"

Kouros pulled a notebook out of his back pocket. "According to his log he picked her and three other passengers up at 1:55 in the morning at the taxi stand, dropped her off at the square in Ano Mera at 2:10, and the other three at 2:20 at the Mykonian Regal Hotel on Eliá Beach. He said he remembered her because she sat in the front seat and was very tall and pretty. He wanted to talk to her but she was on her cell phone when she got into his taxi and didn't get off until just before she got out."

Andreas interrupted him. "Did he have any idea who she was talking to?"

Kouros nodded no. "She was speaking English and he doesn't understand it very well, but from the way she was talking he's pretty sure she was agreeing to meet a man."

"Meet where?" Tassos asked.

"All he remembered hearing was 'Ano Mera' and 'square.'"

"What about the other passengers?" asked Andreas.

"No luck. I checked at the hotel. It's a big place and the owner said unless the hotel called for the taxi—which it didn't—they have no way of knowing who the guests were."

Silence.

"I also checked the bars and tavernas around Ano Mera Square. No one remembers her. I'll try again tonight when the later crowd is there."

Andreas said "Thank you" and Kouros left.

"Good man," said Tassos.

Andreas nodded. "Yes. Hope he keeps his enthusiasm for the job."

"Like us?"

Andreas smiled. "Yeah, like us. Let's get some coffee while we wait for Her Majesty."

"Oh, so you know Katerina." Tassos smiled.

"Only by reputation. A 'pit bull,' I think, is the term most used."

"Even with a pit bull it depends whether she wants to lick or bite. I can't wait until she meets you." Tassos' smile broadened. "If I had to bet, I think she'll work with us on this one."

"Okay," said Andreas. "If you say so." They went to the squad room for coffee.

Ten minutes later Katerina made her entrance into the station: raging red hair, bright blue dress molded onto an impressively augmented five-foot-five figure, and a roaring voice. "Where the hell is that bastard Tassos?"

"In here, my love!" Tassos called out from the squad room.

In she stormed. "What the fuck are you doing ordering me to bring my ass up here ASAP?"

"Katerina, I'd like you to meet Chief Kaldis."

Andreas stood and immediately Katerina's expression softened. She looked him up and down, then gave her most coquettish smile—one no doubt she'd been practicing for at least fifty years. "My, such a young and handsome man to be chief. You must be very good at what you do."

Andreas couldn't help but smile at her hustle. "And you as well, I'm sure."

"Okay, Katerina, start the mating ritual later. This is serious. Let's go upstairs." Tassos took her by her arm and headed toward Andreas' office.

Katerina walked up the stairs ahead of Andreas. At the top she turned and smiled at him. Tassos grabbed her arm again and pulled her toward the office muttering something about "you'll never change."

Tassos sat in 'his' chair, Andreas went behind his desk, and Katerina parked herself on top of it. "So, what can I do for you?" Her voice was still lighthearted.

"Your old client, Manny Manoulis, wants to see you," said Tassos.

Her voice was suddenly professional. "About what?"

Andreas showed her the photograph. "We showed him this picture and asked if he knew her. He refused to say anything more until he spoke to you."

Katerina looked at the photograph, then stood and straightened her dress. "Tassos, you didn't bring me here to talk about Manny doing his jerking-off routine in front of this girl. It has to be something a lot more serious than that."

Tassos nodded. "Always said you're smart. It is more serious. Way more serious. We have to know everything he knows about her."

"Why?" She seemed unmoved.

Andreas spoke. "Her life may be in danger. Anything he knows might help."

Katerina stared at Andreas, then looked at Tassos. "Why do I get the impression there's a lot you're not telling me?"

Tassos spoke. "Because there is; and because there's no reason for you to know any of it. Just take it on faith that this is really serious; and if your client's involved there's nothing you can do to save him, but if he isn't, and you get him to tell us—or you tell us—what he knows, we'll be forever in your debt."

"You're asking me to betray the confidence of a client?" She tried sounding shocked.

"No, I'm asking you to keep an innocent man from looking guilty—the bit about the police being in your debt is only incidental." Tassos smirked.

"Asshole," she said to Tassos. "Let me talk to him and I'll let you know my decision after." She winked at Andreas. "Later, handsome. Don't worry, I'll see myself out. I know my way around here." And she was gone.

"Wow," said Andreas. "I never felt like a boy toy before."

"Believe me, if anyone knows how to play with toys, it's Katerina," Tassos said with a smile. "She's also as sharp and ruthless as they come. We've been doing business together for years. I can't tell you the number of judges she's had eating out of her…uhh…hand."

Andreas smiled. "I get the picture. Do you think she'll let him talk to us?"

"Only if he's not the killer and we agree that whatever he says won't be used against him."

"What if Manny won't talk to us?"

"Oh, that's no problem. If she thinks it'll get him off, and we agree never to expose her as the source, she'll tell us anyway. She calls it 'part of my responsibility to save my foolish clients from themselves.'" Tassos emphasized her words by putting quotes in the air with his fingers.

Andreas shook his head and smiled again.

Twenty minutes later Katerina was back. "Okay, fellas, are you ready for me?"

"I guess that means your boy's going to cooperate," said Tassos.

She looked straight at him. "He picked her up two nights ago just before sunrise at the taxi stand by the harbor, drove her to a beach, then watched her strip, walk naked into the sea, and frolic under the stars. After she finished her little moonlight interlude he drove her back to her hotel. I'll leave to your male imaginations whether he jerked off. But that's all that happened and if she said he did anything to her, she's lying."

Andreas spoke. "If that's what happened, he's got no problem with us. So, why did he call for you?"

"Possibly so we could meet." She smiled. "But apparently the last time you showed him a picture of a girl he recognized you followed up by threatening the shit out of him."

Andreas smiled. You couldn't help but like her style, he thought. "Fair enough. Can we talk with him?"

"What's all this about?" She stared straight at him.

"We're just trying to find a missing person, that's all," said Andreas.

"Yeah, sure." She rolled her eyes and pointed a finger at Tassos. "Don't fuck with me, Tassos."

"I promise you we're not." His tone was solemn.

She looked at Tassos, then at Andreas. "Okay, bring him in and I'll let him tell you what you want to know."

Manny was calmer with Katerina in the room but still clearly nervous. Andreas offered him a cigarette. He took it and that seemed to relax him a bit more. Andreas asked him to "please" tell them everything that happened between the very first and last moment he was with her. Manny said he saw her only that one time and began to tell what he swore was everything he remembered.

Manny said he'd driven her to "the priest's beach." Andreas struggled not to speak but lost the battle after Manny said her naked romp took place directly in front of Father Paul's house.

"Did anyone else see her there?"

Manny sounded surprised at the interruption. "Uhh, no, not that I could tell."

"What about the priest? Was he there?" Andreas' voice was pressing.

"His house was dark, I didn't see anyone. Honest." Manny was getting more nervous, so Andreas backed off and let him finish. It took less than five minutes because according to Manny, after coming off the beach she got back into the taxi, told him to take her to the Hotel Adlantis, and that was it.

"You mean neither of you said a word to the other the entire way back to the hotel?" Andreas sounded agitated.

"Yes, sir, that's right, except—like I told you—'Thank you.'"

Andreas gave him a long, stern look, quickly glanced at Tassos and Katerina, then returned his focus to Manny. "So, what the hell were you doing all that time up there alone in the front seat?" Andreas already knew the answer—a bit of silent self-awareness, no doubt—but wanted him to know he wasn't fooling anyone in the room.

Katerina spoke up. "Now, now, Chief, you know that's not the kind of question you should be asking my client." She smiled.

Andreas gave her a wink.

"Did you ever see her with anyone?" asked Tassos.

"No."

"What about at the taxi stand when you picked her up?" Andreas was back to a calm, friendly tone.

"There was a long line. She was in it."

"Did you see her talking to anyone?" asked Andreas.

"Only Tom."

"Tom? Who's Tom?" asked Tassos.

"The American artist, Tom Daly. He hangs out at Panos' Place."

Andreas and Tassos shot each other a look.

"He was standing with her in line and said good-night to her when she got in. I think they'd been together earlier."

"What do you mean 'been together'?" Andreas heard the excitement in his own voice.

Manny shrugged. "Like they knew each other, that's all."

"How well do you know the artist?" Andreas tried to calm his tone.

"Pretty well. He was teasing me not to rip her off like a tourist when she got into my taxi. He was friends with my father. They used to sit around and swap old mining stories."

"What do you mean by 'mining stories'?" asked Tassos, excitement evident in his voice.

"Before my father had his shop in town he used to work in the mines out there." Manny pointed toward Ano Mera. "And Tom's father was a coal miner in Wales before moving to the States."

"Do you still see him?" Tassos was speaking with obviously forced restraint.

"Oh, sure. Every once in a while I stop by his house, but he doesn't seem to be there as much as when the old mine entrance was open."

Andreas jumped in. "What old mine entrance?"

"The one the church is built on. Tom rents from a farmer who wanted to build a church and thought it made the most sense to put it on top of the mine. That way he wouldn't have to excavate a place for his family's bones. He could just use the old mine entrance as a burial chamber."

A chill shot through Andreas. He looked at Tassos.

Manny's right eye was twitching, and he started rubbing it. "Sorry, it's been a long day."

"No problem. You're being very helpful."

"Where was I? Oh, yeah, so about ten years ago the farmer built his church. Tom was pretty upset because it closed off his entrance to the mines. He spends a lot of time wandering through mines all over the world. He tells everyone it gives him inspiration."

"Inspiration for what?" said Andreas.

"I don't know, something about those tall, blond figures in his paintings." Manny sounded proud of his knowledge of his friend's work.

Andreas glanced again at Tassos. "So, what's he done since the church was built?"

"We really haven't talked about it, but I guess he's found another way in. The mines are too important to him. He calls them his roots."

"Guys, are you done yet?" asked Katerina, looking bored. "I know all this mining shit must be of deep interest to you public-servant types, but those of us who work for a living have to get back to our paying jobs."

Andreas smiled. "Just one more question. Manny, where do you think Tom is now?"

Manny looked at his watch. "I don't know. Probably off in some mine."

Chapter Fifteen

Katerina and Manny had left—but not before she asked Andreas to meet her later that night at a boat leaving for a "pre-*panegyri* party." He said he'd let her know and joined Tassos in kissing her good-bye.

Tassos was shaking his head. "So, what do you think, party boy, is the artist our new number one suspect?"

Andreas ran his fingers through his hair, shrugged, and went to sit behind his desk. "He's sure moved up on the list, but being eccentric doesn't make you a serial killer."

"And everyone who knows him seems to know about his tall, blond-haired nymphs and the mines. Like you said, he could just be our killer's inspiration." Tassos dropped back into his chair.

Andreas stretched his arms out above his head. "We still have to find him—and his four missing potential disciples: Panos, Paul, Ilias, and George."

Tassos patted his chair. "What do you think about Manny?"

Andreas nodded no. "I don't think so, but we've got to keep an eye on him until the deputy minister's niece is found, just to be on the safe side. After all, he's the only suspect around to watch. Be a shame to lose him too." Andreas gave a sarcastic smile.

"I know how you feel." Tassos paused. "Let's head back to the artist's place and check out the church. I know it's not one of Father Paul's, but I still think we should—just to be sure." He put his hands on the chair arms and pushed himself to his feet.

Sure of what? thought Andreas as he stood up and walked around his desk to the door. "Okay, but I think you're just trying to keep me away from Katerina's party."

Tassos laughed. "You know, in the old days—before Mykonos had all this 24/7 nightlife—a *panegyri* was the only place for the locals to party."

Andreas grinned. "Like I said, you don't want me to have a good time."

"It's also where the unmarried met—some even eloped right from a *panegyri*. I'm sure Katerina knows that." He gave Andreas a light tap on the back of his head. "You'll thank me in the morning."

◇◇◇

Echoes of London had been their favorite album for waking up on a gloomy Sunday morning in Peter's flat. John Williams—of all people—made them want to have sex. Annika rolled onto her side to feel him, to stroke him in the darkness. He wasn't there. She wanted Peter; she wanted him very much. She thought he must be asleep on the edge of their bed and stretched out her hand but did not find him. She rolled toward him and reached again. Still no Peter, but she felt something—something familiar, like the music.

Annika ran her fingers lightly along the hard, strong textures—all silky no matter where she touched. She felt no pain. She wanted to be closer and slid on her side to where she could press her body against the one her fingers were exploring. She felt the smooth, cool skin against her own. She pressed and released her breasts and thighs against her companion until the tingle came between her legs, the one she wanted Peter to touch. But he wasn't there. Only their music was with her.

She wanted more. She forced herself to her knees and pressed her body against her newfound lover as she struggled to her feet. Her head was swooning. All she could think of was finding release. She moved to the music as she had so many times before. It felt so good—the firm, cool pressure of his body as she slid along him in a slow, torrid search for what she knew must be there.

She found it in a place perfect for her needs. She gripped it lightly at first, more tightly when she knelt to take it in her mouth. Her tongue fluttered over it until it was as wet as she. Abruptly she stood, then paused trying to make out her lover's face in the darkness. She could not, but no matter, she needed this. She spread her arms and legs and stepped forward to mount him and be taken. Up and down she moved, her nipples as hard as his, her inner thighs wet from how he made her feel. Faster and faster she drove herself until, screaming, she collapsed onto the floor, next to the wall.

◇◇◇

He was a watcher. It was his greatest pleasure. He couldn't remember when he began watching, but it was when he was young. His sister had caught him once, then told on him.

To his mind, the modern world was overrun by an endless rush of words. Far too many for him ever to know what was true and what was not, what was right and what was wrong. In his silent world beneath the earth he only watched—never spoke, never exchanged a smile or a nod of recognition. He showed his tributes no sign that he existed in their world—or they in his. That was how it should be. That was how he wanted it to be. That was how it was.

He touched the scar on the head of his penis. It was a cigarette burn, like the others circling his groin. Marks from his father. For watching his sister, he'd said—or was it for watching them both? Whatever, it didn't matter anymore.

◇◇◇

By the time they reached the artist's place it was early evening. There was no light in the house, but there was a glow about the door frame of the church. They parked by the house, quietly made their way to the church, and listened. They heard nothing at first but after a minute caught the sound of something human. It was definitely coming from inside, yet it sounded far away at the same time. Andreas looked at Tassos and pointed at the door handle. Tassos nodded and pulled his pistol.

Holding his gun in his right hand, Andreas reached for the handle with his left and gently turned it. The door was unlocked, and he crouched and yanked it open.

Tassos' eyes darted back and forth above his raised gun as he scanned the room. Seconds passed, and there wasn't a sound.

Andreas was about to speak when he heard the sound again. It was coming from under the floor, up through an opening partially covered by a marble slab. That was where the light was coming from too. There were shadows moving about in the light below the floor. Someone was down there. They could make out a ladder of sorts anchored to the far side of the opening. It was the way down into the crypt—and what must be the old mine entrance. He whispered, "Should we go in?"

Before Tassos could speak, they heard a sudden, high-pitched wail and a deep, soulful moan rising out of the earth beneath them.

◇◇◇

It was the music that finally got to Annika through the haze that was her mind. Why was it playing here—wherever here was? She felt herself fading away but forced herself back. She thought, I told him, didn't I? I told the bastard all about Peter, about us...about our music. She was fading again and knew she was losing herself to sleep. She moaned to herself, "Water, water. Don't drink water," and passed out.

◇◇◇

It was the third time that day that Catia had called her brother's office, and the third time his secretary said he was in a meeting. In her most courteous tone Catia said she did not want to interrupt her brother but it was "urgent he gets this message immediately." The secretary wrote down Catia's words and read them back at her request. Catia said, "Perfect, dear. Thank you. Please give it to my brother at once. Good-bye," and hung up.

The secretary knew this was not the sort of message she'd dare walk into the deputy minister's office and read to him. She didn't even want it associated with her handwriting. Something about a handwritten message made it easier to kill the messenger.

The gentle *ping* of Spiros Renatis' computer meant he had a new, urgent e-mail message. He quickly glanced at the screen and clicked it open.

Dear Spiros,

When you were a little boy and hadn't done what you were supposed to do, Mother made me look under all the beds in the house until I found where you were hiding. There must be a very big one in your office. WHY HAVEN'T YOU FOUND ANNIKA?

Love, Catia.

◇◇◇

This time he placed the call himself, but still it wasn't to Andreas.

"Hello, mayor, it's Spiros Renatis. How are you?" They'd met a few times but didn't know each other very well.

The mayor had no idea why the deputy minister was calling but guessed it had something to do with raising either funds or hell on his little island. Mainland politicians were always asking for his help in such matters. He never minded because he knew it gave him far more national political influence than any mayor of only six thousand voters could possibly deserve.

"Fine, thank you. How nice to hear your voice, Minister. How are you? Are we going to see you soon on our lovely island?" His voice sounded prerecorded.

"No complaints here and, yes, I'm planning to be there for the August 15 holiday," said Spiros.

"Wonderful," said the mayor. "I look forward to seeing you again. Is there anything I can do to help you with your plans, Minister?" No reason to draw this out, he thought.

"Please, call me Spiros. And thank you for the offer, but we're all set." Pause. "There is one little thing, though, I hoped you might be able to help me with."

Here it comes. "Sure, how can I be of service?" The mayor was at his concierge-sounding best.

Spiros sounded tentative. "It has to do with my sister's daughter. She's on Mykonos for holiday and hasn't called her mother. I left word with your police chief to get her to call, but so far, my sister hasn't heard from her. I can't imagine it would be that hard to find her since I told him where she was staying." Pause. "So, I was wondering if you could give him a call and tell him how important this is to me."

Mihali thought he must be missing something. Spiros was the deputy minister of the arm of government in charge of police. Why was he calling *him* to speak to one of his chiefs? And why wouldn't Andreas call him back? There had to be more to this than the deputy minister was telling him. "I'm surprised to hear that. The chief seems a responsive sort of guy."

Spiros spoke quickly. "Oh, I'm sure he is, and this probably isn't a big thing to him, and to be honest, I think my sister is a bit of an alarmist—my niece only arrived there a couple of nights ago—but after all, she's my only sister and Annika is her only child."

The mayor smiled to himself. This guy's too embarrassed to keep henpecking away at Andreas the way his sister's doing to him. He just wants to be able to tell her he now has both the mayor and the police chief of Mykonos looking for her. "Sure, no problem. Anything specific you want me to tell him?"

"No. He already knows her full name, Annika Vanden Haag—her father's a Dutch diplomat—and that she's staying at the Adlantis Hotel."

It was a very warm evening, but the mayor felt a distinct chill. "What does she look like?" he asked, his voice becoming shaky.

"Your typical tall, blond, blue-eyed, twenty-two-year old Dutch beauty." He sounded proud. "Who just graduated from Yale University."

Silence.

"Are you okay?" asked Spiros.

"Uh, yes, just looking for a pencil." His heart was pounding.

Spiros repeated the information, but the mayor never bothered to write it down. He already knew what it meant. He kept his voice in check long enough to assure Spiros he'd get the chief to address this at once.

He hung up and stared out his window at the sea. His office was on the second floor of the two-and-a-half story municipal building standing at the south edge of the old harbor. It was built in the late 1700s as the home of a Russian count and was the only building on the harbor with terra-cotta roof tiles. It had seen the rise and fall of many ruling powers on Mykonos. The mayor's eyes drifted up to the sky. The sun had just set but the heavens were still bright. He wondered where Andreas was at that moment—and if he knew that the golden red sky was falling in on them.

◇◇◇

At the moment it was the earth, not the sky, that held Andreas' interest. He was the first one into the crypt. He didn't use the ladder, just jumped in. It was only a few seconds more before Tassos was down the ladder but by then Andreas had found his man—and a large brown dog fiercely loyal to the master who'd rescued it from starving Mykonos winters and poisoned baits. Luckily for Andreas, in dog years it was almost as old as its master. Startled, Andreas instinctively ducked to the side as the dog leaped and missed with a midair, snarling lunge for his throat. It crashed and rolled to the floor by the base of the ladder at the feet of a surprised-looking Tassos. The dog never took its eyes off Andreas and scrambled to its feet for another run at him, but Tassos grabbed it from behind and held its snout closed while Andreas turned his attention—and gun—back on the man.

The pounding in Andreas' voice was more because of the dog than the man. "What are you doing down here?" Andreas demanded.

The man was kneeling and seemed surprisingly calm for one just surprised by two men with guns. "It's my church. Hello, Tassos." He looked to be in his seventies, with the craggy face and silver hair of an old fisherman. His well-worn black jacket and dusty fisherman's hat completed the picture.

Tassos nodded. "Hello, Vassili."

Andreas knew it was time to lower his gun. "Sorry, we heard the wailing and moaning and thought someone was in trouble."

The man struggled to his feet. "It's my wife." He pointed toward a small marble plaque on the wall. "She died five years ago and we still miss her." He gestured to the still-snarling animal to come to him. Andreas nodded and Tassos let him go. The dog glared at Andreas but did not snap as it passed him on the way to his master.

"The wailing was mine, the moaning his." He scratched the dog behind its ears. The man now looked to be in his eighties.

"Sorry, sir," Andreas said again.

"If you were looking for me, I don't live here." He didn't sound bothered at all—almost seemed to welcome the company.

"No, sir, we were looking for your tenant, Mr. Daly."

The man nodded. "Tom's not here now, probably off in some mine."

"Yes, we heard he likes old mines," Andreas said.

"Sure does. He was pretty upset when I told him I had to close up that entrance." He gestured toward the rear of the chamber. "But I told him this was where Anna always wanted her church to be." He looked toward his wife's remains. "Tom's a good fella. He understood. Even helped me build it. Did all the work himself, sealing up the old entrance."

Andreas glanced at Tassos, then back at Vassili. "Do you mind if we look around?" He gestured toward the wall sealing off the mine from the crypt.

The man shrugged. "Look all you want."

Andreas took out his flashlight and studied the wall. It was made of two solid, four-foot-wide by four-foot-high slabs of gray-brown granite tightly fitted one on top of the other. He looked at the old man. "Rather unusual construction for a church crypt, wouldn't you say?"

The man shrugged again. "Tom said, 'If we're going to build a church for Anna, let's do it right.' Said he wanted to make sure no one could break in from the other side."

Or into the tunnel from this side, thought Andreas. He beamed his light on the floor by the wall. Nothing there to indicate that the wall swung into the crypt—like the door it resembled—but maybe it swung into the mine. He lowered his shoulder to the wall and pushed, then gestured for Tassos to give him a hand. The two men pushed as hard as they could, first on one edge, then on the other. The wall didn't budge.

"What are you doing?" The old man sounded more curious than annoyed.

"Just making sure it's secure," said Andreas. "Is there another way into the tunnel?"

"I guess, but you'll have to ask Tom. I'm not much for mines. I always preferred the sea myself—until my Anna insisted I take over her family's farm. But I brought her back to the sea when I built her church to Saint Nicholas, protector of sailors." He was rambling off into reminiscences.

"I noticed the blue roof," said Tassos.

That was a courteous way to cut him off, thought Andreas.

The man nodded, seemed to forget what he was saying, and hobbled toward the ladder. He bent over to pick up the lantern and started up the rungs. "You done here?"

Andreas looked at Tassos and nodded. "Yes, sir."

Tassos stood by the ladder waiting for Vassili to reach the top rung and climb into the sanctuary. Instead, the man placed the lantern on the sanctuary floor and asked Andreas to hand him his dog. Andreas stared at the dog, which was staring at him, then looked at Tassos.

"Here, let me do that," said Tassos, grinning. "Vassili, since you built this church, maybe you can answer a question for me."

"What is it?" He took the dog from Tassos, placed it on the floor, crawled off the ladder, and stood up.

Tassos started up the ladder. "Is there anything you can think of that churches built to Saints Kiriake, Marina, Fanourios, and Calliope have in common that makes them different from churches built to Saints Nicholas, Barbara, Phillipos, and Spyridon?"

The old man didn't answer, just stood silently in the sanctuary seemingly waiting for Tassos and Andreas to join him. Finally he spoke. "I wish I could help you, but I'm not a priest."

"I'm not talking about the saints themselves. I'm talking about how the churches are built."

"I know of no differences except of course for the icons." He paused for a moment. "Come to think of it, there might be a difference, but you'd have to check with the archbishop."

He had Andreas' interest. "What difference?"

"I'm not sure if a church has to be built with its front door facing the setting sun on its saint's name day. Though that's the way I built this one." He waved his hand.

"What are you talking about? Everybody knows the front door has to face west so the sanctuary faces east." Tassos sounded impatient.

Vassili shook his head. "No, Tassos, the front door faces the setting sun."

"What difference does that make?"

"I see you're not a sailor." Vassili smiled. "The sun doesn't set—or rise—in the same place all year. It sets along a line running from the northwest to the southwest depending on the season."

"How does that answer Tassos' question about differences between the churches?" Andreas asked.

The man shrugged. "I'm not sure it does, but if a church has to be built with its door facing the setting sun on its name day, the ones in one group face one way and the ones in the other another."

Andreas was puzzled. "Why?"

"The name days for Kiriake and the three saints you said with her all fall in summer—June, July, and August—when the sun sets to the northwest. The others have name days in November and December, when it sets to the southwest. That's about all I can think of. Hope it helps."

If Andreas still had his gun in his hand, he'd have knocked himself out when he smacked his forehead. "Of course! They all have name days falling in the heart of—"

Tassos finished Andreas' sentence. "Tourist season!"

Andreas shook Vassili's hand hard enough to rock him. "Thank you very much. You've been a great help," he said, and raced out with Tassos right behind him—leaving the old man and his dog alone again in their church.

Andreas was running on pure adrenaline, his every muscle tense, every blood vessel pounding. He barely gave Tassos time to close the car door before spinning the tires in the dirt. He knew what this meant. Saint Kiriake's name day was July 7, the day after tomorrow. If they didn't find Annika Vanden Haag by then, she'd be dead. No doubt about it.

◇◇◇

Annika felt weaker than she could remember ever feeling. She must have been drugged. No other explanation made sense to her. She needed something to eat, something to drink, but was certain if she did, she'd be as good as dead.

She tried to get up. That was when she sensed how sore and raw she was down there, and vaguely what she'd just been through. Had she been raped? Instinctively she touched herself to feel for injury, then for fluids. She found no semen there; nor on her belly or thighs. It was a small but precious moment of relief.

What's this? On the outside of her right thigh she felt a swelling. She pressed at it and instantly realized what it was. Ever since childhood her body had reacted this way at the point of an injection. Now she panicked. She realized that whenever she slept he had open access to her body.

She knew she must stay awake to defend herself. It was her only chance at surviving. If she were going to die, she'd go out fighting. She knew her family was looking for her. They had to be. There was still hope someone would find her—if only she could stay awake.

◇◇◇

He'd first used prayer to survive his daily moments of childhood terror, later he developed other, more efficient means for coping with his past. He still practiced both, as his tributes could attest to, had any remained alive.

They were all tall and blond as his sister was—or would have been. He knew just what to say to gain their trust and bring his foreign tributes down into his world among the foreign gods—and what drug to use to control them. Like his tributes, he chose his drugs for a purpose: some drugs for sleep, some for giving pleasure to his gods, some for both. There was no problem finding whatever he needed on Mykonos, this island of open pleasure. All he required lay in the bag by his feet. He was prepared for anything.

Chapter Sixteen

Annika struggled against sleep. The music was soothing and the room warmer than she remembered. Suddenly it hit her; the bastard was piping in heat and music to keep her sleepy.

She smacked at her face with her good hand, but that only worked until the stinging passed; then she felt even sleepier. She thought of her family, but that flooded her with thoughts of how sad they'd be if they couldn't find her.

She needed something to occupy her mind, to keep her awake. She stood up and twisted her head for a few minutes, squatted through a set of deep knee bends, and did some warm-up stretches. Her hand wasn't hurting as much as before. Maybe it isn't broken after all, she thought, or maybe I'm just used to playing through pain. She didn't give a damn that she was naked before an audience. She had to prepare herself.

Her mind was on a brutal, bloody intramural soccer match during her freshman year at Yale. Two older assholes tried knocking her out after her first score. They were relentless but missed their chance; one lost two teeth and the other gained a broken leg while Annika scored two more goals and a "don't-mess-with me" reputation. But that was against adversaries she could see, could challenge with her strength. Now there was none to face but time, and the only victory was not to succumb to sleep.

And so she began: over and over she replayed every move, every feint, every pain, every score; she was determined to win again or die trying.

◇◇◇

He was running out of time.

About thirty feet down the tunnel from her cell was a heap of construction odds and ends. He rummaged through the mess until he found a length of beat-up garden hose and an almost finished roll of duct tape. He carried them back to a World War II–era gasoline generator used for powering light and ventilation. It vented to the outside through an old air shaft. He turned on a flashlight and turned off the generator.

He disconnected the vent pipe from the generator's exhaust and used the duct tape to secure the garden hose in its place. The exhaust connection was about twice the diameter of the hose but the duct tape gave it an airtight fit. Picking up the other end of the hose, he walked back to the cell wall, pulled on his night-vision goggles, and looked through one of the slots. Inside the cell, each slot was faced in the same smooth, painted stone that covered the rest of the inside walls. He'd built them to swing up and into the cell—like mail slots—so fingers pressing from inside would not find them.

She was jumping about naked in a determined little routine. He watched her silently. She kept repeating to herself, "I can beat you, I can beat you." He turned away, slid the garden hose into the end of a wider hose used for drawing fresh air into the cell, walked back to the generator and turned it on.

◇◇◇

The mayor was waiting for them when Tassos and Andreas returned to the police station. He was sitting in Andreas' office and jumped up the moment they walked in. "Have you heard about the deputy minister's niece?" he blurted, nearly apoplectic.

Andreas shot a worried glance at Tassos and looked back at the mayor. "What do you mean?"

"She's missing. The deputy minister called and told me he'd asked you to look for her."

Andreas held up his hand and said, "Calm down. I know, and we're looking for her."

"You know what this means?" Mihali didn't sound any calmer.

Andreas sat down in his chair before answering. "Yes, I'm afraid I do."

Tassos pointed the mayor to the chair in front of the desk. "Sit down, Mihali, we have a lot to talk to about."

Uncharacteristically docile, the mayor now did as he was told. Tassos closed the door and went to sit in the other chair.

Andreas ran his fingers through his hair, then rubbed his eyes. "I figure we have twenty-four to thirty-six hours before she's dead. No more."

The mayor looked like a deer in the headlights. "Why? Why do you say that?"

Andreas spoke as if in a trance. "All of his victims were killed during tourist season. All the bodies were found in churches with saints having name days in tourist season. The coroner set Vandrew's time of death to within twenty-four hours of Saint Calliope's name day—and we found her in Saint Calliope."

"Perhaps you'll recall that the Scandinavian girl supposedly killed by the Irishman"—Tassos paused long enough for the mayor to wince—"was murdered on the name day for Saint Marina."

"Another tourist-season saint," said the mayor.

"And another of Father Paul's churches," said Andreas.

"Do you think he's the killer?" asked the mayor.

Andreas shrugged. "All I'm sure of is she'll be dead in a matter of hours if we don't find her." He leaned forward and picked up a pencil from his desk. "It could be any of several suspects… or all of them…or none of them…and I don't have a fucking clue where any of them are." He threw the pencil against a wall.

"But we know where it'll happen," said Tassos calmly.

Andreas stared at him. "Do you really think with all this heat—and he has to know we're looking for him—he'll still take her to Saint Kiriake? He'd have to be stupid, or suicidal."

Tassos nodded no. "I don't think he'll bring her to Father Paul's Saint Kiriake, but for twenty years something's been driving him to kill in a church on its name day. I think he's going to try again. It's part of his ritual."

Andreas rubbed his eyes again, then ran his hands down his face until his thumbs were under his chin and his fingers clasped about his nose as if he were praying. He paused for a few seconds, looked at Tassos, and dropped his hands to his desk. "I think you're right."

"So, what do we do, guard all the churches named for Saint Kiriake?" asked the mayor.

Andreas said, "We have to be careful not to scare him off. If we do, it'll be too easy for him just to kill her and drop her in the sea."

"Or bury her by the side of the road," said Tassos.

Andreas gave him a "cool it with the Scandinavian already" look.

Tassos switched to his professional tone. "Our best chance of catching him with her is at one of the churches."

"We should check out the mines too," said Andreas.

Tassos paused. "I don't think we should be taking men away from the churches."

Andreas looked at Tassos in surprise and gave him a "what gives" hand gesture. "What are you taking about? We've got at least two suspects running around inside the mines. It's our hottest lead; we have to follow it up. Besides, it won't be cops searching mines. We need men who know them."

Tassos paused again, then nodded. "I guess that makes sense."

Andreas looked at the mayor. "Do you know men we can get to search?"

"At night?" asked Mihali."

"It's always night inside a mine, and we've no time to lose," said Andreas in a tone sharper than intended.

"Sure, I'll have them within an hour," the mayor said.

Andreas looked at Tassos. "Any idea how many men we'll need to put a twenty-four hour watch on the churches—starting tomorrow at sunset?"

Tassos nodded no. "Not until I find out how many churches are named for Saint Kiriake. I'll speak to the archbishop. Thank God she's not a popular saint or we'd have to mobilize the army."

"We still might have to," said Andreas.

The mayor blanched. "You're kidding."

Andreas let out a deep breath. "Let's see how many churches we're talking about before we cross that bridge. All I can tell you for sure is Mykonos is about to go through twenty-four hours of partying without much police protection."

"Syros too," said Tassos, nodding. "I'll have forty men here by tomorrow afternoon."

"Thanks," Andreas said.

"No need to thank me. We're all hanging together on this one." Tassos turned and stared at the mayor. "Right, Your Honor?"

The mayor stared blankly back at them. "Yes." He nodded. "We'll all hang together on this one."

◇◇◇

Ambassador Vanden Haag arrived home a little before eleven. Catia wasn't downstairs as usual. He found her upstairs sitting on the edge of their bed holding a picture of their daughter.

Her eyes were red. "Spiros said he'd spoken to the mayor and the chief of police and they promised to find her, but they haven't."

He sat next to her on the bed. "Do they have any idea where she is?"

She shook her head. "Spiros just keeps saying he's certain she's okay. That she's probably off with some boy." She leaned against him. "I have to go to Mykonos. I have to find her."

He put his arm around her. "I understand. When will you go?"

"Tomorrow morning, I've booked a flight. I should be in Mykonos by the afternoon."

"I'll go with you."

She shook her head. "No, you have that conference tomorrow with the prime minister. Spiros will meet me. Besides, you don't speak Greek well enough to be of much help." She forced a smile and snuggled closer.

"Okay, but I'll come the day after tomorrow—we'll surprise Annika and turn it into a family island holiday. We haven't done that in years."

Catia didn't say a word. She knew it was his way of dealing with the fear gnawing away at their hopes.

◇◇◇

I feel it, I see it...I have the angle, just get the ball back to me. She feinted to the left and moved to the right, then paused for an instant and thrust her body and leg through a vicious kick, followed by a leap in the air that brought her just short of hitting her head on the ceiling. She waved her good hand wildly above her head and yelled, "Score!" Annika jumped about for a moment, then bent over and rested her hands on her knees. She was breathing deeply. That was when she first noticed the odor. The acrid, unmistakable scent of exhaust fumes.

Fear instinctively shot through her body. "He's gassing me!" She struggled to stay focused. "This is just another test, another problem to solve," she kept repeating aloud while hammering away at her thigh with the heel of her good hand. She forced herself to concentrate on what she remembered from chemistry about carbon monoxide poisoning: a sufficient exposure can reduce the amount of oxygen taken up by the brain to the point that the victim becomes unconscious, and can suffer brain damage or even death without ever noticing anything up to the point of collapse.

In other words, if she continued with what she was doing, she was dead. She needed to find fresh air, but how, in this sealed, pitch-black tomb? In the darkness she'd lost track of where she was standing and stretched out her arms to feel for a wall. When she found one she quickly dropped to her knees and began crawling counterclockwise along its base, probing and scratching frantically with her right hand at each bottom stone. She wasn't moving as quickly as she wanted and felt a slight headache. She knew her body was giving in to the fumes and her mind started drifting. She had no idea how long she'd been breathing them in, but she was sure her little exercise at staying awake had intensified its effects. Her only chance was to find what had to be at the base of one of those walls—and quickly.

She found nothing on the first wall and began to struggle as she moved along the second one. Again, nothing but rock. At the third wall she dropped to her elbows and scratched away at its base. She hadn't slept for what seemed days. She was exhausted and wanted to rest, wanted to sleep. The thought of giving in passed through her mind, but she pushed it away, by pressing her toes against the floor to drive her body forward. By the fourth wall the rest of her body was drifting to the floor. Now she scratched out with both hands, grateful for the pain in her injured hand helping to keep her conscious. She had little energy left when she felt what she'd been looking for. She pressed and clawed at the rock until it flipped up into the room. It was the slot in the base of the wall she'd remembered hearing when he'd shoved in the beribboned gift box of chocolates. It was her last and only hope for fresh air.

Annika forced her face into the opening. She sensed a breeze and gulped at what she prayed was fresh air. But was it imagined, was it enough…was it in time? Those were her last thoughts as she fell off into a deep, long-resisted sleep.

◇◇◇

He pressed a switch hidden under a camouflaged plate to the right of the cell door, and a single fluorescent ceiling light slowly flickered on inside the cell. The door was two and a half feet wide and five feet high, made of steel. Three massive industrial hinges anchored it to the stone wall on its left side, and three equally massive sliding bolts along its right side held it firmly to the floor, the adjacent mine wall and the ceiling. It was the sort of door one would expect to see securing the shop of a jeweler, but this one he'd hidden beneath the textures and colors of the tunnel walls.

He slid out the bolt from the wall and pulled at the top one. He had trouble with that one, always had. He hadn't aligned it quite right when he installed it. He thought he might need a hammer to move it but decided to slide the bottom one out first and try the top one again. That did the trick. When he pulled on the door it slid open effortlessly. Not only did it carry the weight of the stone fitted to its inside face, it blended seamlessly into the inside cell walls when closed.

He looked at the girl stretched out along the far end of the wall separating the cell from the tunnel. Her face was pressed into the corner. He remembered his sister as rosy red when he crept into her bedroom that late-winter night to remove the hose from the broken pane by her bed, having just disconnected the other end from their miserable father's truck. Her death was blamed on a faulty space heater. She had been the first of his tributes, though he hadn't thought of it that way at the time.

He still smelled the fumes in the cell, even though he'd disconnected the garden hose and restarted the ventilation system ten minutes earlier. He stood in the doorway and studied her body. Not a flinch. Still, he waited a few more minutes before moving toward her cautiously.

When he felt her pulse he realized there was no need for concern. It was weak. No telling how much longer she might last. That meant he had to work fast. Death must come in a place of his saints of the living, not among his gods of the dead. He rolled her over onto her back and dragged her by the ankles to directly under the light. He straddled her above her waist and stared at her face for a moment before dropping to his knees and easing his naked buttocks onto her breasts. She wasn't rosy like his sister.

Slowly, he leaned forward and stroked her cheek with his left hand, while with his right he pulled a straight razor from behind his ear, snapped it open, and tenderly began slicing away. He was quite skilled with the razor and worked more swiftly as he moved along her body. When he was through there wasn't a hair to be found anywhere.

He made her as bare and smooth as the forty-five-hundred year-old Cycladic marble figurines of elongated, naked females— arms folded beneath their chests—the ancients of these islands sacrificed in place of humans. They'd taken great care to make the sculptures beautiful, a timeless beauty that inspired Pablo Picasso and Henry Moore, then ritually destroyed them in ceremonies honoring their gods. He had little patience for tourists who brought copies into their homes without having any idea of their purpose. Some Mykonians who kept them probably knew, because sacrifice was still among their traditions—the blood of a live rooster must run fresh at the site of a new home to protect all who enter from harm.

He, too, sought to gain the protection of his gods through sacrifice, but he knew that from him they required far more than mere stone or fowl.

His practice was to bind each tribute in symbolic honor to the ancient way before going on to the next step, but this one was so close to death she couldn't possibly put up resistance. Besides, with what he had in mind there was a chance they might be seen before reaching the church. If she seemed drunk or drugged, they weren't likely to attract any more attention than the hundreds of other revelers partying on a *panegyri* night, but if she were bound head to foot, they'd definitely be noticed. It was far too great a risk to take. He'd undertake that part of the rite later.

He left her lying on the floor while he went to do what else was required to complete the preparation. He didn't bother to lock the door. He didn't need to.

Chapter Seventeen

Ninety minutes after his meeting with Andreas and Tassos, the mayor met Andreas at a locals' taverna just off the main square in Ano Mera. Two dozen volunteers were inside. Andreas was impressed by how quickly he'd been able to get so many men to search the mines—and after midnight, no less. Then again, he'd been mayor for almost twenty years, and no one wanted to be on his bad side. Most appeared to be in their early forties, some younger, a few older. Pappas looked like the oldest. Andreas smiled to himself—apparently even the self-described, most important man on the island danced when the mayor played the tune.

The mayor spoke first, and formally. "My thanks to all of you for coming on such short notice in this, the middle of our busiest season, but as I told each of you, it is a matter of life and death. We must find a young woman lost in one of the mines." A few of the men exchanged glances. Pappas didn't blink.

The mayor came up with that cover story at Andreas' office, and even though none of them gave it much chance of flying, they hoped whatever rumors it spawned wouldn't be as catastrophic as the truth. There was a complication though—a very serious one. Volunteers were being asked to help find a ruthless, brutal killer. They had to be warned of the danger in a way that wouldn't blow the whole story wide open. The mayor assured them he'd handle it.

"My friends, we don't know if the missing woman is alone or with someone, went willingly or against her will. But we think she's somewhere in the mines, places you know better than anyone on our island. Just be careful. Prepare for the worst and pray for the best."

Andreas couldn't believe what he was hearing. The mayor planned on sending these men off to look for a serial killer in the dark—literally and figuratively. Where was the warning he promised?

"What do you mean 'prepare for the worst'?" It was Pappas.

Andreas assumed the mayor was agitated by the question, but he didn't show it.

"I think whenever you go in search of someone who might have been taken against her will—and I emphasize might—you should be alert to the possibility that someone may be prepared to do the rescuer harm."

"You mean 'harm' like what happened to that girl up at the church?" Pappas turned to face Andreas, as if directing the question at him.

That had to piss off the mayor, thought Andreas, but still Mihali didn't show it—just hurried to answer before Andreas could speak. "Let's hope not. I repeat, I don't know what happened to her, but I want all of you to be careful."

Andreas noticed he didn't offer his volunteers the opportunity of backing out. Perhaps that's why he wasn't agitated—he knew his audience had no choice.

No one else had a question, and the mayor turned the meeting over to Andreas to organize the search. Andreas described the missing woman and the area to be searched, which included mine entrances by the artist's home and Panos' farm. He said he'd leave it to the men in the room who knew the mines how best to conduct the search, but he insisted they work in groups of no fewer than three and that at least one in each group carry a firearm.

No one said a word. Although military service was mandatory for all Greek men and each probably had several guns at home, for the police chief to insist on guns meant this had to be far more serious than the mayor was letting on.

It was Pappas who said what everyone had to be thinking. "Is that to prepare for the worst?" His tone was sarcastic but he didn't wait for an answer or dwell on his point. Instead, he threw up his hands in a sign of disgust and turned to face the men. "Okay, let's set this up so we're not running into each other inside—because some of you are such lousy hunters you'll be shooting at shadows." That got them snickering. He'd lightened the mood and no one seemed to object to his taking charge—it was almost as if it had been planned that way.

Pappas suggested they divide the area into five sections with groups of four assigned to each section. He and the remaining men—the "old-timers" he called them—would man a command center out of his Jeep on the hillside adjacent to Panos' property. No one offered a better idea, but Andreas insisted that each search group report back at least once every hour, and any that didn't would have police dispatched to their last reported location ASAP.

Andreas noticed the mayor move his head to catch Pappas' eye, and immediately Pappas said, "Okay guys, let's get to work." The men filed out with nervous, resigned looks on their faces, expressions you'd expect to see on men asked to be pallbearers at the funeral of a stranger.

Pappas stopped as he passed Andreas. "How dangerous do you really think it's going to be?"

Andreas put his head down so as not to look him in the eyes. "Don't really know." Then he lifted his head and looked straight at him. "But I'd tell them to be careful, real careful."

Pappas nodded. "Thanks," he said, and left.

"What do you think?" the mayor said to Andreas.

"They know she's not in there on holiday." Andreas sounded annoyed.

"They probably think she was kidnapped by the same one who killed the Vandrew woman." Mihali's voice was calm.

Andreas was surprised. "That doesn't bother you?"

He nodded no. "Not really. Everyone knows a woman was murdered and the killer's still out there. Once they get started, they'll be like farmers chasing a fox with a chicken in its mouth. They won't be thinking about all the other chickens killed by the fox, just the one in its mouth."

"Yeah, and what happens if they catch the fox?"

He patted Andreas' arm and smiled. "We should only be so lucky. If it's okay with you, I have to get back to town."

Andreas didn't want to let the subject drop but could tell the mayor was in "please the electorate" mode. He'd seen it in a lot of politicians. It meant no straight answers.

"Sure, I've got to leave for the mines anyway. I'll let you know if something turns up," Andreas said, although he was certain the mayor would get his news straight from his volunteers, probably before he did.

As Andreas walked toward the door the mayor yelled out in a grandly cheery voice, "Happy hunting, Chief."

Andreas wondered what the hell was going through that man's mind that made him so happy in the middle of this nightmare.

◇◇◇

She hadn't moved from where he'd left her, under the light, flat on her back. He dropped a small beach bag on the floor beside her and stared at her face. He'd seen enough young women die slowly to tell she was still alive. He knelt down and gently lifted her injured hand. Cradling it in his left hand, he gently stroked it with his right. His eyes studied her body for movement, and when he looked at her face his own took on the gaze of a kindly friar. He stared with what seemed only benevolent interest for several seconds before giving her wrist a sudden, violent twist. She winced only slightly.

He placed the injured hand over her right breast, then reached down for her right hand and drew it across her body to rest on her left breast. Then, he sat back on his haunches and reached into the bag for what he needed next, confident the pain he was about to inflict would not wake her.

◇◇◇

Annika was finding peace. The light was bright silver flecked with gold, the air bursting with fresh scents of springtime and mellow sounds of distant songbirds as smiling children in soft white muslin danced around her. They called her "sister" and asked her to join them. From the circle of dancers, a little boy reached out for her hand. She followed him with her eyes but did not reach back. Two young girls with yellow flowers in their hair stepped forward and offered her a soft, white muslin gown. Looking down, she realized she was as naked as the day she came into the world. She looked up and stared into the light. Was this what she wanted to do? Was it time to join her brothers and sisters? Annika was so very tired, and they offered her peace.

She was about to accept the gown when her head jerked violently forward. The children must be pulling at her hair. It hurt. She felt the tugging and touching move along her body to places only her lover had been. These were not children, certainly not any she wanted to play with for eternity. She pushed the gown away and waited for the touching to end.

When it stopped there were no more children or songbirds. Only silence and a blinding light. She was no longer in a place of peace. Had she made a mistake not going with the children? Perhaps they would come back for her. She prayed they would. She'd long ago lost track of time, and now all hope of rescue was gone. She felt abandoned. All she wanted was to find that place of peace.

She felt someone lift her hand. The touch was gentle and comforting. It must be one of the children, returned to show her the way. Now she would take the hand; it was time to go.

Her mind began drifting away from her body. The separation was almost complete when a bolt of pain seared through her left wrist. Although she knew the pain was real, her mind was too detached to trigger a reaction in her body. She knew, too, that whoever did this was not some gentle soul leading her to peace. She grew angry at the pain; it ignited her competitive fire and she longed to fight for control of her body. Her challenge was taken up almost at once.

The new pain didn't seem much at first. It built up slowly. Something was being forced deep within her. Her legs had been pulled apart but it was not a man inside her. It was something else trying to fill her womb. When the real pain came, it was in long bursts of fire. Just when she'd get used to one, another would thrust into her. They seemed to have no end. She wondered if this was the pain of childbirth. In a flash of thought she knew this was the pain of her own rebirth, pain she must endure to survive. She would not let it beat her. She would not let him beat her.

Now "*him*" filled her mind. Him! Him! Annika's conscious mind was returning. She remembered where she was—and her tormentor.

Then a different pain began, in a different place. She felt a burning tear as something pushed into her from behind. Again it wasn't a man—but she knew it was him doing this to her and that was all she needed to bear the pain. If she could regain control of her body, she'd fight him to the death; but she couldn't even open her eyes. Only her mind was working.

Now she felt pain below her eyes. It was being forced into her nose. She couldn't breathe. She was suffocating and face-to-face with the instinctive panic that comes with it. Somehow she must get her mouth to open. It was her only chance for breath. She steeled her will for the seconds left and focused her mind on a single word: *breathe*.

◇◇◇

He was so busy forcing the last of the tampons up through her nostrils that he didn't notice the slight parting of Annika's lips and the first frail draw of breath.

◇◇◇

It was almost sunrise and the only good news from the mines was that the searchers weren't shooting at one another. At least not yet. No one had found a thing, all were exhausted, and most still had day jobs to get to. The mayor promised fresh volunteers "first thing in the morning," which probably meant hours from now in Mykonos time.

What the hell, thought Andreas, it probably doesn't matter much now anyway. All the likely places turned out to be busts— nothing even close to Panos' or the artist's. It was like looking for a needle in miles of buried haystacks. Andreas didn't hold out much hope of finding Annika Vanden Haag this way.

He told Pappas to have the men call it a night. Andreas respected Pappas' knowledge of the mines, but as Pappas told him, "unless you know what the killer has in mind, there's no telling where he might be." Between themselves they'd dropped the mayor's pretext for the search. Andreas let him assume they were looking for the same man who killed Vandrew. He suspected the others had reached the same conclusion.

Andreas thought it might help if he ran through the possible suspects for Pappas, but he didn't dare. Even if the killer were one of those on his list, there were five others he'd be naming as a potential serial killer. God knows how someone like Pappas would use that information against those men—freely citing Andreas as his source for the slander. Not something to do lightly if you valued a career. Still, if they were to have the best chance at finding her, he might have to tell him.

Andreas was standing by Pappas when he heard him radio the last group of searchers to come in. He looked at Andreas. "Any suggestions on where to send in the new guys?"

Andreas nodded no. "Wish I did."

Pappas stared at him and took his sunglasses out of his shirt pocket. "Sun's back." He put them on. "May I make one?"

"Sure."

Pappas walked to the old mining-company maps laid out on the tailgate of his Jeep. They'd used them to keep track of the crews down below. "I think we ought to start looking here," he said, and pointed to an area by the sea. It was at the opposite end of their current search.

"Why there?" Andreas asked.

Pappas shrugged. "I don't know, call it a hunch."

Now it was Andreas doing the staring. "What's your real reason?"

Pappas gave the smile of a shark searching for prey. "Probably about the same as yours for starting us at this end." He pointed again at the map.

"I never told you why I picked there." Andreas' voice was coldly professional.

"Would you have if I'd asked?"

"No." Andreas cracked a smile.

"Look," Pappas said, his tone changing mercurially, "it's late and I'm tired. This is my suggestion. Decide if you want to take it or not, and call me if you do. I have a business to run." He seemed to fall back on that tone every time Andreas almost started liking him, and it pissed Andreas off.

Andreas let his anger pass before speaking. "I'll consider your suggestion. Just tell me where it is. These mining maps have no topographic references I'm familiar with."

Pappas smiled again. "It's a tunnel that opens over there." He was pointing toward the rising sun. "By the priest's beach."

Andreas was pretty sure how he knew to pick that spot. That brought back his anger, though he tried hiding it. "Fine. We'll start there." He knew he sounded abrupt. A few seconds passed and Andreas reached out his hand. "Thanks for all your help," he said sincerely. "We couldn't have done it without you, and I'd very much appreciate any suggestions you can give the new men."

They shook hands.

Andreas' anger wasn't at Pappas—it was at the contractor's friend and benefactor, the mayor.

◇◇◇

"The damn bastard only cares about himself." Andreas was ranting on the phone to Tassos as he drove back to town. "I can't believe he gave him the names."

Andreas heard a yawn. "Ahhhh, start believing. I'm not surprised. Just be happy he's on our side—for the moment. By the way, what time is it?"

"About seven. What do you mean 'on our side'?" Andreas couldn't shake his anger.

"He wants to find the killer as badly as we do. He also wants to keep things quiet, and knows Pappas will keep his mouth shut if he thinks it might jeopardize the island's building boom." He yawned again. "I'm sure the mayor told Pappas what to say at the meeting in the taverna. It made Pappas look like he wasn't afraid to stand up to him, and that way the warning about a killer out of Pappas' mouth, not the mayor's."

Andreas shook his head. "Real smoothie."

"Yeah, so's a snake. Bet when he gave Pappas the suspects' names he told him to get you to tell him too. That way, if anything went wrong, Pappas could name you as the source and you'd believe you were."

"Son of a bitch."

"That's one of his nicknames. Hey, don't worry, no harm's been done, but watch the guy. He's capable of anything, and I mean anything. That's how he's stayed in power so long. He knows where all the bodies are buried—and how to bury them too."

Andreas winced at Tassos' choice of words. "Okay, so, how are we set up for tonight?"

Tassos wasn't yawning anymore, but he still sounded casual. "There are more churches to Saint Kiriake on Mykonos than I thought, but some—like the big one in town—are too public for our killer to use. We'll only have to worry about the out-of-town ones off by themselves."

Andreas' voice sounded doubtful. "Something about this guy makes me not want to take chances."

Tassos' tone turned serious. "We don't have enough men. I don't want a cop sitting alone in the moonlight in the middle of the Mykonos hills waiting for a serial killer to show up. It's too dangerous, especially for the rookies—not to mention the kids still in the academy. We need at least two for every church."

Andreas was serious too. "Can't do it. We have to cover all the churches with what we've got or I'm calling Athens for help. Can't risk it. Not with all our suspects running around loose."

He could hear Tassos' breathing quicken. "What if we get teams to cover the out-of-town churches and uniforms walking beats between the ones in town? That'll give a show of force in town too—and coverup the fact that most of our cops are in the countryside." Andreas knew Tassos was trying to sell him on keeping Athens in the dark, and he wondered if Tassos might be more worried about his pension than he'd let on.

"What time do we deploy?" Andreas' tone was neutral; he would think about the suggestion.

"To be safe, I figure two hours before sunset. They'll be up all night."

"They're young Greek men on Mykonos—they should be used to that." There was mischievous lilt to Andreas' voice.

Tassos laughed. "Yes, but it's harder to stay awake when you're not drinking and dancing."

Andreas laughed too. "Where are you now?"

"Syros. I had to wakeup the archbishop to get his help. I've had a half-dozen men going through the archdiocese's records since three this morning mapping every Saint Kiriake church on Mykonos—everyone they have a record of, that is."

That alarmed Andreas. "How can there be churches they don't know about?"

"As the archbishop told me, we're talking centuries here, and it's possible not every church is in their records. The local priest would know, and certainly the family who takes care of the church would know; it's just that Syros may not have a record of it."

Andreas knew it seemed too simple just to watch every Saint Kiriake church until the bastard showed up. "That's just great. So, how do we make sure we have them all covered?" He knew if there was one person on Mykonos who knew them all, it was the killer.

"We're cross-checking against baptism, wedding, and death records to see if any other Kiriakes turn up."

"How long's that going to take?" Andreas' frustration was building.

Tassos started sounding edgy. "Don't know yet, but it's the best we can do. I'm planning to be in Mykonos by noon with my men. I'm bringing with me whatever information we find by then, and any more will be faxed to your office."

Andreas let out a breath. Tassos had to be as frustrated as he was. "Okay, just try not making too grand an entrance. Forty police arriving at the same time might look like an invasion."

"We're coming in civilian clothes on the ferry so as not to scare the tourists. Where do you want us to meet you?"

"I'll have a bus pick you up at the pier." He thought for a second. "It'll take you to the taverna we went to last night in Ano Mera. We'll use it as headquarters." He ran a hand through his hair. "God, this is going to attract one hell of a lot of attention no matter how quiet we try to keep it."

"I think Mihali's already managed to circulate our cover story to every local on the island. It's our police doing all it can to rescue a foreigner from possible harm. It will enhance the island's reputation for protecting tourists." Tassos spoke with the mayor's pompous, public-speaking cadence.

Andreas smiled and hoped he wasn't about to hear another story about farmers, foxes, and chickens. "Okay, I get the message. See you in five hours."

After they hung up, Andreas decided not to confront the mayor as he'd planned. What's the use? he thought. Each of them, in his own way, was doing the same thing—trying to keep his mind off tomorrow's most likely ending: the deputy minister's niece is found murdered in a bizarre ritual killing and all the world learns that for decades a serial killer has been murdering Mykonos tourists at will.

He headed back to his office, snatched a cot from a cell, and tried to catch a few hours sleep. After all, tonight he, too, would have neither booze or dancing to keep him awake.

◇◇◇

He knew it would be difficult moving her to the church with police looking everywhere for him. He also knew the sensible

196 Jeffrey Siger

thing was to toss her body into the sea and walk away, but he loved his plan too much to abandon it.

Besides, he must complete the ceremony. It was not out of pride that he thought that way, nor was he seeking glory for outwitting the police—certainly not any of a public sort. It was never his desire that the world know of him or his acts. He was not like those others who seemed to crave attention and left some souvenir sign or public message announcing each death. He found all the reward he needed in the many quiet moments he shared with his tributes within the solitude of these walls. No, he must complete the ceremony to honor those who protected him for so long in this foreign place and allowed him all those private moments. Moments like this.

He reached into the bag and pulled out what he needed. With a pencil he carefully drew dark brown eyebrows over the light ones he'd shaved away. Then he dressed her in a loose-fitting, light gray, cotton beach dress. Finally, he lifted her bald head and pulled on a long, dark brown wig. He noticed she was breathing lightly. Good, he thought: she'll make it to the church. He picked up his bag and left to find what he'd need to move her.

This time he locked the door behind him—just in case.

Chapter Eighteen

Andreas had slept longer than he intended. It was almost ten. There was a note on his desk from Kouros. Considerate of the kid not to have awakened him, he thought. He read the note: "Panos never showed up at his restaurant last night. The artist Daly was there for a while but left before we got there. Neither man returned home." Considerate my ass, Andreas realized, he didn't want to tell me in person.

He tossed the note onto his desk and called Pappas. He'd kept his word; the new men had been searching since eight but only enough had shown up to form groups of three. Guess the mayor is losing supporters, thought Andreas. They'd gone in through three entrances on hillsides overlooking the priest's beach and one by a cove just north of it. Pappas said the tunnels ran west through the base of the hills before turning south toward Ano Mera. He said he picked those tunnels because they connected with ones running toward the artist's and Panos' places. Andreas could see his grin through the phone. The shark was still hunting.

Andreas kept his cool. "Let's pray you guessed right."

"They're moving a lot faster now," Pappas reported. "The tunnels last night were some of the oldest and haven't been worked for forty years or so. The men had to be very careful. The ones they're in now were used until about twenty-five years ago. If she's in one, we should know in a few hours."

"What's a few hours?" Andreas didn't want to get his hopes up.

"By this afternoon."

"Early or late?"

"Late."

Andreas thought, if she's in there and he doesn't move her before sunset, at least we have a chance. Once he moves her, all we can hope for is that he sticks to his routine. But he's too smart not to change it. By now every local knows we're searching the mines, so chances are he knows we're looking for him—and that we must know his tactics. But what will he change? What's he thinking—that "sick bastard," he said aloud.

"What did you say?" Pappas sounded angry.

Andreas had been so lost in his own thoughts he was surprised to hear Pappas' voice. "Huh?" Then he laughed. "No, no, not you. I was thinking of the bastard who has her."

Pappas grumbled, "Just don't forget how much you owe me for this."

"Of course I won't." Andreas was back to stroking him. "Please let me know as soon as there's any news—and, again, thanks. We couldn't have done this without you." He hung up, indulged himself with five seconds of dwelling on how much that guy grated on him—despite all his help—and went back to thinking how the killer would try to cross them up.

The only shot they had was if the killer stuck to suffocating his victims in a church on its name day. But maybe he'd bury her—or already has buried her—with enough air to survive until after midnight. He shook his head. Time for coffee.

He got a cup of coffee and brought it back to his office, then sat behind his desk staring out the window and thinking. It was at times like this he wished he had a view of the sea, but land with that kind of view was too valuable for housing cops. No money, no respect, no views. No wonder cops go bad. He thought of his dad. No, he never went bad; maybe that's why he died young—he was too good. He shook his head. "Stop this foolish, stupid thinking." He'd said the words aloud.

Andreas turned his thoughts back to Annika Vanden Haag. If we don't find her in the mines, all we're left with is the churches.

And if he's already buried her in one of them…he let out a deep breath. We have no choice; as soon as Tassos gets to Ano Mera we'll have to send men out to search the churches. My God, I can't believe we're going to be opening every burial crypt in every Saint Kiriake on Mykonos in the middle of preparations for tonight's *panegyris*.

He dropped his forehead into his hands. Andreas could just hear the screaming priests and families. This was going to be one giant public-relations nightmare. Time to get His Honor the mayor back in the fun.

◇◇◇

Andreas enjoyed watching the slight twitching at the outside corner of the mayor's right eye expand across his eyebrow as Andreas explained what he intended to do. "With any luck we'll find her before dark," he said trying to sound enthusiastic.

The mayor spoke in a measured tone. "Don't you think your plan is a bit too aggressive? Watching churches is one thing, but opening tombs is…" He searched for the words. "Quite a different matter."

Andreas took the formality of the phrase to mean "insane." "We don't have a choice. We can't take the chance he's already buried her alive in one of them."

"But how do we know? She could be anywhere." His voice cracked.

"Could be, but the churches are our best guess, and if she's in one and we don't check…" He paused. "I don't have to tell you what that means."

The mayor stared at him. "No, you don't have to remind me." He got up from behind his desk, walked to the window, and stared out.

He has a view of the sea, Andreas thought.

Still staring out the window, the mayor said, "There's no way he could bury her in a busy church during preparations for a *panegyri*. There are too many people around." He turned to face Andreas. "Why not do a thorough examination of the busy ones for anything unusual and save your digging for the less public ones? After all, isn't that where he's likely to take her?"

The mayor was doing his political thing—looking for compromise—and his approach would attract a lot less attention and aggravation, but Andreas nodded no. "I understand where you're coming from—I had the same thought—but we can't risk it. This killer's smart enough to have figured some way of getting her into any church he wants, no matter how many people are around. We can't forget that he's probably been studying our churches for years with just this sort of thing in mind."

"That's *my* churches, Chief." His fangs were showing. "I'm the one who has to live here after you've desecrated who knows how many final resting places of our citizens' ancestors."

Andreas let him vent. He knew the mayor had no choice but to go along with him. This was nothing more than Andreas giving him the chance to put his best political spin on the search.

The mayor let out a breath and walked back to his desk. "Let me speak to the archbishop. I think I can get him to cooperate as long as it's clear there's only going to be a quick look under floor slabs and no one's planning on knocking down any walls looking for her in a wall crypt."

"Unless there's a sign of fresh cement on a wall, I can go along with that," said Andreas. It was a minor compromise, one to let Mihali save face.

"Fine, just don't start digging before I speak to him. Give me an hour."

Andreas looked at his watch. It was almost noon. Time to meet Tassos. "Okay, one hour."

That seemed to satisfy the mayor's deal-making nature. "By the way, I got a call from a friend of Ilias' who wondered if I knew where he was. He said Ilias borrowed his boat a couple days ago and hasn't returned it. I guess that means he could be anywhere."

Yeah, him and everyone else, thought Andreas.

◇◇◇

It was a small yellow motorbike. One of thousands that seemed to sprout everywhere during tourist season and contributed greatly to the orthopedic practices of the island's doctors. Tourists who rented them seemed to share hallucinogenic visions of invulnerability to injury and drove more wildly than they would ever think of doing at home. He'd found this one about a quarter of a mile from the mine entrance, not far from where his own motorbike was hidden in the brush. The key was still in it. He listened for sounds but heard none. He scanned the hills above and below the road for movement. Again, there was none. Whoever left it wasn't nearby—or was being very quiet. He listened longer. Still no sound.

He turned the key to unlock the front wheel and slowly pushed the bike forward along the road without starting the engine. He pushed faster and faster until he was running beside it. When he stopped he was breathing heavily but not as much as you'd expect for a man of his age.

He turned the front wheel and carefully pushed the bike toward the downhill side of the road. Slowly, he eased it over the edge. The bike started to get away from him but he used his strength to hold it back. It was a tough fifty yards down the hill to the mine entrance. You couldn't see it from the road. He was halfway there when the weight of the bike and the angle of the hillside combined with the sandy, dry dirt to overcome his strength. His feet slid out from under him. He struggled to keep his balance but couldn't. He was sliding out of control toward the boulders below, still holding the bike. He wrenched it onto its side and fell behind it, trying desperately to stop their slide. Both stopped about thirty yards on when the bike hung up on a huge wild rosemary bush—and he slid knee first into the motor housing. He cursed.

He was fifteen yards below and to the side of the mine entrance. He steadied and lifted the bike, angled it toward the entrance and dragged it. Limping because of his hurt knee, he cursed again.

By the time he reached the entrance, almost forty-five minutes had passed since he'd left her. He stood catching his breath and looked down at his pants. They were torn by the rocks when he fell and there was an ugly gash along the side of his thigh. His knee was throbbing. He looked like a tourist who'd been in a bike accident. Perhaps this wasn't such a brilliant plan after all. Dumping her at sea was beginning to look better all the time.

◇◇◇

Catia's plane to Athens arrived right on time, leaving her a bit more than an hour to catch her connection to Mykonos. Plenty of time for a call to her brother and a coffee. He wasn't in his office. She left word that she was at the Athens airport and would call him when she got to Mykonos. She bought a coffee, walked to the gate, and sat in one of the plastic and metal chairs anchored in rows to the floor. Looking at her watch, she saw that it was after one. She'd be there by two-thirty—the time Annika most liked being on the beach.

She covered her eyes with her right hand and tried to keep from crying.

◇◇◇

As usual, things didn't go as planned. It was almost one-thirty before Tassos and his men arrived in Ano Mera; but the delay did give the mayor enough time to obtain a letter from the archbishop "blessing" a search of the churches. Though built and cared for by local families, churches were holy properties under the control of the archbishop. The letter was all the legal authority Andreas needed. He didn't want to think about what the mayor must have promised to get that letter; he was just happy at the result. The last thing he needed at this moment was a battle with the Church; he'd worry later over what part the mayor undoubtedly had him playing in their deal.

Within an hour, sixty plainclothesmen working in teams of three and carrying a copy of the archbishop's letter, a photograph of Annika Vanden Haag, and descriptions of the possible suspects were on rented motorbikes heading to every known church in the countryside named for Saint Kiriake. Teams with more than one church to cover were assigned churches as close as possible to each other, with at least one team member stationed at each one. Team members were ordered to remain in open radio contract with one another at all times until relieved. Five uniformed two-man teams, in marked cars, were assigned specific areas of the island to serve as backup, just in case. All were told to be polite but firm and, if asked the reason for the search, to state only that they were acting with the permission of the archbishop and to show the letter.

Seventy cops were now dispersed throughout the Mykonos countryside. Another dozen were walking beats among the churches in town. Tassos said it might have been the biggest show of force on Mykonos since World War II. It couldn't help but attract attention from the locals. Still, it was the best plan they could come up with under the circumstances—at least that's what Andreas hoped.

◇◇◇

He limped all the way down the tunnel, wheeling the bike. When he reached the cell he leaned it against the wall and opened the door. The tribute lay exactly where he'd left her. Still breathing, too. As he went inside, he stooped to pick up a water bottle on the floor. He walked over to her, dropped his pants to his ankles, and sat next to her. The floor was cold. He stared at the ceiling for a moment, as if in prayer, then at her as he poured water on his thigh and rubbed at the blood and dirt in his wound. He poured on more water but his eyes were back on the ceiling, as if he was waiting for a sign.

It was the pinging that caught his attention. Very high-pitched, like metal striking metal. It wasn't a natural sound in a mine. He leaped up and pulled on his pants. Sweeping her up in his arms as if she weighed no more than a doll, he carried Annika out of the cell. The sound was getting closer. He lifted her onto the bike so that her legs straddled the frame and her chest leaned forward over the handlebars. Looking down the pitch-black tunnel, he determined that the sound was coming from there. Behind him was the entrance he'd just used, which led into daylight at the middle of the island.

There was no other way to go but toward the sound. In that direction two tunnels branched off to the right. The one he wanted was the second, less than three hundred yards from where he stood. The other was only a hundred yards away, and the sound seemed to be coming from that one. He pushed the bike ahead into the darkness. There was no time to get his night-vision goggles or anything else. It didn't matter. He knew his way from here in the dark and that he'd better hurry.

He was almost to the first tunnel when he saw a faint flicker on the wall ahead of him to the left. Someone was coming down the tunnel. He heard the noise again, then voices. He had to get past the opening or they'd find him for sure. He pushed the bike faster, and at the change in momentum, her body unexpectedly slumped away from him. The bike began to tip. He grabbed for her with one hand and steadied the bike with the other. He was almost at the first tunnel. He held his breath and listened. He saw more flickers, brighter but still random as if no one was paying attention to what was up ahead. Again, he held his breath, seemed to immerse himself in deep prayer, and pushed the bike and the girl across the opening.

◇◇◇

The three men had been walking in the dark since eight in the morning, stumbling over, under, and around boulders, timbers, and all sorts of debris without finding a sign of anything but snakes and feral dogs. As far as they were concerned, they were on a dusty wild-goose chase into a dilapidated and dangerous hole. No one in his right mind would walk around in here—least of all a young tourist woman.

For the first few hours they'd been careful to be quiet. They weren't trying to surprise anyone; they just didn't want someone to hear them coming and set up an ambush. After a near miss from a surprised—and striking—viper, they decided a little noise was a better risk than startled dogs and snakes. None of them had any plans of becoming a hero or doing any more than was required to keep the mayor happy and themselves on the municipal payroll.

The oldest of the three had worked in the mines thirty years ago and the other two—both in their twenties—had to put up with his stories of the "good old days" of six-day work weeks, sleeping next to the mines in five-man tents and living off the food he'd carried back from town on his one day off. At first they listened to kill the boredom, but when he started talking about ghosts haunting the mines, they told him to "shut the hell up." He didn't. Instead, he began pinging away with the butt end of his sheath knife at the miner's tool he carried. "To ward off the spirits," he said. It also kept his weapon handy. Something they all did—just in case.

They'd gone in through an entrance on a hillside above the priest's beach and walked west for two hours before turning southwest into a connecting tunnel. That was several hours ago. Now they were coming up on a T. If they turned right at that spot and walked two hundred yards they'd be at the beginning of a mile-and-a-half-long tunnel running north to the sea. If they went left, they'd end up outside about a quarter-mile away, just below an old mining road. The oldest searcher said that heading left was very dangerous—the tunnel was almost impassable—and they should take the tunnel to the right to get out.

"Bullshit," said the youngest, who was out in front. "I'm not walking another couple miles in this shit if I can get out in a quarter mile. Have some other assholes check out that tunnel over there." He swung his head to the right to indicate where he meant, and the light on his miner's helmet turned with it.

"Hey, keep your light pointed where you're headed," said the oldest. "I don't want to have to carry you out of here because you trip over something." He kept his own eyes on the fifteen feet in front of him, regularly glancing farther ahead to see what to prepare for next. "That's how you get through dangerous places like this." He'd told them that over and over.

"Yeah, yeah," said the youngest. "Hey, I see the T, there it is." He pointed and started walking faster.

The oldest shook his head. "Take it easy, and remember, take the right. We're going back the safe way."

As the youngest reached the merge he looked back over his left shoulder, threw an open palm at the oldest—the Greek equivalent of the middle-finger salute—and turned left. He froze in midstep. "Jesus. Look at that." He was pointing straight ahead.

The others ran up to him. A hundred yards straight ahead, light was streaming into the tunnel. There appeared to be an open door. They looked at one another, checked their weapons, and crossed themselves. They seemed like frightened rabbits about to confront a hound. Cautiously, as if in prayer, they headed toward the light, their eyes fastened to it, their ears perked for sounds ahead, beyond the crunch of their own boots on the earth.

By the time they reached the door the man holding his breath in the dark—ten feet to the right of where they'd turned left—had finished his own prayers and slid deeper into the darkness. Only the faintly perceptible sound of wheels under weight turning slowly in the dirt could be heard—if someone were listening for the sound in that direction. But no one was, so no one ever heard him or saw him—or her.

Chapter Nineteen

The first report in to Andreas was "they found her." He was so relieved at the words that he hugged Tassos. On their way to the mine entrance closest to where she'd been "found," he'd learned the truth. The plunge from great joy to deep despair took only the time it took to hear a single missing word: what they'd found was "her hair."

Andreas stood at the edge of the road, staring down the hill toward three of his men waiting by the mine entrance. His face looked bloodless. He wondered if this was how his father felt when facing the end of his career. No, Andreas knew it must have been a lot worse for his dad. He'd been betrayed by someone he trusted. Andreas would never do that—trust someone—or so he kept telling himself.

"Pretty deserted out here. Guess that's why he picked it." Tassos sounded like a cheerleader. "We're just over the hill from Panos' farm and less than a mile from the artist's place."

"And this tunnel ties in to an entrance above the priest's beach." Andreas kicked a rock down the hill. "Pick one."

Tassos shrugged and watched the rock tumble until it disappeared. "Any news on the suspects?"

Andreas nodded no. "A few people saw Father Paul having lunch on Paradise Beach two days ago with some woman from California, but we can't find him—or any of the others."

They started down the hill. Now neither seemed very enthusiastic.

"Hey, look at this." Tassos pointed at gouges in the dirt. "Something big slid through here recently."

They followed the marks.

"Looks like another motorbike accident," said Andreas. He pointed to a few bits of bloodstained fabric near the end of the slide and moved toward a large wild rosemary bush. "The bike and driver ended up here." He looked around. "I don't see anything, do you?"

Tassos nodded no. "The driver must have dragged the bike back up to the road. Guess it wasn't serious. Damn lucky. Could have been a lot worse." He started toward the mine entrance.

Andreas grabbed his arm to stop him. "Wait a minute." He drew a line in the air running from their feet to his men at the entrance. "Those are tire tracks. That's where the bike is."

Andreas yelled to his men. "Is there a motorbike in there?"

"A what?" a man yelled back.

"A motorbike," Andreas barked.

The men looked at one another then back at their chief. "No sir."

Andreas and Tassos followed the tracks up to the mine. The entrance was crisscrossed with boards warning of danger in three languages and signs depicting stick figures falling off a cliff. The tire tracks went inside. They maneuvered themselves through the maze of boards by following the tracks and, with flashlights blazing, found the reason for the warnings. About fifty feet inside the entrance, an ugly, jagged gash in the floor opened into an abyss. The tracks ended there. Andreas pointed his flashlight into the hole. "My God, do you think the driver and bike are in there? I can't see the bottom."

Tassos angled his beam across to the other side of the gash, then onto the ceiling and back along the walls behind him. Andreas sensed he wanted to say something. "What is it?"

Tassos seemed reluctant to speak. "I don't think so. Take a look at the ground on the other side."

The tire tracks picked up again, about two feet from the edge.

Andreas was amazed. "It's at least fifteen feet to the other side of this! How the hell did he get over there?"

Once more Tassos paused before speaking. "He had some ancient help." He directed his light on the floor at their feet. "Our guy knows his island history."

"What are you talking about?" Andreas was getting impatient.

"I'll bet our killer is the one with the bike." He pointed into the light at their feet. "The tracks end about two feet from this edge and resume about two feet from the far edge. And there's a three-foot wide impression in the dirt between the tire tracks and the edges on both sides."

Andreas wanted him to get to the point. "Great, this hole to hell keeps the curious away from his hiding place, but how'd he get across?"

"That's where he turned to the ancients."

Andreas' voice was rising. "What the hell are you trying to tell me?"

Tassos didn't answer. He simply pulled at a timber about five feet back from the edge of the hole. It looked it was holding up the roof—not a timber you'd want to move.

Andreas instinctively looked up. That's when he saw a huge plank coming toward him. It was part of the ceiling spanning the chasm, but it wasn't falling; it was slowly descending, suspended by ropes at each corner. The near end rested at his feet precisely within the impressions in the dirt.

"Amazing," said Andreas.

Tassos spoke like a teacher delivering a lecture he'd given a hundred times before. "Actually, this sort of thing wasn't all that rare on the islands in ancient times." He paused as if considering whether to continue. "Every island built secret tunnels to hide from pirates and invaders. Sometimes, an earthquake created an underground abyss—such as this one—across a tunnel. The ancients took it as a sign that the gods would protect them if they reached the other side. Trouble was, a permanent bridge made it easy for their enemies to reach it, too." He pointed to the timber he'd pulled. "Ingenious how they did it. The timber secures the whole system in place. It works sort of like a castle's drawbridge, except this bridge drops straight down."

"This can't be that old," said Andreas.

"It isn't," said Tassos, who no longer showed any reluctance to speak. "Whatever caused this hole happened after the mine was built, and this setup uses modern ratchets, weights, and pulleys to lower and raise the plank. The timber keeps the ratchet from allowing the plank to move." He pointed to the other side. "I'll bet somewhere over there's a ratchet for moving the plank from that side. My guess is this was built by our killer—he knew what he was doing."

Andreas didn't feel like complimenting the killer, no matter how obvious his skills. "It's time to get over there."

Tassos gave a slightly nervous look over the edge. "Heights aren't my thing. After you, Chief."

Andreas patted him on the back and winked, then briskly crossed over the plank. "Just keep your eyes shut." He was beginning to sound like himself again.

Tassos let the three officers cross before slowly inching himself along the plank, shuffling—not lifting—his feet to the other side. He started breathing again when he stepped onto solid ground. The others were fifteen feet ahead staring at a mound of debris blocking their way. It looked impassable. "A little labyrinth, I see," said Tassos.

Andreas pointed at the tire tracks. "And here's Ariadne's cord to lead us through it," he said, just to let Tassos know there were a few things he too knew about ancient Greece and its myths.

Tassos grumbled, "Yeah, and maybe at the other end we'll get lucky and find Theseus ready to slay our version of his youth devouring Minotaur."

Andreas decided to leave Tassos with the last word on that subject.

They followed the tracks and fifteen minutes later were standing with the men who found the cell. Each swore none of them had gone inside. Andreas stood at the door and stared at the mound of blond hair in the middle of the floor. Near it was a bag, a beach tote. Andreas tried not to think of what she had been through—and was going through. He just wanted to catch the bastard before…He noticed a puddle on the floor and carefully stepped into the cell. He knelt down and examined the liquid. "I think we have some blood here Tassos."

"It's probably his, from that slide down the hill," said Tassos as he stepped over to the bag. "At least now we have DNA to work with."

Andreas stood up. "Pretty sloppy of him, wouldn't you say?"

"Probably had to leave in a hurry." Tassos was carefully probing around inside the bag with his flashlight.

"Just what I was thinking." Andreas yelled to one of his men to get forensics here ASAP.

"Look at this," said Tassos. "It's a regular drugstore in here."

Andreas crouched back down to look in the bag. "Bet it's crystal meth in that one." He pointed to a vial. "And the syringes over there are how he delivered it."

"Yeah, and next to them is all the equipment you'd need to cook up a shot." Tassos pushed the light around a bit more. "I can't tell what's in those other vials, but the pills in the bubble packaging—they're roofies. Our friend Panos' favorites."

"And that?" asked Andreas, pointing.

Tassos poked at the item with his flashlight. "An eyebrow pencil."

"First he shaves them, then paints them? I can't figure him out." He shook his head and started to stand. As he did his eyes caught a glimpse of the ceiling. He froze. "Tassos, look."

For a moment neither said a word. They just stared at the ceiling.

Ringed around the outside of a circle containing four groups of tiny, roughly drawn figures were six carefully painted images. Each image in harmony with the others and posed as if ascending from hell to heaven.

"My God," said Andreas pointing. "Those four are images of saints from the churches where the bodies were found!" Instinctively, he crossed himself.

"And those figures in the middle." Now Tassos pointed. "They look like…like blondes with wings."

"Someone's idea of angels I'd guess…or nymphs," said a somber sounding Andreas. "And if I'm counting correctly, the figures grouped next to each saint correspond to the number of bodies buried in its church—including one for the Scandinavian under Saint Marina."

"He's keeping score?" Tassos' voice cracked.

Andreas looked down, paused, and let out a breath. "What about the two other images? I don't recognize them."

"I do." Tassos looked down. "One is Serapis, the ancient god who ruled the underworld, the other is Anubis, the guardian of entrance into the underworld—and who some worshipped as the god of embalming and protector of the mummies."

"He thinks he's binding them like mummies? What the hell is going through this guy's mind?" Andreas spoke without emotion and without looking up.

"I have no fucking idea." Tassos shook his head and looked at Andreas. "What do you think, is the artist our guy?"

Andreas stared back at the ceiling. "I don't know. It doesn't look like his style. More like someone imitating old icon paintings—and the drawings are just scribbled on."

"Yeah, but whoever did this had talent."

Andreas headed to the door. "Time to stop this bastard from making any more drawings."

Tassos followed.

Andreas waved and smiled to the three searchers as he stepped back into the tunnel. "Good work, guys."

"Thanks," said the oldest.

"Did you see or hear anything after you found the room?" Andreas asked.

They all indicated no.

Andreas turned to Tassos. "Why the hell the motorbike, and where's it now?" He aimed his flashlight down the tunnel at the tracks. Both the light and tracks disappeared into darkness past the first tunnel entrance.

The only sound was a hum from the generator.

"Uhh, Chief, I might have heard something." It was the youngest and he sounded nervous. His voice was cracking. "When we got here and saw the…uhh…hair, they"—he gestured at the other two—"ran up that way to get the walkie-talkie to work." He pointed toward the entrance Andreas had used. "I was scared being here alone, and started singing to myself." He took a deep breath. "I didn't even think about it until you said 'motorbike,' but I might have heard a motor. Down there." He pointed toward the second tunnel entrance. "It was very faint, and I didn't hear it very long. I told myself it must have been the generator."

Andreas turned to his two remaining officers. "Follow those tracks—and be careful." To Tassos he said, "That's why he got the bike, to get her out of here. Damn it, we just missed him." He kicked the dirt.

A pebble ricocheted off the cell wall and landed next to a small, broken ceramic urn lying against the opposite tunnel wall. Andreas turned his light on the urn and said, "Why the hell is that here?" He started toward it.

Tassos stopped him. "Let's get these men out of here. Forensics will take care of this. We've got him on the run, and we'll find him from his DNA."

Andreas looked at Tassos. "He must know that too. He might just dump her and take off."

"The good news is he hasn't. Yet."

Andreas nodded. "You're right. Just hope he sticks to his craziness. Okay, let's get out of here and over to where that second tunnel comes out." He had no time now for old pottery.

As soon as they were outside, Andreas gave orders to tell the men watching the churches that their suspect—whoever he was—was on the move with the missing woman.

The question was, to where?

Chapter Twenty

Catia's plane to Mykonos landed on schedule. That seemed like the last thing to go right. At the town hall she learned that neither the mayor nor the chief of police was anywhere to be found, and when she called her brother for help, he too was unavailable.

She raged across the harbor front to the taxi stand, jumped into a cab ahead of two waiting tourists, and told the driver to take her to the hotel where her niece was staying. The driver started to object, but she cursed him in Greek and he said, "Okay, okay."

Fuming, she started venting aloud. "No one in this town is where they're supposed to be. I'm here to meet with your wonderful mayor, and he's gone. I try to see your chief of police, he's gone. I fly all the way from Holland, and neither of them bothers to show up for our appointments." She really didn't have appointments, but it gave better currency to her anger.

Tentatively, the driver said, "I'm not a big fan of the mayor and, as for police, they give taxi drivers grief, but I wouldn't take this personally. They're busy, very busy. The whole island's filled with cops—they're looking for a missing girl."

Catia shivered for an instant, shut her eyes, and took a deep breath. Her brother really did use his influence. She'd underestimated him. Her voice was its old courteous self. "Have you any news of how the search is going?"

His eyes darted between the mirror and the road. "Just that they're searching the old mines and a lot of churches."

Catia was puzzled. "Why are they looking there?"

The driver was concentrating on crossing a very dangerous intersection. "I don't know about the mines but I guess the churches because that's where they found another woman's body."

Catia thought she was going to faint. She couldn't seem to breathe. When she finally spoke, her hands were shaking and her voice was very weak. "Please...please take me there."

"Where?"

She spoke between drawing nervous breaths. "Where they're looking for my daughter."

The driver jerked his head around, his eyes seeming to swell in their sockets. "Your daughter?" He crossed himself.

She simply nodded and didn't speak or lift her head for the rest of the ride.

◇◇◇

Even in a four-wheel-drive SUV Andreas almost slid off the road twice. Tassos yelled what the two cops in the back had to be thinking: "Slow down before you kill us!" They were on the beat-up, mountain dirt road that ran past the church where they'd found the Vandrew woman's body.

Andreas wasn't listening. "Son of a bitch is just too lucky. Can't believe he got away from us back there."

"If you keep driving like this there won't be anyone left to catch him." Tassos had his hand braced against the roof. The SUV was careening back and forth maddeningly close to the edge every time it hit one of the deep ruts cutting across the road.

About a quarter mile past the church the road turned to the right and plateaued for about thirty yards before starting downhill. Andreas slowed down slightly and pointed across his body with his right hand. "Over there, see, that's where the tunnel comes out, down on the other side of that hill." It was about a half-mile away, another brown hillside flecked with green and gray.

Andreas knew he had to drive faster if there was any chance of catching them.

◇◇◇

He drove the motorbike onto the crumbling, rusting pier. There was no choice. The police would be there any minute, he was sure of it. His eyes scanned the cove and its ridges for any sign of them—or anyone else. It was, as usual, gray and deserted everywhere he looked. Gray from the color of the barite once loaded onto ships from this spot and deserted because of its ugliness. Even Boy Scouts from their camp in the cove just to the west never hiked here. Too much beauty elsewhere to bother with this place. That's why he chose to hide the boat here last night. It was a gray, medium-sized Zodiac inflatable—a common summer sight in the Aegean.

He put the girl down on the pier next to a rope tied to the Zodiac and pulled on the line until the front of the boat was close enough to slide her onto the bow locker. She slumped forward, obviously still out of it—despite forty-five minutes of bouncing along with him on the motorbike through the tunnel's maze of debris. He'd built the maze and other, more menacing surprises, to discourage the curious from his business inside—such as moats and dens baited with food for attracting feral dogs. They'd worked—at least until today.

He knew his DNA would be all over the tunnel, but that was only part of what police would find to tie it all to him. One of them, at least, would piece it together.

He pushed the motorbike to the end of the pier but hesitated before letting it fall. Maybe he should tie her to it and dump them both? Why wait any longer?

He stood perfectly still holding the bike, then abruptly opened his fingers and watched it fall into the sea. No, it wasn't yet time.

He got into the boat, undid the line, and started the engine. Annika was in front of him, lying on her belly with her head turned forward at the windiest part of the boat. He couldn't see her face but would be able to tell if she moved.

As he headed east out of the cove he kept looking back to shore, expecting any moment to see the police.

◇◇◇

They were less than a quarter mile away when Andreas sped into a blind, descending, right-hand curve. Just beyond his line of sight the right wheels hit another deep rut, but this one ran parallel to the road—not across it—and channeled the SUV's wheels as if set on tracks. Andreas jammed on the brakes and twisted the steering wheel hard to the left—the perfect scenario for a rollover. But it didn't roll over because the rut wouldn't let go, and no matter how hard Andreas braked or steered, the SUV kept sliding head-on into—or over—the hillside, depending on where the rut took them.

The killer wasn't the only lucky bastard that afternoon. At least that's what Tassos was calling him when the SUV finally stopped. They'd hit the hillside, but only hard enough to be bruised.

Andreas jumped out and looked at the damage. "It's not that bad. We can push it back onto the road."

"Only if I drive," said Tassos.

Andreas was angry only with himself, but his tone didn't show it. "This is serious, we have to get there *now*."

"I know, that's why I'm driving," Tassos repeated.

Andreas didn't object, just gestured for the others to help push. It took five minutes before they sufficiently untangled and dug out the mess around the front wheels to get the SUV back on the road. It took another five minutes of careful driving by Tassos—and cursing by Andreas to go faster—before they reached an utterly impassable road. The cove they wanted was at the end of it. Tassos turned off the engine. "The rest of the way's on foot."

"If he came this way, we'd have seen him," said one of the cops.

"Unless he was able to make it back to the main road and swing east before we got here," said Tassos.

"He'd have to be on a motorcycle to do that," said the same cop.

Andreas gave him a sarcastic look and started running toward the cove. "Stop all this bullshit and let's get down there."

They'd parked just west of a cluster of deserted, one-story, gray concrete-slab buildings. About 150 feet to the west, on an adjacent hillside, was a mine-shaft entrance covered over with weather-battered boards and warning signs marked DANGER. Everywhere and everything was gray. The place looked abandoned to ghosts.

Tassos was moving more like a scurrying duck than a runner. "That was the mining company's offices." He pointed to the buildings. "Looks sort of like someone nuked the place, doesn't it?"

The road was utterly unusable, so Andreas and the two younger cops led the way traversing the hillside, more sliding than running. They came to a narrow plateau covered with thousands of spent shotgun shells and pieces of broken black and blaze-orange ceramic. They kept running but Andreas yelled back to Tassos, "What the hell is this?"

Tassos was panting. "It's where locals do skeet and trap shooting"—he caught a breath—"practicing for bird and rabbit hunting." Again he paused. "It's the only place deserted enough not to worry about hitting tourists sunbathing in the bushes."

Just beyond the shooting range they met back up with the road and followed it for a few hundred feet between two hillsides. It looked like it was about to end at a cliff falling off into the sea. Instead, at the very edge of the cliff the road made an unexpected hairpin turn back onto the hill to the right and ran a steep two hundred yards straight down to the cove. Andreas stopped at the turn. You could see it all from there: the mine entrance, the beach, the pier, the sea.

"Looks like we're late again," said Andreas.

"Maybe he's not here yet. Maybe he's still in the mine," said one cop.

Andreas pointed to motorcycle tracks running from the mine to the pier. "Maybe, but I doubt it."

Tassos finally caught up to them. "Looks to be something yellow in the water at the end of the pier."

Andreas looked. "I'll take the men down for a look around. Why don't you stay here and watch our backs for anyone who might come along."

Tassos smiled. "Thanks. I wasn't looking forward to hiking down there and back."

Andreas winked and started down.

◇◇◇

The sunlight was blinding. Annika's eyes weren't used to it. She could sense the sea. Everything was moving faster now, not just jolts and vibration like before. She could feel the breeze growing stronger. Her face was right into the wind, but hard as she tried, she couldn't smell it, couldn't breathe through her nose. She tried to taste it. It was whipping its way between her lips, forcing her to breathe more deeply.

◇◇◇

It wasn't hard for Andreas to guess that whoever came out of the mine had been riding the motorbike now lying off the end of the pier; but where did he—hopefully they—go? The logical explanation was a boat, but that meant the killer had one waiting for him. Did that mean an accomplice? Maybe they'd walked to another car or bike nearby?

He told his men to search along the shore for footprints coming out of the water. Sure enough, they found a pair of man-sized sandal tracks on the end of the beach farthest from the road. Andreas told one man to stay by the mine entrance—just in case—while he and the other cop followed the tracks. They led along the shore, out of the cove and around to another small beach.

There they found matching arriving and departing tire tracks, signs of a boat dragged into—but not out of—the water and the same man's sandals in the middle of it all. They took some quick pictures just in case the wind got there before forensics.

They made their way back to the cove just in time to see the two cops who trailed the bike emerge from the tunnel. They'd found nothing but tire tracks. *Good*, thought Andreas. *She's still alive.*

"You must have seen something besides tracks," he said.

"Sure, a lot of rocks and things you'd expect in a mine," said one cop.

"And tools by some of the places they're digging," said the other.

"What do you mean digging?" said Andreas sounding annoyed. "That tunnel's been closed for twenty-five years."

The first cop looked eager to impress the chief with his thoughts on the second cop's observation. "It's more like an archeological dig."

The second cop didn't seem about to cede credit to the first for his own find. "Except these digs are all over the place, some in the walls, some in the ground, some old, some new. It looks like professionals, not weekend amateurs looking for potshards."

Andreas thought of the broken urn by the cell. Looked like their killer was into robbing antiquities as well as lives. It was a high-paying racket that had Greece and a lot of other plundered nations suing Western museums for the return of their treasures. Billions of euros were involved; and that was only the publicly known plunder. There was no telling how much was in private hands. But that was someone else's problem. His job was finding Annika Vanden Haag. They started up the road toward Tassos.

This time it was Andreas panting when Tassos started talking. "You found something over there?" He pointed to the far end of the beach.

Andreas nodded and told him what they'd found on the beach.

"Any idea how old the tracks are?" asked Tassos.

Andreas nodded no. "Since we don't have tides in this part of the Mediterranean they could be old."

"But we do have wind," said Tassos.

Andreas nodded. "Yes." He pointed to the motorbike tracks on the beach below. "They're older than those." His breathing was regular again. "Looks to me like our killer brought a boat out here early today or late yesterday, probably tied it up to the pier, walked through the water to cover his tracks, got to his vehicle, and drove away."

"That means he planned on using a boat all along." Tassos sounded surprised.

"Sure seems that way." Andreas kicked a stone. "I guess we're following in his footsteps more than chasing him." He sounded frustrated. "We need to check out the boats and beaches and coves and—"

Tassos stopped him. "We don't have enough men to do that. We can't pull them off the churches. You know they're still our best bet."

Andreas nodded. "I know. I'll ask the port police to help out. The shoreline is their jurisdiction anyway—and they've got a helicopter."

"Where do we tell them to start looking?" asked Tassos.

"I'd say our killer could be an hour away from here by now," Andreas said.

"That means they could be anywhere on Mykonos," said Tassos.

"Which is exactly where I'm going to tell them to start looking—any place they can think of where someone in a boat might try to hide from police."

Tassos rolled his eyes. "Sounds simple enough."

"Yeah, like everything else in this case."

Andreas' cell phone rang. It was Kouros. "Chief, you told me to call you on your mobile if I couldn't reach you on—"

Andreas interrupted him. "It's okay. What's up?"

"I have news on the jeweler."

"Did you find him?"

"No, but he's not where he's supposed to be."

Great, thought Andreas, just what we need, another missing hot suspect.

Kouros continued. "One of his salesmen has outstanding DUI warrants, so I pushed him to tell me where his boss was."

Good work, thought Andreas.

"He gave me a number in Athens for the jeweler's girlfriend. When I called and asked for him she started screaming before I even identified myself. Said he wasn't there and if I wanted to know where he was I should call his wife—because that's where he told her he'd be staying this trip to Athens. So, I called his wife."

"Let me guess," said Andreas. "She had no idea where he was."

"Yes, she thought he was still on Mykonos, but when I said he wasn't and identified myself, she suggested I call the girlfriend."

"She what?"

"Didn't even seem angry, just told me to call her. I told her I already had."

Andreas couldn't help but laugh at the image.

"That's just what she did, sir."

"What?"

"Laugh. She said, 'Good, now the bastard's cheating on both of us.'"

Andreas laughed again. "Okay, but does he have any other family you can check with?"

"No, sir. The salesman told me he has no other family. They've all passed away."

Andreas hung up and shook his head as he told the story to Tassos.

"I wonder where he is?"

Andreas shrugged and turned to the other cops. "Okay, let's get back to the car."

They concentrated on breathing rather than talking as they walked up the hill to the SUV. When they got there Andreas used the radio to call the chief of the port police. Tassos leaned against the driver's side fender and looked off to the west. The sun had fallen below some of the nearby hilltops, sending their shadows out into the valleys.

Andreas finished his call, walked over, and leaned on the fender next to Tassos. "He'll have the chopper in the air in thirty minutes, and his boats will be looking for Vanden Haag—with a shaved or covered head—in the company of a man fitting the description of any of our suspects. Probably in an inflatable boat but not necessarily—he could have pulled a switch on us."

Tassos seemed in a trance. "Sunset is my favorite time of day," he said, and let out a sigh. "But I'm afraid it's coming on a might too quickly for me today." He turned his head toward Andreas. "You know, in a couple of hours it's going to be too dark to hunt by helicopter, and if they try chasing him down in the dark by boat, it's way too easy to toss her overboard."

Andreas nodded his agreement and reached for his cigarettes. "The boys found something else inside the mines."

Tassos didn't say anything; he was back to staring at the sunset.

"Relic digs. I think our killer's involved in the stolen-antiquities market."

Tassos seemed unphased. "Not surprised. These hills are full of them—many stolen centuries ago from Delos and hidden, misplaced, or simply reused as building materials here. Not sure how valuable any of them are." He paused but didn't move his eyes.

Andreas joined him staring west. "I wish I knew what's behind all these…these human sacrifices. I'm sure his serial-killer traits are off the charts, but why the ritual-sacrifice angle? And how do those paintings on the ceiling of saints and underworld gods tie in to all this? Do you think there's a connection to the relics?"

Tassos' tone remained the same. "Don't know, but in today's world some movie or TV program on human sacrifice in some ancient civilization could have set him off." He paused. "Maybe that Mary Renault book did it—the one about your lady with the cord, Ariadne, getting mixed up in human sacrifice on Naxos." He gestured toward that neighboring island. "Or even a news story on those crazies still doing it in parts of India and Africa." He paused again. "He's probably twisted so many things up inside his head even he doesn't know what's driving him anymore. I don't see much of a chance of us ever knowing what pushed him over the edge, but I do think we'll identify him. It's only a question now of when."

Andreas offered him a cigarette, and Tassos took one. "Do you remember the story of Saint Kiriake?" Andreas asked.

"She was a young woman martyred by pagans who tried torturing her into denying her faith."

Andreas lit Tassos' cigarette and then his own. He drew in a puff and slowly let it out without saying a word; when he did, he sounded like a preacher. "Yes, but what first attracted the pagans' attention was her extraordinary beauty. No matter what tortures or guiles they tried, she wouldn't give in. God protected her and healed her wounds—even destroyed a pagan temple and a few of her tormentors in the process."

Tassos took a puff on his cigarette before speaking. "Sounds like a plan. Let's just hope Kiriake can get some of that action working for Vanden Haag tonight."

"Amen to that."

Chapter Twenty-One

When it came to schmoozing, the mayor was one of Greece's best. Once he locked on, there was no graceful escape from his bottomless pit of conversation. Catia was learning that firsthand. He'd not left her side since she introduced herself as the sister of the deputy minister. Despite all the mayor's words, he hadn't told her much more than that the police were doing everything humanly possible to find Annika and expected to do so soon. When she said she appreciated all that he and her brother had done to organize the search, Catia caught what she thought was a puzzled look on his face, but he quickly offered lengthy praise for her brother's help and commitment to the search.

No matter how many ways she asked whether Annika was in danger, his answer always was "I sincerely hope not." The mayor dismissed the taxi driver's reference to "another girl's body" as a product of "uninformed village gossip" growing out of an "isolated, unrelated crime" involving some of those "wrong types" now allowed into Greece. He was certain a woman of Annika's "obvious character" would not associate with such a "bad element" and with "hundreds" of police searching by "land, sea, and air," she'd be found "before too long." When she pressed him for a more definitive time line, he shrugged and said, "Soon."

Her impatience at his stalling was about to erupt when a fast-moving helicopter suddenly shot over the taverna. Without looking up, the mayor smiled broadly. "See, it's like I told you.

It's the port police flying out to find your daughter. It's only a matter of time. Trust me."

It was the perfect phrase for turning her impatience into alarm. She must call her brother immediately.

◇◇◇

The pilot and copilot were told to look for a middle-aged man and a kidnapped young woman in—probably—an inflatable boat. That hardly narrowed the search. Practically every yacht afloat used inflatables, and the idea had caught on. Now everyone could act like part of the yachting set for the price of a blow-up boat. They had a lot of hovering to do before sunset.

They swept north out of the airport over Panormos Bay and its popular, clothing-optional beaches. Even late in the day, the beaches were packed with partiers. The pilots took a quick peek at the bodies on the beach and moved on to hover over the occupied boats anchored offshore. There were a lot of naked bodies in those boats and a few explicit acts going on undisturbed by their presence. One couple in a Zodiac even waved at the chopper in the midst of their humping. The guy looked middle-aged and the brunette looked young, but from the way they were going at it they seemed happy enough. Besides, there was another middle-aged man/young woman couple doing the same thing at the same time on the deck of a nearby sixty-foot sloop. Just another typical summer day in the air over Mykonos beaches.

The chopper flew out of the bay, turned east, and ran along the north shoreline in the direction of the mines. They decided to search the rarely used coves and beaches along the north and east coasts first. Then on to Tragonisi, a tiny, deserted island two thousand yards east of Mykonos, once favored by pirates and still by smugglers for its secret caves and hidden inlets. That was where they were betting their man would feel safe. Time to surprise the bastard.

◇◇◇

He kept thrusting for a few minutes longer just to be sure. He stopped and listened. No rotors. He turned his head and scanned the sky. Nothing. He sat up and looked around at the other boats, then down at her. She was breathing faster and stronger than before. He couldn't believe their brief, adolescent dry-humping session was bringing her around.

He'd had her lying atop the bow cushions on her stomach—as if sunbathing nude—when he heard the helicopter. He'd done the first thing he could think of to hide—be obvious. He'd pulled off his pants and lifted her to the floor. Then spread her legs, gripped his fingers in hers, and did what he could to make it look convincing—even lifted one pair of interlocking fingers in a wave. It worked.

Now what to do? They were anchored far enough out not to attract attention from shore, and the other boaters were into their own thing. Still, he wanted to get out of here. She could wake up any minute, and he had no drugs to give her. He'd left it all back at the cell when he ran. He wanted to tie and gag her but didn't dare in daylight—too many people around.

His original plan was to hide in one of the caves to the east—or on Tragonisi—until it was time to take her to the church. He'd started off in that direction but changed his mind. Being chased by police wasn't part of his plan, and those caves were the logical first place they'd look. He'd decided to turn west and hide in the open among tourists who still believed all was perfect in paradise.

He looked at the sky. It would be hours until dark. He wanted to move out to sea but knew he couldn't with that helicopter still searching for them. If she woke up here, she'd start screaming. He sat quietly staring at her. Slowly, and with great care, he covered her with the gray dress, stood up, put on his pants, and went to fetch the bowline. He improvised a garrote and placed it next to her throat. If she slept until dark, she lived; if she woke, she died.

◇◇◇

Deputy Minister Renatis had no idea what his sister was talking about: a massive search for Annika? He asked to speak to the mayor. The mayor was his usual political self—all words, no substance.

"Minister, you must know your niece is very important to us and we're sparing nothing in our search to find her." He smiled at Catia.

"What's all this about another body—and what's that got to do with my niece? I want to know *now*." He spoke like an angry boss.

The mayor lowered his voice—presumably so Catia couldn't hear but possibly as a supplicant to the deputy minister. "A young tourist woman was found murdered a few days ago, and the police are concerned the same killer may have your niece."

The phone was silent for so long the mayor must have thought the connection had failed.

"Why wasn't I told?" Spiros asked in a voice as cold as stone.

The mayor paused. "Didn't the chief call you about it? I thought he had."

Spiros didn't answer. He was certain the mayor was just another politician instinctively trying to pass blame, but he remembered that he'd been avoiding Andreas' calls. Perhaps that's what the chief was calling about. He asked to speak to his sister.

"Catia, I'm leaving immediately by helicopter to be there with you. Don't worry, we'll find her."

Silence.

He tried sounding reassuring. "Our very best men are on this. We'll find her. I promise. You must believe me. I'm leaving now for the heliport." He looked at his watch. "And I should be there in forty-five minutes. Around nine."

He heard a meek "Okay, I'll be waiting for you."

He was angry at himself for ducking Andreas, but that didn't excuse what was going on in Mykonos without the knowledge and authority of his ministry. Heads were going to roll. He'd see to that personally. But first, he must get to Mykonos and take charge of this mess.

◇◇◇

Andreas and Tassos personally checked every church to Saint Kiriake located outside of town. None of the police at those churches had a thing to report. There was nothing in or under the churches and no sign of the woman or a potential suspect. Andreas wondered if the men sensed how wound up he was. Tassos didn't seem much better. They barely spoke as they drove from church to church. Now they were headed to town.

The crackle on the police radio made them both jump. Andreas answered, "Kaldis here."

"Andreas, where are you?" It was the mayor and he sounded panicked.

"About five minutes from the harbor." Andreas put the radio on speaker so Tassos could hear.

"I am at the taverna in Ano Mera. Get here as soon as you can. We have a problem."

Andreas looked at Tassos. "What sort of problem Mr. Mayor?"

"The missing woman's mother is here, and her brother—the deputy minister—is on his way from Athens by helicopter. He's supposed to be here by now."

Andreas' voice was flat, though his blood pressure must have soared. "Thank you. Tell them I'll be there as soon as I can."

"But—"

Andreas switched off the radio.

"Guess we should get over there," said Tassos.

"First we have to check out the churches in town. Getting reamed out by the deputy minister isn't going to help find his niece." Andreas seemed in a trance.

"Okay, but let's do it quickly. No reason to piss off our executioner—His Honor the deputy minister—any more than we already have."

◇◇◇

Annika felt the cold in the wind off the sea. The sky was black except for the stars and a bit of moonlight. She'd been curled up

230 <J Jeffrey Siger

on her side on the floor of the boat for what seemed forever, but she knew it was only since he'd raped her—or tried to rape her. She wasn't sure. She'd been groggy and had no strength when he'd pulled her to the floor, but she tried to resist—at least she thought she had. Now she felt bloated—pain too—everywhere down there, and couldn't breathe through her nose. Her wrist was hurting again too. The good news was her senses were back.

She was facing forward and knew he was somewhere behind her. Her instinct was to turn and confront him, but she could hardly move, let alone fight. Besides, she was still alive and untied; probably because she'd been unconscious. Things can only get worse once he knows I'm awake, she thought. She considered pulling herself overboard but doubted she had the strength to do it and certainly not enough to make it to shore— wherever that was. She decided to lie quietly and listen. She'd make her move when she had more strength—or no other choice.

◇◇◇

It had taken about an hour in the dark to get the boat from Panormos Bay to where they now sat. She'd never woken up, even when they crossed in front of the frenetic Mykonos harbor in full view of two idling police boats. He'd gambled on a lot of small boats heading in the same direction at the same time, making him just another anonymous little duck on the pond. He had been right.

His voice was very soft when he began talking to her. He spoke in Greek as if he knew she was conscious but wouldn't understand a word of what he was saying. He was wrong about that.

◇◇◇

There was nothing in the town's churches. Now it was all wait and see. As they pulled up to the taverna, Andreas wondered what the hell he was going to tell her mother. He wasn't even thinking about what to say to her brother, his boss.

Tassos was the first one out of the car. Andreas looked at his watch: ten-thirty. A woman was walking quickly toward them.

She had to be the mother. Andreas got out and walked over to meet her.

He could tell she'd been crying. "I'm sorry to be late, Mrs. Vanden Haag," he said, trying to sound confident and professional, "but I had to make sure everything was ready."

She grabbed his arm. "Please, tell me what's happened." She didn't have to say she was worried to death.

Her brother and the mayor walked over, and Andreas nodded an acknowledgment. "I'm sure the mayor has told you—"

She squeezed his arm. "No, please, you tell me. Tell me everything."

He looked into her eyes, then down at the ground for a moment before looking at Tassos. It was just the five of them. "Sure," he said, and looked her straight in the eyes. It took about fifteen minutes. He told her everything, as if he were confessing. No one interrupted him, and when he finished, Catia was silent.

It was her brother who spoke, his voice rising. "You think my niece is being held by a serial killer who's been murdering tourist women on Mykonos for almost twenty years?!"

"Yes," Andreas answered crisply.

"I think you're insane!" Spiros screamed. He stared at Tassos. "I suppose you're going to tell me you agree with him."

Tassos looked straight at him. "Yes."

He turned to the mayor. "Is every cop on this island crazy? Greece has never had a serial killer." He looked back at Andreas. "What you're saying is impossible!"

"There are eighteen dead bodies saying it's not," Andreas said, an edge in his voice now.

Catia spoke softly. "Spiros, I don't think this is the way to talk to people who are trying to help us."

Spiros struggled for control as he glared at Andreas. "I want the names of every suspect. I want them rounded up and interrogated immediately."

"Can't find them, except for one who showed up on his own—with a lawyer," Andreas said calmly.

"I don't give a damn about lawyers. I want his name!" He was screaming again.

The mayor blurted out Manny's name.

Andreas shook his head in disgust and looked at Spiros. "What are you going to do, have somebody blowtorch him so you can make yourself think you're doing something?"

Spiros was a bureaucrat not used to challenges from subordinates. "You're way out of line, Chief." He was shaking with anger. "I want your men out of those churches and rounding up suspects for interrogation. That's how we'll find my niece. And no more of this rubbish about ritual killings or serial killers. *Do you understand?*"

Andreas' look was deadly serious. "Yelling doesn't make your thinking any clearer, sir. Watching those churches is our only chance of finding her." He paused. "Alive."

"That's it, Kaldis, you're off this investigation." Spiros raged. He turned to Tassos. "You're in charge."

"I won't be doing anything differently, sir." But Tassos' tone was deferential.

Spiros' face was red. "Fine." He gestured to a man standing just out of earshot. He was one of the men who'd accompanied him on the helicopter from Athens. "Mayor, this is Captain Leros of Special Operations in Athens. He'll take over the investigation. I expect you to give him your complete cooperation."

"Certainly," said the mayor with a smile.

Spiros barked at Andreas and Tassos, "I want the two of you out of here now. And I mean now!"

Andreas looked at Catia. "Sorry, Mrs. Vanden Haag," he said, and walked away with Tassos.

Catia waited until they were out of earshot. "Spiros, I know how upset you are."

"Damn right I am." He was biting at his lower lip.

"And those men weren't respectful or appreciative of your ideas," she said softly.

He drew in and let out a breath. "I'm only trying to help you and Annika."

She hugged him. "I know. I know you'll do everything possible." She paused. "My only thought is, it's almost eleven and probably you won't be able to find those suspects tonight, unless they're home in their beds—which means they couldn't be with Annika."

He nodded. "That's right."

"So." She hugged him again. "What's the harm in leaving the policemen at the churches for the rest of the night? There's nothing more for them to do until tomorrow."

He looked at her and smiled. "You've always known how to work me."

"And it wrecks any claim by Andreas or Tassos that their plan might have worked if you'd listened to them," added the mayor in a solemn voice. The others seemed to have forgotten he was there.

Catia glared at him coldly. "Sir, I really don't like you," she said and walked away.

Spiros watched her leave. Both men let Catia's remark pass. "Do you realize what would happen to Mykonos—to all the islands—if those two are right about a serial killer?" Spiros was using his professional voice.

The mayor was all but kissing Spiros' feet. "Yes, yes—if it ever gets out—absolutely. I kept telling them the same thing, over and over, but they wouldn't listen."

A glare returned to Spiros' eye as he watched Andreas and Tassos drive away. "Those two will wish they had. I'll personally see to it that their lives are over." For the moment, he seemed to forget that his niece's life could be ending that night as well.

Chapter Twenty-Two

It was his practice to talk to his tributes when he brought them out into the light from the silence below; to educate them on what they were about to become part of. He considered it an opening rite of the sacrifice, as important to him as prayer. None of his tributes understood, of course, because he spoke to them only in Greek. That did not matter to him because he believed ~~that, in life, most prayers went unheard.~~

He spoke softly and paused often, in the style that had once so charmed his tributes.

"The traditional *panegyri* actually begins the day before the formal celebration. That's when family and friends begin contributing goats and lambs to the church for slaughter in preparation for the next day's cooking. Other contributions are wine, bread, salads, fruits, vegetables, and special local dishes and desserts. It's all part of the sacrifice honoring a saint. Tonight we honor Saint Kiriake.

"The men in charge of the slaughter arrived yesterday with their own food—and wine. Lots of wine. They were followed by friends who showed up to help, bringing more food—and more wine. Somehow they always manage to get everything done on time. It is, as they say, the Greek way.

"Guests at tonight's *panegyri* will have taken a piece of bread blessed by the priest and a cup of broth. Then would come the real food: tables full of goat, lamb, appetizers of every kind, salads, black-eyed beans and dandelion greens, and wine—lots and lots of wine.

"The boiled meat comes next; then the *yahknee* stew, and later, pastries, custards, yoghurts, and fresh fruits. All this accompanied by music, dancing, and more and more wine, until the morning church service. After that, they sober up and finish off what's left of the food at an after-church lunch.

"That's when the *panegyri* traditionally ends. But tonight we have a different sort of *panegyri*. A special one, just for you."

◇◇◇

That the man intended to kill her didn't surprise Annika. Nor was she surprised that he still didn't realize she was Greek—and had been to more *panegyris* than she cared to remember. What surprised her was that he knew she was conscious. Or was he guessing? She hadn't moved, at least didn't think she had. He always seemed to be one step ahead of her.

She felt her stomach tighten in fear—fear that she was making a mistake. Maybe she shouldn't risk trying to escape? Perhaps she should just confront him now—in perfect Greek. That certainly would surprise him, and once he knew who her uncle was, he'd know he wasn't as smart as he thought.

She struggled for the right words—ones sure to have the maximum impact. What she came up with was "You've made a big mistake. My uncle is Spiros Renatis, Greece's deputy minister of Public Order in charge of all police. Let me go now and I won't tell anyone. If you don't believe me, leave me somewhere that will give you time to escape." She rehearsed the words silently to herself until she had them just right—down to a properly nonchalant tone—drew in a breath, and…FUCK, am I crazy? she thought. I sound like one of those naïve, airhead girls whining at the bad guy in a horrible B movie just before he kills her.

She decided to follow her father's advice and keep her fluency in Greek to herself. That seemed her only advantage at the moment. So, she stayed as still as she could and listened to him ramble on in Greek about the Mykonian tradition of *panegyri*, honoring the ancient gods of the underworld for treasures revealed to him beneath the earth and paying tribute to the saints of neglected churches.

◇◇◇

Andreas and Tassos had driven into town from Ano Mera. They were having coffee on the waterfront, exchanging jibes with a few port police and some locals who had no idea how powerless they were about to become. Andreas kept thinking there was something he was missing. Something simple. It always was something simple.

"Well, my friend, let's pray they find her," said Tassos. "The deputy minister would be so happy taking all the credit he'd almost forget about cutting off our balls. Probably just force me to take my pension and make you miserable for the rest of your life—that is, if you decide to stay on the force."

"And that's the good news." Andreas forced a smile.

"Yeah." Tassos nodded. "But, if God forbid they don't—"

Andreas cut him off. "Don't bother telling me, I can guess." He imagined the sort of headlines: Like Father, Like Son. At least I'll be alive to read them, he thought; Annika Vanden Haag won't be.

Andreas changed the subject. "You know, all this time I've never asked if you're married, or have a family."

Tassos was quiet for a moment. "No. I'm a widower."

"Sorry."

Tassos at first seemed reluctant to say more. "She died during the birth of our first child." He paused again. "A son. He didn't make it either."

Andreas didn't know what more to say.

Now Tassos changed the subject. "Maybe we deserve what's coming to us and maybe we can't help Vanden Haag, but it pisses me off that bastard mayor giving up Manny like he did. We know he's not the killer, but those sons of bitches are going to beat the shit out of him anyway." He sounded disgusted.

"Sure are. That's what Leros is known for, his interrogations," said Andreas.

"I've got an idea," said Tassos. "Shouldn't his lawyer be informed if he's taken into custody?"

"We can't get in much deeper shit. Go ahead, knock yourself out."

Tassos flipped open his cell phone, dialed, put the phone to his ear, and waited. "Katerina, it's Tassos. Call me back as soon as you get this message. It's very important."

"Let's hope she calls back." Andreas looked at his watch. "It's after two in the morning. Where can she be?"

"She's at some *panegyri*, don't you remember her invitation?" Tassos grinned.

Andreas smiled. "How can I forget? But that was for last night. I was supposed to meet her at some boat." At the word *boat* Andreas bolted out of his chair. "A boat! Why the hell did she need a boat to get to a *panegyri*?"

He ran over to one of the port police. "Is there a *panegyri* tonight you can get to by boat?"

Tassos was right behind him.

The cop looked at his watch. "That's the only way you can get there, Chief, but it should be over by now."

"What are you talking about?"

"The *panegyri*. On Delos. It's the big one, but it ended at two." He gave a knowing wink and said, "Personally, I think that's so the guards can sleep off their drunk before tourists show up in the morning. It's their annual chance to party at work with their buddies from Mykonos."

Andreas' stomach was churning. "This is serious. What are you talking about?"

The cop's tone turned professional. "Around two years ago permission was given to a Mykonos family to build a tiny church on the remote northeast side of Delos. They're allowed to hold a *panegyri* once a year, and a flotilla of boats travels to Delos from Mykonos to celebrate what they call their once-a-year opportunity to party with the gods. But everyone has to be off by 0200 hours."

"And the reason for the *panegyri*?" Andreas held his breath.

The port cop seemed surprised. "It's the name day for the church they built there—Saint Kiriake."

Andreas grabbed Tassos by the arm. "That's where he's taken her." He was waving to the port police lieutenant standing by a boat. "Let's see if his boat's as fast as he's been bragging."

In less than five minutes, Andreas, Tassos, and three port police were streaking toward Delos. With luck they'd be there in twenty minutes, and with greater luck, Annika Vanden Haag would still be alive.

◇◇◇

"We're lying close to the island of light, the birthplace of the gods Apollo and Artemis and of a civilization going back more than two thousand years before Christ. For six hundred years a center of commerce and cosmopolitan life for the ancient world, a place of great temples, festivals, and sacrifices honoring the gods and drawing emissaries from throughout the known world."

She knew he was talking about Delos. Everybody on Mykonos talked about Delos—as if being less than a mile from so sacred and important an archeological site justified Mykonos' relentless party life.

"The ancient Mykonians honored their pagan gods in a far simpler way. They danced and feasted on sacrifices of goat and lamb. The same as today's Mykonians do at a *panegyri*." He paused. "Today the Greeks worship new gods, different ones. Today they call them saints."

He paused again. "It is important to honor the saints, to honor them for what they have done for you in the past, for what you may pray to them to do for you in the future. No saint should ever be neglected, not a single one."

His voice grew louder. "But what of ancient, long neglected gods? The gods who answered my prayers, allowed me to live among them and flourish. Are they any less worthy of honor than the saints?" Another, longer pause.

"Could the moment be more perfect? We're about to honor Saint Kiriake as we sit by the heart and soul of ancient pagan Greece."

He said nothing for several minutes, the silence more threatening to Annika than his voice.

"Time to join the *panegyri*."

The motor roared to life and the boat moved again.

Annika thought, wherever we're heading there'll be people. Like he said, *panegyris* go on all night. That's when I'll run—when he's close to shore. I'll jump and scream in Greek to everyone I see. That'll be his one mistake, and when he makes it, I'll be ready.

The last surprise will be mine.

Chapter Twenty-Three

Annika felt the boat slowing down. She thought an hour had passed since they started moving again, but it could have been ten minutes. She'd lost track of time. Suddenly, the engine cut off and she felt a change of weight at the stern. He was moving forward! This was it. Either make her move now or give up.

"Never!" she shouted, and forced herself to her knees—but he already was up to her. He grabbed her neck from behind. "No!" she screamed in Greek and drove the heel of her good hand hard into his crotch. Whether he was startled by the word or the pain, he let go.

She crawled toward the side of the boat but too slowly to get there before he recovered. He lunged at her, but on this side of Delos even a calm sea had waves generated by distant, passing ships, and at the instant of his lunge, a wave hit the gunnels behind them, knocking her to the floor and him over the side into the sea. She heard the splash and looked up. They were thirty yards from land. She could see a church on a rise about fifty yards up from shore. There's the *panegyri*, she thought. She crawled onto the bow locker and shouted in Greek, "Help! Help! I've been kidnapped. He's trying to kill me! Help me, please help me!"

The boat abruptly jerked to one side. His hands were on the gunnel. He was pulling himself into the boat. She shouted louder. No one seemed to hear her. I'm too far away, she thought.

He was back in and charging forward. She did the only thing left for her to do—she rolled off into the sea.

It was deeper than she expected—and colder—but calmer than above. She floated more than swam beneath the surface toward what she thought was the shore, her dress billowing about her as gracefully as a medusa drifting above its tentacles. Suddenly, something moved across her forehead covering her eyes. She panicked and tried to stand. Her body burst through the surface and she ripped the creature off her face.

Her eyes long ago had adjusted to the night, and she looked at the mass in her hand. It was hair. She touched her head and for the first time realized she was bald. She spun around looking for shore still holding the wig. The water was waist high and the boat twenty yards away. She heard the engine start. He must have seen her and was coming for her. She dropped the wig and tried to run toward shore. Her legs wouldn't move. She heard the engine slowly, deliberately closing in on her.

She thrust and kicked and willed her legs to carry her to shore. "I will survive," she kept repeating to herself. "I will survive."

◇◇◇

Andreas told the port police lieutenant to head straight for the church. No time for the protocol of landing only at Delos' port. He was damn sure the killer wasn't observing it.

Tassos called the guard station on Delos but no one answered. "The port cop was right," he shouted to Andreas over the noise of the engines. "They're all probably passed out dead drunk by now."

Andreas kept trying to reach the deputy minister and the mayor. Neither took his calls. "Assholes," he said aloud. He phoned Kouros.

"Yianni, it's the chief." Andreas wondered if he knew how shaky that title was.

"Yes, sir," Kouros answered, respectful as always.

"Do you know where Minister Renatis is?"

"Yes, sir, he's here at the station with Captain Leros and the mayor. They're waiting for Manny to get here."

"Did they find any of the others?"

"No, sir." He added with a hint of satisfaction, "And they only found Manny because the mayor told the taxi dispatcher to get him here."

Bastard, thought Andreas. "I need you to get a message to the deputy minister."

"Yes, sir." He sounded like a player anxious to hear his coach's winning play call.

"Tell him the killer has his niece on Delos, probably at the church to Saint Kiriake. And tell him to get as many men as he can there ASAP." His voice sounded urgent.

"Yes, sir." There was a tentative tone to Kouros' voice.

"What is it, Kouros?"

Even more tentatively, he said, "I'm not sure the deputy minister will listen, sir."

"Why?" Andreas was abrupt.

"Uh, I got a call from Manny's lawyer. Said she's on her way here and to tell whoever's interrogating Manny what she'll do if anything happens to him. When I gave the message to the deputy minister, he started cursing you."

Andreas was quiet for a moment. Katerina had returned Tassos' call as they were leaving the harbor. "Good point, Yianni. Is the girl's mother there?"

"Yes sir."

"Give her the message."

"Will do, sir."

Andreas hung up, his expression stern. He muttered to himself, "Screw 'Hell hath no fury like a woman scorned'; I'll bet on a mother protecting her young any day."

◇◇◇

Annika didn't feel the pain at first. Her focus was on reaching shore ahead of him. She'd succeeded, but her bare feet were bruised and bleeding from her stumble through the rocks in the shallows. Now she was struggling to climb the grade toward the church and her wrist was killing her. She kept tripping on the front of her wet dress, and her feet kept finding the rocks and sharpest thistles on the hillside, but she didn't stop. She looked back and saw the boat at shore. Thank God it wasn't a completely dark night, she thought. The moon gave her enough light to make out shapes and movement. She tried moving faster; the pain didn't matter anymore. She looked back again. He was out of the boat and undoing the rope on the bow.

She was halfway to the church and shouting again for help. Still no one answered, and no one was in sight.

"Annika." He was close enough to her that he didn't shout.

She was frantic to reach the top and kept yelling for help.

"Annika…" The voice was soft, emotionless, and getting closer.

She yelled louder, "Help, help me, please! Please, someone help me!"

All she heard was his droning on in Greek. "You did surprise me, Annika. I never thought you were Greek. I never planned to sacrifice a Greek. It never seemed wise before. Fascinating how the ancient gods managed for you—a Greek beauty—to be here on their island on the name day of the Greek beauty who defied them." Now he was closing quickly. "Seems ordained, don't you think?"

She was almost to the church. It was tiny, no more than eleven by nineteen feet. He was right. There was no one in sight. It was deserted. Fear again. She looked back. He was less than thirty feet away, walking parallel to her toward a gully just below the south side of the church. He was moving steadily, the rope looped and swinging in his hand. She stumbled up to the rear wall of the church by its corner with the north wall. Just beyond the north wall was another rocky rise leading up to a steeper hillside. She knew she couldn't make that climb and pushed herself along the north wall—leaning on it for support—toward a pile of rocks just beyond the front of the church. She had to get there before he reached her. She just hoped he wasn't already at the front of the church, waiting for her.

◇◇◇

He knew she was headed to the pile of rocks; it was her only choice. It wasn't really a pile so much as a fallen ancient wall. He wanted to get there first and angled himself toward it for a run up the side of the gully. He was almost to the top when a sudden sharp pain in his injured knee made him stumble. His feet slid out from under him and he tumbled to the bottom of the gully.

He cursed in English, stood, and took a step. He felt the pain again but limped as quickly as he could to the top.

He reached the southwest corner of the church and stopped. Not a sound, and nothing was moving. She still must be on the other side of the church, he thought. He stepped out to cross in front of the doorway and surprise her at the other corner. He was almost there when the first rock hit him. The pain in his shoulder was instantaneous. The second rock whizzed by his head and ricocheted off the wall, striking him on his back. The third rock struck him in the chest, possibly breaking a rib. He groaned and stumbled back toward the south wall for cover, shielding his head from the hailstorm of rocks.

"Take that, you miserable bastard!" she screamed.

The rocks kept coming even after he'd found cover. She was dangerous, this one.

Each rock had to weigh at least five pounds. Any one of them could have killed him.

He waited a few minutes, then carefully peered around the corner. He saw no movement at the pile. Perhaps she'd run away. He waited a few more minutes. Not a sound. Quickly he jumped out from behind the wall. A rock sailed by him, and he jumped back to cover. Again, more rocks flying.

"Come on, you cowardly, motherfucking bastard! Come on out so I can kill you."

He knew she would too. He'd have to come up with a different plan—or let her be.

◇◇◇

Annika was breathing so quickly she thought she'd hyperventilate. An eight-pounder was in her hands above her head—as if ready to throw in at a soccer match. No longer feeling the pain in her wrist, she was waiting for him to come out again so she could kill him. She knew she'd hurt him. She wanted to hurt him. She wanted to kill him. If she'd taken more care with her aim the second time, instead of just grabbing and throwing everything she touched, maybe she'd have hit him in the head and knocked him out. She'd take better aim this time. Then, when he was down, she'd beat him to death. Her face twisted with rage.

Not a sound from behind the wall. Maybe he was playing her game: staying quiet and waiting for the quarry to move. She kept her focus on both corners of the church, just in case he sneaked around to the northwest side. That corner was less than twenty feet away from her. If he came at her from there, she'd have no time to grab a rock and aim. She had to be ready with a rock in her hands, but her arms were aching from the weight. Her adrenaline rush was over. She lowered the rock to her chest. She was feeling weak.

She glanced quickly to her right and left. Ten yards behind her was a stone wall. It was about ten feet high and ran for only twenty feet or so to her left before ending at the top of some rough stone steps starting somewhere between her and the end of the wall. To her right, the wall seemed to run on forever. She glanced at it again. It wasn't like the walls she was used to seeing on Mykonos. These rocks were flat and layered on their sides in staggered piles, like books. This was more like a wall from Delos.

She looked again at the walls and back at the church. For the first time she noticed little stars looming in the distance behind the church, but they weren't stars and they weren't in the sky. They were lights on a hillside across the water—on Mykonos! Suddenly, it all made sense.

There were no people here, and there wouldn't be any until sunrise. She had no idea what a church was doing here, but she was certain this was Delos—its most deserted part, at the very northeastern edge of the ancient stadium. There was no place to hide here, and if he reached the footpath that ran along the top of the wall behind her, she was as good as dead. She was by the top, northeast edge of this cigar-shaped island and had to move south, toward its broader center and the heart of the ancient city's ruins. There she could find a place to hide until dawn—when people would come and she'd be safe.

Slowly, she edged out from behind the pile and along the wall to her right. The rock was back above her head, her muscles twitching from the weight. Carefully she moved, wondering when the charge would come. She'd have to make sure the rock struck his head. She stepped again, her heart pounding but her breathing steady. She almost was at an angle to see along that southern wall. Just another step…

He was gone! No one was there. She panicked. Where was he? Had he gone into the gully to the south or swung around to the north up the hillside? Either way he could get—or already was—above her. She couldn't stay here. She lowered the rock to her waist and staggered south along the wall toward the main ruins. They were at least a half mile away—over mostly open ground—but it was her only chance. After a few yards she dropped the rock. It was too heavy, and besides, if he was waiting to ambush her up ahead, it wasn't likely to help, only slow her down. All she could do was pray to find a place to hide before he found her. She knew for sure that the next time they met one of them would die.

◇◇◇

Andreas saw the Zodiac before he noticed the church. "Over there!" he shouted. "In that cove." The lieutenant sped up and threw on his searchlights. They lit up everything in their path, but there was nothing in the water and nothing to see beyond the Zodiac except barren land and the church. The lieutenant brought his boat as close as he could to shore. Andreas and the others jumped into the water and waded the few yards to dry land. The lieutenant kept the boat at idle, and the light beamed on the men racing up toward the church.

The church blocked the light from reaching its front side, and by the time Andreas got there, glare had wiped out his night vision. He was the first to reach the front door and the first to trip over rocks scattered everywhere. He fumbled for a flashlight. The door was locked. No sign of anyone. He knocked, not expecting an answer. He yelled, "Police, open up!" Still no answer. He tried to force open the door. It was built to resist those with bad intentions and all the time in the world to break in to an isolated church on a deserted island.

He gestured for the others to step back, pulled out his gun, and put two rounds into the lock. Then he kicked in the door. He saw nothing inside but the expected.

Tassos' light flooded across the foot-square marble floor tiles. "No burial crypt in the floor, but wouldn't expect one in a new church." He lifted his fist to knock on a wall. "Bones go inside the walls in most of the new ones," he said, and pounded twice. Two dull, solid thuds. He knocked again at another place. Same result.

Andreas knocked on the opposite side wall. "They're solid. There's no place to bury anything in here," he said, sounding confused.

Tassos looked around, then smacked his forehead with his hand. "Of course, there's no place to bury anyone in this church—we're on Delos!"

Andreas gave him a blank stare.

Tassos sounded frustrated. "Since, like the fifth century BC there haven't been bones buried on Delos and no one's been allowed to give birth or die here. All the bones are buried over there." He was pointing west. "On the neighboring island of Rhenia, the one the locals call Big Delos."

"Do you think he's taken her there?" Andreas, asked alarmed.

Tassos spoke with a simmering rage. "I don't know. My gut says no—and there's that boat behind the church—but he knows there's no place to bury her in this church. I'm sure of that."

Silence.

Andreas yelled to the two men outside, "Check around the foundation for signs of fresh digging." He looked at Tassos. "Maybe he buried her under the church?"

Tassos shrugged but said nothing.

"If he knew he couldn't bury her here, he must have planned to bury her somewhere else on Delos. Where in the hell could that be?"

Tassos shrugged again. "I think he'd go for the spectacular. He seems the sort."

"But where?"

Before Tassos could answer, one of the port police shouted from outside, "Chief, I've found something!"

He was standing behind a pile of rocks next to a wall.

"There's a puddle of water here, and footprints in wet dirt."

Andreas stared at the footprints and pointed his light at the front of the church. The whitewash was riddled with gray and brown marks—the same color as the rocks he'd tripped over. "I think our girl's giving him a fight. Looks like she got away and was throwing rocks at him. Don't think she got him, though; and he didn't catch her. At least not here."

"Why's that, Chief?" asked the officer.

"No body," said Andreas, "and the same pair of bare feet moving back and forth behind this pile, then heading south— toward the center of the island. They're all the same footprints," he repeated as he pointed into the light, "except for these, a pair of sandal tracks heading south and overlapping the bare feet."

He looked at Tassos. "It's the sandals from the cove where we found the motorbike. Looks like he came down those steps"—Andreas pointed the light north— "and is following her tracks—something we've got to start doing right now." His voice was urgent.

Andreas told the other port cop to get their brightest portable lights off the boat. "We want him to know we're looking for him."

Tassos said, "I think your two rounds into the door did a pretty good job of that."

Andreas wasn't sure if Tassos was making a joke. "Let's get going," he said to Tassos and the officer who found the tracks. To the cop heading back to the boat he yelled, "Catch up to us with those lights and tell the lieutenant to keep an eye on the Zodiac—just in case he doubles back." He held the beam of his flashlight snug against his chest so Tassos could see his face. "Maybe she's still alive."

"Maybe." Tassos' voice held no enthusiasm. "Then again, there's a reason the guy brought her to a place where no one's been allowed to die for twenty-five hundred years." His light moved to the rocks scattered by the door. "That's ending tonight."

Chapter Twenty-Four

Annika's move south along the narrow dirt footpath from the church to the upper path was taking much longer than the few minutes she thought it would. She'd gambled that he'd gone north because the church was Delos' northernmost structure and he only had to climb a low hill to reach the path above her. If he'd taken the gully to the south, there was the Stadium Quarter's maze of excavated walls, wells, and foundations to negotiate in the dark just to reach the path she was on. Going north was the obvious choice for someone in a hurry. Still, her heart jumped to her throat every time she inched past an excavation. She knew he could be waiting for her in any one of them.

It seemed a lifetime before she reached the upper path and was on open ground in familiar territory. It was as close to a sense of relief as she'd felt since her nightmare began. She could see if someone was in front of her, avoid places where he might be hiding, and move faster—if only her legs would respond beyond a drunken stagger. She couldn't seem to run no matter how hard she tried—nor could she breathe through her nose. She'd been so focused on escaping she'd forgotten all about that—and the pains in her belly and below.

Without stopping, she worked her fingers at her nostrils until she found an edge to get at with her nails. She pulled slowly. She didn't know what to expect but, in the surreal tale that her life had become, was not surprised at finding tampons in her nose.

She didn't care about the pain—just wanted to breathe—and pulled them out as best she could.

Annika noticed something else. She was cold, very cold. Even in July, Delos was cold at night, particularly out in the open with the wind picking up as it had. What made matters worse was the soaking wet dress. She pulled it off as she stumbled forward and wrung it out as best she could. She thought of putting it back on, but it still was too damp to wear. Fitting the shoulder straps over her head, she wore the dress down her back like a cape. It would dry faster in the wind that way.

She was between the stadium and the northeast corner of the Lake Area ruins, headed south toward the middle of the island, when she came upon a half-dozen or so houses about a quarter-mile from the center of the ancient town. They were built as a concession to the modern practicality that those working Delos' archeological digs and protecting its sites from plunderers and mischief makers needed housing. Newer ones were built more out of sight, on the southern tip of the island. One house sat only about twenty-five yards to the east of her, beyond a low stone wall running along the eastern edge of the narrow dirt road the footpath had become. It curved south toward the Archaeological Museum, a quarter-mile away. The other houses were to the west across flat, open ground, with the nearest forty yards away and the rest at least twice that.

There wasn't a light or sign of life in any of them. Maybe everyone was living in the new ones to the south? She thought of yelling but doubted she'd be heard above the wind blowing in from the north—even if anyone was there to hear her. The only one listening for certain was him. He was back there somewhere, and she knew it was only a matter of time—possibly minutes—until he found her.

The houses were her only hope of finding help before dawn—but that choice could lead to catastrophe. If she went for the houses and they were empty, she risked him catching up to her before she reached the high ground that she thought gave her the best chance of holding him off until the morning.

Morning seemed an eternity from now...and that place was another quarter-mile past the museum, at the far southeast side of the ruins.

She took a deep breath and decided to gamble on the houses—but on the ones to the west. Even though they were farthest away from the road she wanted to stay on, there were more of them, so the odds seemed better. She did a quick scan behind her, saw nothing, and headed toward them. She was almost at the first one when she heard two gunshots. They came at her on the wind from the north, from the direction of the church—and the way he'd be coming. Certain they'd been aimed at her, she fell to the ground for cover.

Her mind was racing but her body didn't move. He has a gun! She waited for the next rounds but heard only the wind. Slowly, she lifted her head and looked toward the houses. Not a single light had come on, not a sound from a door or window opening. Maybe the wind had swept the sound away from them—or maybe no one was there. Then she thought, if he has a gun, I'm not safe in those houses even if people are there. I must get to where I can defend myself—against him and his gun.

She stared north, looking for movement—and found it coming steadily south on the road fifty yards north of where she'd left it. "It's him!" She said the words aloud into the wind. She watched him start to run. He'd seen her. The road was no longer a choice. She had to get away, had to start moving. She crawled up into a crouch and moved as fast as she could to the west, away from the road. She was headed into the ruins over a half-mile from where she wanted to be. It was Delos' flattest and most indefensible part.

◇◇◇

It felt like hours that she'd been stumbling over walls and excavations—looking over her shoulder on every step, until she found herself standing amidst the fabled marble lions of Delos, on the western side of the ancient city. She stared southeast over the ruins of its Sacred Lake and largest building, the Agora of the

Italians. Somehow, she'd have to cross southeast through the heart of the ruins and climb east along Mount Kynthos, Delos' most prominent height, without being caught. She was as far away from where she wanted to be as she could imagine.

She was tired, she was cold, she was hungry, and she was naked. Worse yet, she had no idea where her pursuer was. She hadn't seen him since he stopped at the place where she'd heard the gunshots. He must be ahead of me, she thought, waiting for me to cross the ruins. I know he's out there, waiting to kill me. That thought led to another, a bizarre one that made her smile: I can't believe this; here I am, in a cradle of ancient Greece, being forced to compete for my life and I'm perfectly dressed for the occasion! Naked as all those Olympian boys. She put her hand over her mouth to keep from laughing. She was afraid if she started, she'd become hysterical—and lose it all.

She stared off toward Mount Kynthos. Fitting, too, she thought, was the place she'd chosen to make her stand: it was what remained of a temple built to honor the pagan deity on Delos probably closest in kinship to Saint Kiriake. Annika was on her way to the hillside Temple of Isis, the magical Egyptian goddess of protection and healing and a modern symbol of female power. Some claim worship of Isis ended only when her many temples were renamed in honor of another hallowed female icon, the Virgin Mary.

◇◇◇

Andreas and Tassos let the port police officer lead the way. They stayed ten yards behind, scanning from side to side for signs of doubling back—or anything else that might be helpful. They found it in discarded tampons. Now they were certain they were following Annika.

The cop did a good job of tracking her bare feet through the dirt—even after they left the road and headed west. Andreas thought she was headed to some houses, but her tracks abruptly veered south just past where she seemed to have fallen. Hopefully the cop was as good at following tracks over ground pounded almost to stone by thousands of tourist feet a day, because that's where they were headed—to the heart of tourist Delos.

"Chief, we have a problem." The cop stopped about ten feet past the place of her fall.

"What is it?" asked Andreas.

"The sandal prints turn back toward the road."

The prints had been in step with Annika's since the church. Andreas looked toward the road. "I wish your buddy would get here with those damn lights." Frustrated, he looked at Tassos. "Why'd the killer suddenly stop following her?" He looked at Tassos.

"Doesn't make any sense, does it," Tassos said, as a statement, not a question.

The cop said, "Maybe he heard your gunshots and decided to take off?"

"Maybe," Tassos said somberly. "Or maybe he knows where she's headed."

"How could he know?"

Tassos shrugged. "My guess is he's spent a lot of time here and probably knows most of Delos' secrets. She's trying to hide in his backyard. Who knows what she said or did that helped him figure out what she's likely to do now. One thing's for sure: he has something in mind." He paused. "And he's not afraid of us or"— he gestured toward the houses—"the drunks in there sleeping off the *panegyri*." He pointed to the sandal prints. "I think I'll follow these."

"Do you think it's a good idea tracking him alone in the dark—especially if he knows this place as well as you think he does?" Andreas obviously didn't like the idea.

Tassos' voice was firm. "One of us has to follow him, and I know this place pretty well myself. The ancients didn't just build temples here. They were practical businessmen and had ways to escape from invaders and pirates. The official version is that all their secret tunnels and hideaways were destroyed or simply collapsed over time." He paused. "I don't believe it. Too many smugglers still use this island. Smugglers don't go where there's no place to hide—and with our guy liking tunnels as much as he does"—Tassos shook his head and repeated himself—"I think he's up to something."

"Okay, but what makes you think you can find him?"

In the dark, Tassos sounded like someone speaking in a trance. "A few years back, antiquities illegally removed from Greece and some other places started turning up in the newer acquisitions of prominent European museums. It wasn't just embarrassing for the museums, it was expensive; they had to return what they'd acquired to the plundered countries without getting their money back. The museums and their insurance companies wanted the source cut off and raised holy hell with Interpol to do it." He paused. "Interpol traced the operation to the Cyclades but couldn't find the bad guys. I did—right here on Delos."

"That's the favor you called in?"

Tassos nodded.

Andreas let out a breath. "At least wait for the kid with the lights."

Andreas made out another nod in the dark.

"We'll follow her." Andreas gestured for the port cop to start moving. "Hopefully, one of us will find who we're looking for before they find each other."

Tassos started walking. "I'll follow these tracks back to the road and wait there for the lights."

By the time Andreas and the port policeman reached the edge of the ruins by the Lake Area, they were sure Annika knew she was being followed. Her sudden shifts in direction and dramatically shortened stride were what you'd expect from someone ducking and crawling to evade a pursuer.

What Andreas couldn't figure out was why the killer had called off the chase. He probably knew she'd spotted him, but why would he stop when he was so close? Unless he didn't want the chase to end—at least not yet…or not here.

He scanned the ruins. Nothing. He turned to the cop. "Okay, let's get back to the tracks—and switch to the red lens on your light, it'll make them easier to see on this hard stuff." Andreas knew that no matter what the bastard had in mind, he wasn't likely to give up on his plan, whatever it was—and Annika didn't seem likely to give up on hers either, whatever it might be.

Perhaps Tassos was right and she did have a plan…one the killer had figured out. That meant any minute she could be dead. Andreas preferred to think the killer had turned away because he was afraid to fight her face-to-face after the rock-throwing back at the church—and her tracks would lead Andreas to a place where he'd find her safe and sound. But Andreas hadn't believed in fairy tales in a very long time. He knew they had to find her fast.

◇◇◇

Annika had left the lions and moved toward the southeast beyond the dry lake bed that once was the reservoir of Delos. She moved tentatively, conscious of every shadow and alert to every sound. She passed through the crumbled former marketplaces for slaves, goods, and grain and by the monuments, temples, and other ruins of Delos' central area. It was here that the people of Delos erected the Sanctuary of Apollo to honor the son of Zeus who, myth held, they helped by allowing him to be born on Delos in exchange for his father's promise that the island would prosper. Now it was Annika asking for their help.

She was jittery as she came to the Theater Quarter—the ancient city's most opulent shopping and living area. Everything had been too quiet, and there was no sign of him. Something was wrong. She turned east, toward an area of more ruined sanctuaries—these, though, to foreign gods. She was headed for a western foothill of Mount Kynthos when she saw the tightly clustered mass of fig trees and bushes. It was the perfect place for him to hide. But she had no choice; she had to pass through there to reach the ridge she must climb to the Temple of Isis.

She held her breath—and two large rocks—as she crept toward the greenery. Although she heard nothing, she was certain he was in there, listening to the pounding of her heart. As she stepped onto the narrow dirt track that wound around the mass, she realized this was just what he expected her to do, so he could surprise her as she went by. She paused for an instant, then charged from the path into the heart of the bushes and trees screaming in her mind, *I'll kill you!*

Immediately, she found herself amid a swarming rush of sounds and movements, fur and feathers, jumping and flying. Wild rabbits and birds were as unaccustomed to creatures of her sort on their island at this hour as she was to being here. She dropped to her knees, her body shaking. She let the stones fall from her hands, bowed her head, and thanked God her tormentor wasn't there. The adrenaline rush had passed, followed by exhaustion. But still there was a climb to make. She struggled to her feet and trudged toward the hillside.

The climb made her dizzy, and halfway she gagged as if to vomit—but there was nothing to come up. She crawled the rest of the way in a daze. At the top she collapsed. If he found her now, she was as good as dead.

When she looked up, it was all as she remembered. It was far different from any place she'd passed through below. A headless statue of the goddess Isis stood framed within the four entrance columns and crowning horizontal entablature to a small, 2,200-year-old Doric temple. Though no more than seventeen feet wide, nineteen feet from floor to cornice tip, and thirty-six feet deep, it had once boasted a magnificent entrance, which had been painstakingly resurrected from scattered remnants. Now—as before—the Temple of Isis stood facing west toward the sea astride a foundation of stone five feet higher than the path leading to it.

A beautiful place...the perfect place for her...to wait to ambush him. "My God," she said aloud. Her heart skipped a beat. He could have taken the road past the museum and be inside waiting for her. Her eyes darted about in the dark—or he could be hiding behind the temple's walls. Her heart was racing.

Very carefully, Annika climbed to where she could peer between the columns. She wanted no more surprises. There was nothing inside but the statue of Isis and several large pieces of carved marble a few feet from the far left corner. They stood tall and wide enough for him to hide behind. She picked up a rock and held her breath as she carefully edged along inside the right side wall to where she could see behind the marble pieces. Nothing there. She let out a breath and made her way out of the temple to search behind its walls.

Unlike most of Delos' ruins, the Temple of Isis had had its stone rear and side walls rebuilt in their original place. Although not as tall as the originals, they were more than high enough to hide behind. From its highest point at the edge of the temple's front cornice, each side wall descended abruptly to where it leveled out a little more than halfway to its intersection point with the eight-foot high rear wall. Annika slowly circled the temple walls twice—first counterclockwise, then clockwise. She found no sign of him. She climbed back into the sanctuary.

For a moment she stood quietly staring at the statue of Isis, the rock still in her hand. She walked back to the front of the temple and set the rock next to a pillar. From here, she could see across Delos to the sea and anything moving below.

Annika had wondered when she worked here how any being—even a betrayed king—possibly could possess rage deep and bitter enough to reduce such an extraordinarily vibrant civilization to this tragic island of rocks. She no longer wondered; she knew.

Her mind raced over her plan. If he came for her, she'd see him and bombard him with rocks as he climbed. She could kill him from here—even if he came with a gun. If he tried to flank her from the other side of the hill or from Mount Kynthos, she'd have plenty of time to escape along the ridgeline to any number of paths to other places filled with stones to throw. If he kept after her, she'd find her way back to Isis along another path and start the cycle all over again. Yes, that was her plan. If only her body would cooperate.

Annika knew she'd picked the obvious place for what she had in mind. Anyone familiar with the island could figure that out, but so what? There was no sign of him anywhere. She was here first, and that was all that mattered. This was where she'd fight until help arrived—or one of them was dead.

For the first time, Annika felt prepared for whatever he might try. She stretched out her arms and yawned. The dress she wore as a cape whipped about her face in the wind. She'd become so accustomed to the cold, and her feet so numbed to the pain of the stones, that she'd forgotten she was naked. She touched the dress. It was almost dry. Only parts around her neck were still damp. She pulled it over her head and wrapped it around her neck so the wet ends trailed behind her like a scarf. The wind would dry them quickly.

She wondered how much longer until dawn. Not much, she hoped. Her mind wandered to how it would feel standing as a mortal—a mortal woman no less—with the goddess Isis as first light fired across the legendary birthplace of the god of light, Apollo. It was an enchanting thought—but one that ended abruptly with a flash of light from the base of the hill. Someone was there.

Instinctively, she stepped back. It was a natural reaction to fear, and she knew how to handle it. From the movement of the light, she could tell he was climbing quickly toward her. Annika took two deep breaths and focused solely on how best to kill him before he made it up the hill. It was a mistake she'd realize too late.

Chapter Twenty-Five

Andreas and the port cop had an easy time tracking Annika to the hillside. From the way she was moving, she seemed determined to get there as fast as she could and didn't care who knew. At the bottom of the hill by the House of Hermes they stopped to look up. "She has to be up there somewhere," Andreas said. He took out his flashlight and ran it along the hillside toward the ruins above.

"There!" the cop yelled.

Andreas had seen it too, a figure jumping back into the shadows of ruins, some 250 yards away. "Tell Tassos and your buddy we found her and we need those lights here, *now*. Stay here and show them where to shine them."

Andreas started running up the hill toward the ruins along an old dirt path and rough-cut stone steps. The wind was howling down the hill; after a few moments he couldn't even hear the cop shouting on his walkie-talkie for the lights. Andreas thought of yelling up the hill, but it was useless to try in this wind. He knew that had to be Annika, but would she be alone? Not having heard from Tassos, he knew the killer could be anywhere—including up there, in that place with the four pillars. All he could do was move as fast as he could to get there—and pray for no surprises.

◇◇◇

He limped toward his destination. It was a long climb, one he'd not made in years, but he remembered the way. Very few even knew the tunnel existed, and probably none alive had explored it as he had.

He hadn't heard a sound but his own footsteps for almost an hour, but now there was whistling. It was the wind rushing between the loose-fitting stones of the foundation walls of the place just above. He made his way around the last of the maze of boulders and dead-end passages and pulled himself out into a stone-walled space not quite high enough for him to stand fully upright. He still carried the rope.

It was a place built by ancients to hide from pursuers and, if necessary, escape through the mountain tunnel to the sea. He wondered how so many, over so many centuries, had so wrongly guessed the real purpose for its construction. They thought of it as merely the foundation for a sanctuary built to honor three foreign gods: Anubis and Serapis from the Land of the Dead, and Serapis' wife from the Land of the Living.

He moved to the left rear corner of the space and ever so carefully removed two square feet of stone from above his head—and from the floor of the Temple of Isis, wife of Serapis, ruler of the underworld.

◇◇◇

Annika knew her time had come. She saw how close he was getting, even sensed it. She had to move. She drew a deep breath and started forward. Her foot brushed against the rock she'd left by the pillar, and without slowing down, she knelt to pick it up. As her hand touched the rock she heard the violent crash of stone against stone only inches above her head and felt a body falling over her from behind.

She'd knelt at the exact instant of the killer's murderous downward swing. He'd picked up the rock after climbing in behind her through the far left corner of the temple's floor. It was meant to shatter her skull but struck the pillar instead and his momentum sent him tumbling forward over Annika and out of the temple.

Annika froze. Where had he come from? She saw him getting on his feet to her right and in panic threw the rock. It missed but made him duck, giving her just enough time to leap out of the temple to her left.

She landed stumbling to her knees, the effort to regain her footing almost too much for her. As she stood, something jerked at her throat, yanking her off her feet again and onto her back. My dress, she thought, struggling to regain command of her limbs. He'd grabbed the tail of her dress.

He slammed his fist into the side of her head, wrenched her over onto her belly, and with his knees pressed firmly into her back, twisted the fabric closed around her neck.

He said not a word to her as he rode out her struggle to throw him off her back; and in the silence she felt his strangle hold intensifying as she lost her strength. Tighter and tighter he twisted the dress about her windpipe. She felt she'd be gone to the darkness in seconds. That was when she heard the words. They came in a harsh, breathless whisper from lips pressed tightly against her ear. "Your destiny is here. On this altar to Isis. Among my gods. Overlooking our neglected saint."

Then he kissed her.

With the knowledge that she was about to draw her last breath came a flash of blinding white light.

Was this death? No, she still felt his weight on her upper back. And then, for an instant, he relaxed the noose.

It was only a glimmer of a chance, but she snatched it. Sheer will bowed her back, as she summoned strength to thrust off from the ground, gain her knees, and buck him flying over her head. He landed still holding one end of the dress and yanked at it, but she'd expected it this time and spun out of the dress as he pulled. Her hands found a rock. Adrenaline was back; she was ready to finish this.

The rock hit him hard. She picked up another and flung it but realized she could no longer see him. The blinding light had returned and grown brighter. She threw rock after rock in what she thought his direction, toward the blinding light. She kept hearing her name. She couldn't see but knew he'd keep coming for her no matter how much she hurt him. She had to kill him.

If only she could see, if only…suddenly she felt his grip on her injured wrist. She tried pulling away, but she had no more strength. Then she heard a gunshot. He pulled her closer to him. She tried punching him with her free hand, but he grabbed it and butted her head with his. A second shot, louder. She felt him wince. He jerked and twisted her so she was between him and the light.

He pressed his face to hers, stared into her eyes and whispered, "Later, Annika. There's a promise to be kept." And then he was gone.

She didn't know what to do anymore. So she started to spin around in the light…and scream…and scream…and scream.

◇◇◇

Andreas reached the ridge ten seconds after the lights went on. He was thirty yards from her. She was throwing rocks wildly in every direction. He saw someone crawling toward her, beneath the aim of her throws. Andreas yelled, "Annika!" but she didn't seem to hear and didn't stop throwing. He pulled his gun. He wanted to shoot the crawling bastard but didn't dare, because Annika was directly beyond him, in the line of fire. He started running toward her but had to stop when within range of her rocks. He called her name again. Still no reaction.

Suddenly, the killer sprang from below her and grabbed her arm. Andreas had no choice now but to fire. He didn't dare aim for the killer's center of mass, they were too close together. He aimed just to hit him. The first shot missed. He adjusted and fired again. A hit! Better yet, the killer let go of her and was heading to where Andreas had a clear shot. Andreas refocused his sight picture and started to squeeze off a round "Damn it," he said aloud, and pulled back his gun. Annika had stepped right into his sights. She was spinning and screaming.

There was no choice to be made. He ran to her and let the killer run. There would be no place for him to hide in that temple.

Chapter Twenty-Six

Catia was the first to see the lights shining on Mount Kynthos. "Over there, Spiros, over there!"

The helicopter had flown west from Mykonos directly to Saint Kiriake. The pilot nodded and veered south toward the lights. Catia was holding her breath.

"Look, up there, by the Temple of Isis," shouted the mayor, sounding as excited as she was.

Catia saw two people—a naked, bald woman and a man holding a gun. She screamed, "There's Annika." The helicopter came in for a closer look, and the man waved as he took off his jacket and put it around the woman.

"Land, please land." Catia was frantic.

"There's no place to land up here, Mrs. Vanden Haag. We have to land by the museum," said the pilot.

Everyone seemed to be waiting for Catia to decide.

Her eyes were glued to her daughter. She saw another man join them. He was in uniform. He took Annika's arm and walked her away from the temple in the direction of the museum. "Okay, land there." She watched as the jacketless man walked—gun still in hand—toward the temple.

◇◇◇

There were no signs of life inside. Nothing. Andreas had seen him run in there and there was blood on the floor. It led to the left rear corner and disappeared. No doors, no windows—hidden or otherwise—just marble. He stomped on the squares in the corner. Solid, no give in them at all. He looked at the carved marble pieces next to the corner. That must be it, he thought. He'd climbed them to get over the wall. Strange, though, no bloodstains on them or the wall. Whatever, we'll tear this island apart after daylight. He's not getting away, certainly not now that we know who he is.

Andreas heard his name on his two-way radio. "Yes."

"Did you find him?" It was Tassos.

"No, he just seemed to disappear into the Temple of Isis, but don't worry, we'll find him when the sun comes up."

Silence.

"Tassos, are you there? Tassos, Tassos." He was yelling into the phone.

"Chief?"

"Yes, who's this?"

"It's Kouros, sir, I flew over on the deputy minister's helicopter."

"Where's Tassos?"

"I don't know, sir, he just handed me the radio and ran off." Andreas could hear Kouros shouting into the phone trying to be heard above the wind.

"Where are you?" asked Andreas.

"By the museum."

"I'll be right there." What the hell was going on now?

◇◇◇

Catia and Annika were crying in each other's arms when Andreas reached the museum. A medevac helicopter was on its way from Athens.

The first thing Andreas did was find the port policeman who'd been tracking the killer with Tassos. "What happened? Did you find anything?"

"Yes, sir, we followed his tracks to there." He pointed to the south end of the museum. "That's where they turned toward the sea. We followed them until they disappeared in the water. We walked back and forth along the shore looking for more tracks but didn't find any. That's when we came back—and were walking south toward Mount Kynthos. We were almost up to you when I got the call for the lights."

Andreas paused. "You must have found something. Something that made Tassos take off like he did."

The cop shrugged. "He was interested in some caves over there that open onto the sea." He pointed to the southeast, beyond Mount Kynthos. "But there were no tracks, just wet rock."

"Did you go into the caves?"

He nodded. "There were no tracks but a lot of passageways. 'Perfect hiding places for smugglers,' he told me."

That must be it, thought Andreas; Tassos is looking for a tunnel entrance. One that leads up to the temple. "Officer, I want you to take me there now," he said firmly.

"Yes, sir."

At that moment he felt a hand on his shoulder. He spun around, still a little edgy from it all. It was the deputy minister.

"I guess I owe you an apology Chief."

Andreas' mind was elsewhere—he had to help Tassos. "Fine, no problem."

"No, really, please come with me. My sister and niece want to thank you."

Andreas felt trapped. He looked at the cop. "Stay here, I'll be right back."

When Catia saw Andreas, she ran to him, threw her arms around his neck, and kissed him. "I cannot thank you enough. I will pray for you every day."

Andreas didn't know what to say; he just smiled and said, "I'm glad she's safe."

"I told my brother that if he didn't listen to what Officer Kouros told me I would never speak to him again. Thank you, thank you, thank you." She kissed and hugged Andreas again. "Come, I want you to meet my daughter."

Andreas wanted to say, "No, later," but how could he? She led him to the helicopter where her daughter sat huddled under a blanket.

"Annika, this is Chief of Police Kaldis. He's the man who found you."

The woman looked at him and said not a word. Andreas stared into her eyes. Neither spoke. Andreas felt as if he were in church. He bowed his head. She reached out and gently touched his hand. "Thank you, sir, and bless you."

He was about to say something when he heard the shot. Instinctively, he pulled his gun and swung around to stand between Annika and the direction of the sound, but it was too far away to be of any risk to her. "Tassos!" He ran to the cop. "Take me to those caves."

Two more shots; five seconds apart.

"Hurry!" Andreas was praying as he ran—and thinking of his father's death.

◇◇◇

Tassos met them just outside the caves. The grim look he'd worn when Andreas last saw him was gone.

"Are you okay?" Andreas was out of breath from running.

"Yes." His voice was easy.

"What happened?"

Tassos looked at the port cop. "Why don't you go back and tell everyone everything's okay." He waited until the cop left.

"Our killer's gone." Tassos sounded as if he'd won the lottery.

"As in gone gone?" Andreas asked, still panting.

"As in gone dead!" Tassos replied, his voice as jubilant as if Greece had just won the World Cup.

"What happened?" Andreas asked, confused.

"I waited by the caves. I knew he had to come out of one of them. That's where the old-timers always said the secret tunnels must be."

"You guessed right?" Andreas sounded surprised.

There was unabashed enthusiasm in Tassos' answer. "Yes." He nodded. "He came out right in front of me."

"Did he have a gun?" Andreas asked.

"No," Tassos replied, sounding unconcerned.

"But the shots?" Andreas said, his concern mounting.

Tassos shrugged. "Mine. The first took out his kneecap. I didn't feel like chasing him."

"And the other two?" Andreas asked, not really wanting to know the answer.

"I decided to move the process along," Tassos said.

"'Move the process along,'" Andreas repeated, shaking his head and staring at the ground between them. Now Tassos was pissing him off.

Tassos smiled. "You know he did it, I know he did it, the court would know he did it, and every inmate in prison would know he did it. Even though there's no death penalty in Greece, sooner or later someone on the inside would kill him. So, I just moved the process along."

Andreas kept staring at the ground. He couldn't believe what he was hearing. "And the body?"

"It's back in one of those deep holes inside the cave. He'll never be found—at least not by mortals." Tassos smiled again and punched Andreas on the arm. "How do you like that, he gets to be buried with the gods."

Andreas looked up at Tassos' face and wondered if he'd flipped.

A deadly serious look suddenly replaced Tassos' smile, and he spoke now through clenched teeth. "May they enjoy torturing that bastard's black soul for all eternity."

Maybe he has lost it, thought Andreas. "What are we going to tell the deputy minister, the mayor?" Andreas paused, "And everyone else?" After all, an unarmed prisoner in custody had just been murdered by a chief inspector.

Tassos' voice resumed its nonchalance. "I don't know. I'm sure we'll figure something out on the way back." He patted

Andreas on the back, linked his arm through his and started them walking toward the museum.

Too many moral questions for such a short walk, thought Andreas.

◇◇◇

By the time they reached the museum the medevac helicopter had landed and taken off with Annika and Catia. Spiros and the mayor had stayed behind.

Spiros spoke first. "Again, gentlemen, thank you for finding my niece."

Tassos and Andreas simply nodded.

"So, how do we catch the man who did all this?" Spiros asked.

Andreas looked at Tassos to answer. "Well, sir, I don't think that's going to be necessary," said Tassos in a calm professional voice.

"What do you mean?" Spiros' voice seemed about to head toward its high-pitched anger range.

"Like I said," Tassos said in a tone that let him know who held the cards, "it won't be necessary."

Spiros was glaring at him, but before he could say another word the mayor jumped in. "Tassos, are you saying the problem has been—uhhhh—resolved."

"Precisely, Mr. Mayor," said Tassos as if patting a precocious child on the head.

The mayor smiled. "Uh, Mr. Minister, I think this means we don't have to worry about a trial."

Spiros' eyes darted between Tassos and the mayor, and outrage spread across his face. "But there has to be a trial—we can't let the man get away." Suddenly, his expression changed and he focused a look of understanding on the mayor. "Oh, I see," he said, nodding.

Andreas knew it was his time to speak. "You two will have to decide how you want to handle this. There are at least eighteen families who don't know their daughters are dead, and Mykonos still thinks a killer is running around loose." Silence. "I have no choice but to tell the truth about the Vandrew woman's killer.

He was pursued and killed. His body will never be recovered." His voice was coldly professional.

Tassos quickly added, "He was an itinerant worker." He glanced nervously at Andreas, as if unsure how he'd react to the lie.

Andreas said nothing, just looked at the ground.

"An Albanian," the mayor said. "He'd only been on the island a short time."

Spiros added his own embellishment. "And he was in the country illegally."

Unbelievable, these politicians, thought Andreas. Now that the killer's dead, they don't care who he was. They don't want the truth; they just want someone to blame who fits their personal political agendas. No wonder Tassos wasn't worried that he killed him. He knew all along that's what they wanted.

"And what about the other victims? What do you tell their families?" Andreas asked, unable to keep the belligerence from his voice.

Spiros shrugged. "It's been so long, why add to the suffering of those innocent families by opening everything up and subjecting them to an uncaring media only interested in sensationalizing the death of their children?"

The mayor nodded in agreement.

Fucking, disgusting politicians, thought Andreas. He looked at Tassos.

Tassos didn't return the look. He simply asked, "So, how are you going to explain the sudden disappearance of such a well-known man from Mykonos?"

The mayor and Spiros gave each other a puzzled stare.

Tassos continued. "Let's not jerk ourselves off here. I'm talking about the man who really kidnapped your niece—and killed at least eighteen tourists on Mykonos." He paused and, as if to remind them of the tremendous favor he'd just done them all, said, "I'm talking about the killer, who won't be getting the chance to enjoy all the publicity of his trial. What are you going to say about him?"

"Who are you talking about?" asked the mayor.

Tassos stared at Andreas. "They don't know?" he asked, surprise in his voice.

Andreas nodded no. "He was gone before they got here. They never saw him."

Tassos laughed out loud. "I don't believe this. You two really don't know who the killer is." He laughed again and looked at Andreas. "I don't think we should tell them. That way, if something nasty happens to us down the line—like my forced retirement or"—he pointed at Andreas—"bad assignments for you—we have another way to make a living."

Spiros started shouting. "Don't you dare threaten me with what I can or cannot do to you. I can do anything I damn well please."

Tassos winked at Andreas. "Somehow, I don't think his thank you was sincere."

Andreas didn't respond. He honestly didn't know what to do, what side to take—if any. What would his father have done? He decided to stay out of it for the time being. He could always do something later, after he'd had time to think. After all, the killer was dead, Annika was safe, and Mykonos was secure again—except from its politicians.

Tassos looked at Spiros. "I'm glad we had this little chat. In an hour, this place will be filled with Mykonians honoring Saint Kiriake on her name day and tourists visiting from Mykonos—possibly even a few journalists. It will be my great honor to announce to them—and the rest of Mykonos—that after twenty years Mykonos is free of its serial killer." He turned to Andreas. "I think that's an appropriate way to resign from the force, don't you?"

Andreas only shrugged.

"And move on to CNN, BBC, and a book and movie deal," Tassos said, smiling.

Veins were popping on Spiros' forehead. He was cornered.

"You'll destroy our island's reputation!" Now it was the mayor's turn to be hysterical. He looked at Andreas. "Chief, do something!"

Andreas hated the devious little shit as it was and wasn't about to be drawn into his mess.

"I said do something!" the mayor screamed.

The mayor had succeeded in pissing Andreas off, which is why Andreas said more than he intended. "Not my problem. As you once reminded me, I'm from Athens and don't belong here." He smiled and finished with the unstated punctuation: *asshole*.

Spiros' face lit up. "Yes, you're absolutely right." He turned to the mayor. "I think the chief has earned a promotion back to his old unit—as head of his old unit—in Athens. Don't you agree, mayor?" He made it sound as if the mayor's opinion mattered.

The mayor did not hesitate. "Absolutely." He looked at Andreas. "Do we have a deal?"

Andreas didn't know what to say. This wasn't what he'd meant. Yet he was being offered the very thing he most wanted—for a price he never thought he'd consider…but…the killer was dead, Mykonos and Annika were safe…

"Well, do we have a deal?" Spiros asked.

Andreas drew in a deep breath and shut his eyes. Fucking politicians. "Yes." He'd become one of them.

"Good," said Spiros, and turned to Tassos. "And you?"

"No retirement," said Tassos waving a finger.

"No retirement." Spiros nodded.

The mayor let out an audible sigh of relief.

"So, who's the killer?" asked Spiros.

Tassos looked at Andreas. "I don't think we should tell you. Of course, if you really want to know, all you have to do is check up on which of our distinguished suspects never shows up again on Mykonos. But do you really want to know?"

"Why wouldn't we?" Spiros seemed surprised more than angry.

Tassos looked at him. "Because, if you don't know—as far as you're concerned—none of this ever happened, and isn't that what you want to believe?"

Silence.
Heads began to nod.
"Yes, that's right," someone said.
More silence.
"None of this ever happened," said another.
It was dawn. Mortals were back on Delos.

Chapter Twenty-Seven

A week had passed since Annika's rescue, and Andreas was getting only good news. Not a word had come out about Annika's ordeal other than that her unidentified abductor was dead. The police had no questions for her, and she refused to talk about it with anyone but her doctors. That was fine with her parents. They were just thrilled at how well she'd recovered from the carbon monoxide poisoning. It was a miracle of healing, one doctor said, and Annika apparently agreed. She planned on returning to Delos next year for Saint Kiriake's name day. It was a pilgrimage she vowed to make every year for the rest of her life in thanks for the miracles performed by her healers—and protectors—from the world beyond, Saint Kiriake and the goddess Isis.

If everything's so great, thought Andreas, why am I on a ferry on my way to Syros? Certainly not for pleasure, because on Syros tourism is envied, not cultivated. He stood at the bow. It was one of those beautiful Aegean days when the sea seems painted along the bottom of the sky in parallel bands of blue—from indigo and lapis at the horizon—to aquamarine and opal at your feet, with sapphire, turquoise and so many other shades filling in between. He tried to think of things other than the purpose for his trip—like resuming his hunt for Athenian dope-ring assassins, or finding the right girl and settling down to start a family.

When the ferry docked, Tassos was waiting for him. Andreas had called yesterday to set up the meeting. He hadn't told him the purpose, just that he had to see him.

"I thought it best we have a coffee away from the office," said Tassos.

Andreas nodded. If his instinct was right, Tassos must have guessed what the meeting was about, so he'd let him pick the venue. It was a cozy little taverna just off the port and set away from a relatively quiet, marble-paved side street by a line of oleander and tamarind. Tassos chose a table away from other customers and told the owner to keep it that way. They chatted about Annika's health until the coffee came.

"So, what's up?" asked Tassos.

Andreas stared at his coffee. "I think you know."

Tassos smiled. "Maybe."

Andreas looked up. "Why the fuck didn't you tell me?" His voice was angry but low. "You risked that woman's life."

Tassos held up one hand. "Honest, I never suspected him until we found that bridge in the tunnel, and by then there was nothing left to do but catch the bastard who had her—whoever he was. And I still wasn't sure it was him." He didn't sound the least bit defensive.

"But why?"

Tassos shrugged. "It's a long story I don't want to get into."

Andreas stared at him.

Tassos stared back. "Hey, what are you so upset about? He's dead, she's safe. No harm, no foul." Now he actually sounded offended.

"That's not the way I see it," said Andreas, his voice rising.

"Well, maybe you'll see it differently when you're back in Athens at your new job as chief of your old unit."

Andreas kept his cool. "I really missed all the signs, didn't I?"

Tassos looked away.

"It never hit me you might be covering for a suspect."

Tassos didn't look at him this time, and when he spoke his voice reflected a different sort of anger. "I never thought he was the killer. I've known him for years, never suspected a thing."

"Yeah, you seemed to know everything about everybody in the Cyclades except for the one guy who turns out to be our killer. That's what started me thinking. And then I remembered when I told you I'd chased him into that temple you didn't even ask who he was. You already knew."

Tassos shrugged, his eyes still avoiding Andreas'.

Andreas leaned forward, still staring. "So, I did a little checking. Interesting what I found out. Did you know he once was under investigation by Interpol?" Andreas' eyes didn't move from him.

Tassos' face tightened, but he still made no eye contact.

"Seems they thought he was involved with stolen antiquities, but the investigation ended when the real dealers were found by a certain Inspector Stamatos. Two Albanians, both died trying to escape—from some caves on Delos."

Tassos kept looking away.

Andreas struggled to keep his voice down but did nothing to hide the simmering rage of a blood betrayal burning in his eyes. "You miserable bastard. You knew he was taking her to Delos all along."

Tassos met Andreas' glare with a look of remorse such as Andreas had never seen before and never wanted to see again. "I swear on the graves of my wife and son I had no idea. Our deal was he'd stay off Delos—and I never knew there was a church to Saint Kiriake there. That night on Delos, I tracked him over by the caves to where the secret tunnels run into Mount Kynthos, but there was no sign of him or the girl. I didn't know where they were until you told me about the Temple of Isis. Then I knew." He dropped his eyes to his hands. He seemed on the verge of tears.

"That's why you killed him. To keep your little arrangement quiet." Andreas was struggling to regain his composure.

Tassos said nothing. His eyes didn't move.

"Isn't it?" Andreas pushed the words out between clenched teeth.

Without lifting his head Tassos answered. "Six years ago I caught him and the two others red-handed at the caves on Delos. They'd been digging artifacts out of the tunnels. He offered me a deal. He'd make me his partner and promised no more digging on Delos or dealing with Europeans. Nothing to let Interpol think the old ring still operated."

"Did your deal include killing the two Albanians?" Andreas' voice seethed with anger.

"I didn't kill them. I just said I did. No idea what happened to them. Their bodies were never found." His voice was emotionless.

Sounds familiar, thought Andreas.

Tassos looked up. "What's so bad?" he asked. "Mykonians plundered Delos for centuries. Stolen artifacts are all over—and under—Mykonos. Our deal was simple: he'd find them in the mines or wherever and sell them to his Asian, Middle Eastern, and American contacts. Just keep away from Delos, and no customers from Interpol countries."

He wasn't even trying to hide the truth.

"His work required a lot of traveling—or so he said. I never thought anything of it for him to be away for days at a time. When I saw the bridge, I remembered he'd told me he'd built something like that to keep the curious away from where he was digging." He paused. "I never went into the mines. That was all his thing." He looked down again. "I just covered for him."

Silence.

Tassos looked up and stared directly at Andreas. "Do you think if I thought he was killing those women I'd have covered up for him?"

Andreas said nothing. He wasn't looking at Tassos. He was thinking of his father—and how one betrayal begets another.

"Do you?" There was genuine pain in Tassos' voice.

Andreas looked at him. "No."

A shroud seemed to lift from Tassos. He reached across the table and squeezed Andreas' forearm. "Thank you."

"But I'm not sure where that gets us with everything else." Andreas found it easier now to sound professional.

Tassos shrugged. "Oh, I don't care about that. Do whatever you feel you should. I just wanted to be sure you didn't think I'd let that bastard kill them." His anger flared only on the last words.

Andreas looked surprised. "You really don't care?"

"No, why should I?" he said, sounding utterly nonchalant. "You sound like your dad. And I really did like him. When I joined the force, I worked at the prison on Yaros." He gestured toward an island between Syros and Tinos. "It was where the Junta kept its more prominent political prisoners, ones who later rose to power." He smiled. "I always was nice to them, and they've always been nice to me."

Tassos called for the check. "The worst I've done is make black money from someone dealing in stolen antiquities and killed a very bad man. Making that sort of money isn't something anyone's likely to come after me for, and as for killing him…" he gave a dismissive wave of his hand. "Besides, first they have to prove it—then convince someone to prosecute. I know the prosecutors—that's not going to happen. No one wants the story to come out. No one. Worst case, some internal disciplinary proceeding costs me my pension. But, thanks to you know who, I really don't need it anymore."

Andreas' head was pounding. Not from anger, from this rush of reality.

Tassos paid the bill and they both stood up. "Andreas, I really like you, so do what you think best for your conscience. I'll be fine. I'm like a Mykonian: I'm used to living in a bordello—filled with police." He smiled, gave Andreas a hug, and left.

Andreas sat back down at the table and watched Tassos cross the street and disappear around a corner. He looked down at what remained of his coffee, then up at the sky. To that bright blue, cloudless Aegean sky he said aloud, "I don't know, Dad, I just don't know."

All he knew for sure was that a South African jeweler from Mykonos—reported in Athens as missing by his wife and girlfriend—was dead. Or so he hoped.